MW01077403

Melanie A. Smith

Published by
WICKED DREAMS PUBLISHING
info@wickeddreamspublishing.com
Boise, ID USA

Cover design, editing, and interior formatting by Wicked Dreams
Publishing

eBook ISBN: 978-1-952121-78-4
Paperback ISBN: 978-1-952121-72-2
Discreet Paperback ISBN: 978-1-952121-73-9
Hardcover ISBN: 978-1-952121-74-6

RECKLESSLY IN LOVE

A STEAMY SMALL-TOWN FORCED PROXIMITY ROMANCE

ALPINE RIDGE

MELANIE A. SMITH

WICKED DREAMS PUBLISHING

CONTENTS

CONTENT WARNING

Recklessly in Love is a small-town forced proximity romance novel that includes elements that might not be suitable for some readers. If you are sensitive to any of the following, please put your mental health first:

Attempted drugging
Mention of sexual assault of women/minors (off-page/non-graphic)
Abusive parents (emotional/mental)
Explicit language
Graphic sexual activity

CHAPTER ONE

JOANIE

"You got fired for having sex with one of the junior partners in the copy room?" Mia gasps, parroting back the words I'd just used in the form of a question.

I grin, getting the exact amount of shock value I hoped for.

"During business hours," I add. "If it'd been after hours, it would've just been a slap on the wrist." I don't bother mentioning that's probably because they'd have to fire everyone if that were the rule.

"Where do I even start with that?" Mia says with a sigh. "At work, Jo? Really? While anyone could walk in?"

I snort. "That's part of what made it such a thrill," I respond. "Unfortunately, as hot as he was, the sex was awful."

"So, you got fired for having bad sex. At work."

"That about sums it up."

"And what about him?" she asks, a note of suspicion in her voice.

"Oh, don't worry, he was fired too. No sexist double standards there, at least."

"Well, that's … good? I have to say, you don't sound upset about losing your job," Mia points out.

I shrug, even though she can't see me over the phone. "I knew it was a possibility. Again, that's kind of what made it stimulating."

"Why do I get the feeling you hoped it would happen?" Mia asks.

I can't help my shit-eating grin. "Ah, Mia, darling, you know me so well."

It's precisely what I'd been banking on when I seduced the poor bastard into fucking me not just in the copy room but on the copy machine itself. Maximum noise. Maximum evidence. Too bad it didn't live up to the fantasy of during-work sex. And photocopying a dick isn't nearly as entertaining as I thought it would be, either. Still, the encounter served its purpose.

"Well, that's one way to get the holidays off work," she replies drily. "Were you that desperate for a break? Because you know you could've just taken an actual vacation. It's been almost two years since we went to Hawaii. You certainly deserve one. But like this?"

I snort. "I'm not you, Mia. I wasn't *overwhelmed* by my job; I was *done* with it. The same stupid cases over and over. Defending corporations facing criminal charges for their shady business practices was getting tiresome. I want something different. Something that's a challenge. But now that you mention it, a vacation sounds divine."

My mind drifts back to that week in Hawaii and the

two hot local surfers I'd spent it with. The original intent was for Mia and I to each have one guy to keep us company that week, but when she had to leave suddenly to take care of her Gran — on day one of our vacation, no less — they both seemed interested in sticking around. And there was lots and lots of sticking around if you know what I mean. That was a first, even for me. One that still features prominently in my fantasies. Maybe a few new "firsts" wouldn't be such a bad idea. And since Mia found hunky Nate in her Gran's tiny mountain town — and herself while she was at it — it ended up working out well for us both.

"That reminds me. We're reviving the Alpine Ridge Winter Festival. With the bakery doing pretty well and Nate's practice getting off the ground, it'll be a good opportunity to capitalize on the seasonal traffic to Leavenworth. You should come to stay with us and join in," Mia offers.

I wrinkle my nose. "Snowy mountain town wholesome goodness isn't exactly my idea of a fun vacation," I reply hesitantly.

"Come on, Jo, you've only visited *once* since the bakery opened, and that was only for a day. I miss you," Mia pleads.

"It's not like you haven't seen me at all. You've come here to Seattle a couple of times, too. Hell, we could go on vacation together. Let's do something crazy. How does Thailand sound?" I counteroffer.

"I may be able to take off a day or two here and there, but I can't leave the bakery for weeks while traipsing off to a foreign country," Mia points out. "Trust me, it'll be fun. Just for starters, I'm making cocoa and gingerbread macarons to go with Rae's hot mulled wine and apple cider, plus there will be all sorts of fun activities like ice skating, snow sculptures, concerts —"

"All right, all right, you had me at gingerbread macarons," I agree with a sigh, even though the rest sounds like it's straight out of a Hallmark Christmas movie, which is definitely not my scene. "Will there at least be some hot guys?"

"There are some single guys in town," Mia hedges.

I quirk an eyebrow at the lack of qualifying their attractiveness. "Well, that's a start. Are any under fifty? Because you know I cap it at fifteen years older than me. Any more than that, and it treads into 'daddy' territory." I shudder at the thought. I may be wild at times, but that's one kink that's a hard no for me.

"I mean, sure, there are, but …" Mia trails off, and I roll my eyes.

"What, am I too worldly for your small-town boys? Are you worried about your harlot friend tainting your perfect mountain paradise?" I tease, reading between the lines.

"Honestly? Yes. A little," Mia says with a chuckle. "I'm not sure the guys here are ready for Hurricane Joanie."

"That sounds an awful lot like a challenge," I reply.

Mia groans, and I laugh.

"Nate is going to be furious with me for talking you into this," she jokes.

"I guess we're both going to be on the naughty list this year," I joke back. "Welcome, Mia. It's so much more fun than the nice list."

The following weekend and a two-plus-hour drive finds me bundled up against chilly air and piles of snow, yet still freezing my ass off, while I stand next to a radiant Mia and her smoking hot fiancé Nate, staring at a tree.

Yep. A tree.

Those gingerbread macarons better be damn good.

Granted, the tree is humongous and right in the center of what I suppose qualifies as "downtown" Alpine Ridge. Mia's bakery is just down the road behind us, next to Nate's shop and the grocery store. And I see a sign for a bar and restaurant across the main drag. There's also an unmarked building behind the tree, plus a couple of other buildings further up the road from where we stand. All done up in the same rustic wood with wagon wheels style. Quaint, if not a little trite. But that's about it. Alpine Ridge is a small town.

"So, this is where all the fun will be?" I ask drily, shooting an equally dry look at Mia.

She responds with a dramatic eye roll. "This is where the tree lighting ceremony will be. But many of the activities will be inside —" she points at the unmarked building "—at the community center."

I smirk. "A community center, huh?" I tease. "I

wouldn't have thought the town was big enough to have one."

Mia slips her arm into mine and starts to lead me toward the building. "Real funny. Maybe keep those kinds of comments to yourself around the locals, hm?" Mia hums.

I look pointedly between her and Nate. "I guess that means you don't consider yourself locals?"

Nate snorts. "By the usual definition, sure. I mean, we live here full-time. But by Alpine Ridge definitions? Not even close. If you weren't born here, you're not local."

I raise an eyebrow. "Is there even a hospital here where you can give birth?"

Mia suppresses a smile. "Not yet. But you know what he means; many people in town have lived here their whole lives." She pushes the heavy door to the building open, and we head inside.

The small entry alcove has a desk to one side and opens to a larger room behind it. A hallway leads off to the right behind the desk.

My head swings around, trying to take in the massive amounts of knotty pine. Paneling. Beams. Even the damn desk is made of it.

"Well. This is ... rustic," I mumble, following Mia into the larger room. Long tables are arranged against the walls. And then my eyes land on a bent figure in the corner. And the spectacular ass pointed in my direction.

"Hey, Greg," Nate calls toward the ass. I mean, the guy. Because there is obviously a guy attached to that splendid backside. A fact that becomes startlingly clear when he rises and turns toward me. Because the guy is just as spectacular as the ass.

At about Mia's height, short for a dude but perfect for my tiny self, he's all lean muscle, rugged five o'clock shadow, and full lips on a mountain man face. The face of a man who can rough it or rough you up in bed — in the best way possible, of course.

"Nate," he returns, heading over and slapping Nate on the shoulder in greeting. "Perfect timing. Know anything about rewiring wall heaters?"

Nate follows him over to the corner to work on his heater issue. And I turn to Mia, shooting her a meaningful look.

"Girl, you were holding out on me," I accuse her in a low voice.

Mia's brows scrunch together. "Greg? Really?" she whispers back.

I raise my eyebrows incredulously. "Yes, *Greg*," I snap back. "Holy hotness, Mia. What's his deal? Is he married?" I curse myself for being too tangled up in fantasies of that scruff scraping along the insides of my thighs to notice whether he was wearing a ring.

Mia shrugs. "Nope. He runs this place. He and Nate work out together a few times a week, and he also helps at the wellness center sometimes. He's a good guy. Quiet. I wouldn't have thought he was your type."

I huff a breath out of my nose. "Hot isn't my type? Yeah, okay, Mia."

A faint smile plays over Mia's lips. "I've got Nate. I don't even think about whether other guys are hot anymore. I mean … look at him." She sighs wistfully as she eyes her man. And it's not like I'm going to deny that the towering hunk of muscle matched with the brains of a former doctor isn't fucking hot. At least to myself. To my best friend about her fiancé? That's a no.

"Eh. You don't think about other guys; I don't think about guys who are taken." I shrug — such a lie. I'd totally do a threesome with them — just sex, of course. I'm not into polyamory by any means. Just a good time. But I know even suggesting anything like that would probably make Mia's head explode.

She graces me with a smirk that says she knows anyway. "Well, you'll see a lot of him while we're here. Just … don't break him, okay?"

I snort. "No promises."

And with a flip of my long, dark hair over my shoulder, I tug Mia toward the boys. Scratch that — men. Definitely men. So sayeth my tingling girlie parts.

"Greg, this is my friend, Joanie," Mia offers as we stop beside them. "She lives in Seattle but will join us for the festivities."

Greg's gaze turns to me, and his cornflower blue irises meet my ice blues. And I never knew it was possible to be jealous of the shade of a man's eyes.

"Nice to meet you," he says, offering a hand.

I slip mine into his, shaking it firmly. He's noticeably surprised.

"Joanie is a lawyer too," Mia offers as if in explanation. I'm a little surprised at the "too" since she's not technically a lawyer now that she's given that life up to run a bakery in the middle of nowhere. But that's neither here nor there.

I look back at Greg to find an "aha" look on his face, and I fight the urge to roll my eyes. Yes, tiny girls can have firm handshakes — and law degrees.

"Well, that's impressive," Greg says with a smile that may have just melted my panties off.

I can't tell if he's sincere, so I smile sweetly. "Thank you. And it's nice to meet you too, Greg," I say, pointedly giving Mia the stink eye. But then, if he's the kind of guy who is easily intimidated by a strong, intelligent woman, I guess I wouldn't be interested anyway.

"Feel free to put us both to work," Mia offers with a nod in my direction. "I know there's a lot to do before the festival opens next week."

Greg smiles that devastating smile again. "Be careful; I may just take you up on that. It's a lot of dirty work."

I purse my lips. "Well, good thing I'm always up for getting dirty," I reply in as suggestive a tone as I can manage. And in case he doesn't get it, I wink at him for good measure.

Greg looks mildly shocked, and I can't help grinning. Nate shakes his head and laughs, and Mia rolls her eyes. "And that's why you're on the naughty list, Jo," Mia says.

My grin grows to Cheshire-cat proportions, and Nate facepalms. He walks past Mia and mumbles just lowly enough for only Mia and me to hear, "Well, if he wasn't interested before, he is now."

Hours later, I'm fluffing a fake, silvery Christmas tree in the entry alcove when Greg finally approaches me. Mia has been doing her best to keep me decorating so I wouldn't have time to pounce on him immediately. The joke's on her because I always give them a few hours minimum to get a look at the goods first. And I've caught him checking out my ass more than a couple of times this afternoon.

"You're a pro at that," he says, leaning against the knotty pine desk. Once again checking out my ass.

I turn and bat my eyelashes at him. "I'm a woman of many talents," I assure him.

He laughs, and his dimpled grin sets Bev aflutter. Yes, Bev. My beaver. My lady parts. What? Guys name their dicks, so I figured I should name my pussy.

"I'll just bet you are," he murmurs, his eyes sweeping over my frame. "So, how are you liking Alpine Ridge, Joanie?"

I step off the stool I'd been standing on and turn toward him. "It's fine," I reply succinctly. "But let's just cut to the chase, shall we?"

He raises an eyebrow, looking intrigued.

"I do like a good chase," he responds in a low voice.

I bite into my bottom lip to keep from grinning too widely. Now we're talking.

"Mmm," I murmur noncommittally, reaching up and running my hand down his chest — and holy shit. The muscle tone I feel under his dark plaid work shirt is no joke. "But the catching part is much more fun, isn't it?" I look up at him from under my eyelashes, giving him a coy smile.

He chuckles, low and deep. Damn, I just want to eat this man for Christmas dinner. Yum.

"It can be," he allows. "But —" he leans in, his hot breath tickling the shell of my ear "— anticipation can be pretty fucking hot too." His nose grazes my lobe, sending tingles shivering down my entire left side. He straightens up and, with a wink, is gone.

I'd turn to watch his ass as he walks away, but I find that I've lost control of myself. My whole body has turned to Jell-O from the husky, dirty promise in his words.

Well, this vacation just took a turn for the better.

I'm pulled from dreams of all the ways I want Greg's wicked tongue teasing me by something big and soft landing on my head. I blink my eyes open against the light shining through a crack in the guest bedroom's door to find half of my head covered by a pillow.

"Good morning, sunshine," Mia calls from the doorway.

I pull myself into a sitting position. "I knew I should've stayed at the B&B," I grumble. But it used to be Mia's Gran's house, and now that she's gone, that would be a different type of torture. So pillows in the head at an ungodly hour it is.

Mia laughs. "And that's why I threw the pillow from

here. So pleasant in the morning, aren't you?" she asks wryly.

"What the fuck time is it?" I ask, scrabbling for my phone on the nightstand.

"It's almost six. Normally, I'd have been at the bakery for hours by now, but I let you sleep in." Mia strides into the room and sets something down on the nightstand in the spot just vacated by my phone.

Notes of coffee and hazelnut hit my nose, and I inhale deeply. "Your offering of caffeine is accepted. But baked goods better be next."

"Don't worry. Rae and Penny are at the bakery, so I'm sure there are fresh donuts by now. Up."

I mock grumble as I get out of bed, and she leaves, but she had me at hazelnut-flavored coffee. Though there isn't much I wouldn't do for fresh donuts, too.

When I make it downstairs, it's to a shirtless Nate fondling my best friend in the kitchen. Said best friend's tongue looks like it's getting very familiar with his tonsils.

"You two are disgustingly cute," I grumble.

Nate tries to pull away, but Mia won't let him, flipping me off while she finishes mauling her man. When she finally pulls away, I get one of the rare glimpses I've had of Nate's torso, and I can't say I blame her for being hot for him even after a year and a half of coupledom. The man has the definition *and* the bulk. Plus, he has a penchant for grey sweatpants that leave nothing to the imagination about the ginormous dick he's packing. On top of already knowing — only from prying it out of Mia — that he's a beast in the sack and that he adores her, I have to admit she's hit the jackpot. You know, if committing yourself to one dick for the rest of your life is your thing. The jury's still out for me. It'd have to be one spectacular dick.

"So, what's on the agenda besides eating my weight in baked goods?" I ask as I drain my coffee mug and set it in the sink.

"Well, after we get a head start on macarons, cookies, and pies, we're going to help Rae bottle her wine and cider," Mia responds.

Nate makes to walk past me out of the room. "What about you, muscles?" I ask, poking him in his ridonculous bicep. "Are you baking with us babes?"

"Nope. I'm helping Greg set up the snowshoe obstacle course." And with that, he leaves the room, presumably to find a shirt and pants that'll keep that lovely dick from freezing off.

"All right, let's do this thing," I say resignedly.

Mia's eyes flick to the door.

"Don't worry, we'll be bringing the guys lunch later," she says with a smirk, her eyes flicking back to mine. "It won't be all girl time."

I don't even try to pretend like I'm not relieved while we pack up and head out. Because hanging with the ladies is great and all, but Bev is as hungry for cock as I am for donuts right about now.

CHAPTER TWO

GREG

Nate groans as we lay the last humongous tire in place for the final leg of the obstacle course in the field behind the community center.

"All right there, old man?" I joke as we straighten up.

He shoots me a look. "Just ready for lunch." He jerks his chin toward something over my shoulder, and I look back to see an SUV that's appeared next to his truck in the parking lot back by the building. "Looks like the girls are here."

I nod casually, trying not to show too much interest. Because I think I may have overplayed my hand with that Joanie chick already. But fuck if she isn't hot. And I'm not just talking about the body I couldn't stop staring at to save my life. It was how *forward* she was that threw me for a loop. I've never found that attractive before. But with Joanie … well, it was *such* a turn-on that I'm afraid some long unused parts of me took over my brain. But this time, I'm determined to play it cool until I figure out if going after her would be a good thing or a bad thing.

After all, we are on my territory, so if things go south, that'd be hard to escape, especially since I don't know how long she'll be around. There's a reason I don't date girls in town. I like it here, and small-town plus breakup equals bad news for everyone, including Joanie's Alpine Ridge resident best friend. The last thing I want to do is create friction between Mia and me because of a hookup with her best friend that has gone wrong. Something that didn't occur to me until after my dick ran my mouth when we met.

Bringing myself back to the present, I focus on keeping calm as we trudge back through the deep snow, though it's just far enough to keep the sweat coming under my thick jacket and gloves … yeah, the nervous excitement has nothing to do with it. That's what I'm telling myself, though I know it's bullshit.

When we get to the building, we knock the snow and mud off our boots and pants before heading indoors. It's nice and toasty inside, but as I strip off my jacket, gloves, and hat, goosebumps spread over my skin.

At first, I think it's just the air hitting my sweat-soaked T-shirt, but then my eyes flick up and meet Joanie's ice-blue stare. Just like the first time, I feel her sharp gaze X-raying me. I can't help the grin that pulls at my lips. I swear my body has a fucking mind of its own when it comes to this chick. Because it's sure as hell not listening to my decision to stay cool around her.

Now done stripping out of his snow gear, Nate doesn't

seem bothered by his sweaty shirt. Or the sexual tension that's suddenly thickened the air. He starts heading toward the girls but gives me a look when I don't follow.

I only see it out of my periphery as I don't actually look at him, unable to look away from Joanie despite my determination to be cool. "I'm going to change my shirt in the office," I say in Nate's direction. It takes all my willpower to tear my gaze away and head down the hallway.

I half hope she'll follow, then kick myself at the thought. That definitely wouldn't be feeling her out first. Well, there'd be feeling something, but ... I mentally slap myself as my mind starts to picture feeling Joanie up. Jesus fucking Christ.

Changing my shirt cools me down but does nothing for the thoughts racing through my head. So, when I return to the room, keeping my eyes to myself is way more difficult than it should be. I look only long enough to notice Mia and Nate seated on one side of the table, with Joanie standing near Mia, chatting.

Food, Greg. Focus on the food. You're hungry, right? As my eyes settle on the spread of sandwiches, sides, and desserts, it does help divert my focus a little as my stomach rumbles in anticipation. Between the meatball subs dripping with marinara and melted cheese and the array of clearly fresh-baked sweets, it smells fantastic in here. Way better than stale air and sweat, which is what it usually smells like.

But my focus is abruptly broken since I'd been

standing there admiring the food a hair too long as Joanie saunters between me and the table. Her tight little ass nearly grazes the front of my jeans as she picks up a plate and starts loading it with sweets before settling in one of the chairs on the other side of the table.

"You know, I made meatball subs just for you," Mia grumbles to her friend.

Joanie pops a jam tart in her mouth and grins around it. "Sorry," she mumbles, making an exaggerated yum face. Except it looks pretty much like an O face, so there goes my determination to focus on the food. Though, I may still be drooling, for different reasons now. Not helped at all by Joanie licking her lips and blowing me a kiss.

The little vixen knows exactly what she's doing.

I smirk and shake my head at her, grabbing a plate for myself and loading it up with a bit of everything before sitting down in the chair next to her, across from Nate.

Food.

Focus. On. The. Fucking. Food.

"I'm on vacation. I'm allowed to eat dessert first," Joanie declares.

I look over at her without thought, and her eyes move from Mia to meet mine. I hold her gaze as I continue eating. She grins.

"And you did just lose your job. If I were you, I'd eat whatever I wanted, too," Nate agrees. My eyes flick over to him. She just lost her job? Well, that's interesting. Then he adds with a thoughtful face, "Actually, I'm pretty sure that's exactly what I did when I moved here after quitting my job." He looks at Joanie with concern. "Just ... uh ... don't do it for as long as I did."

Joanie laughs. "What, did your body fat get above ten percent for the first time, hot stuff?" she teases.

Nate blushes, and I hold back a laugh. He was a little softer around the middle back then. Like she heard my thoughts, Joanie's attention shifts back to me.

"So, Greg," she says, leaning toward me and wrapping her lips around a cookie. I watch, mesmerized as she licks the crumbs off her lips before continuing. "Tell me all about your mountain man life. Lots of chopping down trees? Skinning animals to sell their fur? Swimming naked in remote lakes?" She bats her eyelashes.

I set down the sub I was working on and wipe my mouth, trying to hold back the smirk. "Yeah, exactly," I reply. "Just like I'm sure you spent your days lying to defend remorseless criminals and getting paid exorbitant amounts of money to play the justice system." I meant to point out that she was applying ridiculous stereotypes to me, just like I'm sure people do to her. But as soon as the words are out of my mouth, I realize they may have come off as harsh and judgmental.

To my surprise, she grins and points her fork at me. "That is actually pretty accurate." Then she takes a bite of the cheesecake on her plate, licking the fork clean. Of course. My eyes track the movement despite trying to pry them away. If she wants to turn me on ... well, I'd be lying if I said it wasn't working. Honestly, I'm just relieved I didn't offend her.

"All right then," I concede. "No, I don't skin animals to sell their fur." I raise an eyebrow, then add with a shrug, "But the rest?" I smirk, leaving her to imagine me chopping down trees and swimming naked in remote lakes.

Just by the look on her face, I know she is. Just like I was imagining feeling up those perky little tits earlier. I shift in my seat, trying to give my dick some relief from the pressure it's suddenly under.

"Well," she says, a bit breathlessly. "I hope tree chopping and naked swimming are part of this whole winter festival crap. Because if they are, I may be warming up to the idea."

Before I can peel an acceptable response from the dirty ones floating through my brain, Mia offers, "There is the Freeze Your Buns Run." I suspect she's mostly just trying to move on from talk of naked swimming. I should be grateful. It's not a great time of year for that. But if it was *Joanie* swimming naked … I shake myself. You'd think I was eighteen again instead of thirty-eight with all these horny little fantasies.

"Oh?" Joanie asks with interest. "Does that require nudity as well?"

I almost choke on a chip. This woman is going to be the death of me. I cough and take a swig of beer before answering her. "Almost, but not quite. It's an undies run. In the snow." I decide to screw with her just a little to get back at her, so I wink at her. "Think you can handle that, city girl?"

She gives me a challenging look. "I can, if you can,

mountain man." She lifts her chin, pink staining her cheeks, presumably in embarrassment at the rhyme.

Nate busts up laughing, but I try my hardest not to since a laugh at her expense seems like a bad idea. Mia looks at Joanie sympathetically, and suddenly, Joanie laughs, too. Relieved, I stop holding back my laughter.

"Good," I respond. "Because it's next weekend. Better start practicing." I finish my food, drink what's left of my beer, and then give her a wink.

She raises a brow in answer. "Better ease up on the meatball subs and beer if you want to be light enough on your feet to beat me."

I raise a brow in return, leaning back and lifting my shirt, patting my flat stomach. "Oh, I think I'll be fine."

I don't miss for one second the hungry look in her eyes as she looks at my abs. So, when her gaze rises to meet mine, I give her another wink. She purses her lips. And though I wasn't lying to her before — I usually like the chase — the anticipation is already killing me.

I don't catch more than a few glimpses of Joanie throughout the week. I'm busy organizing the Freeze Your Buns Run, checking the ice-skating pond, and building a platform for the musicians playing Christmas music for the tree lighting ceremony and other events throughout the festival. Nate switches between helping me and going with the girls to post signs, managing decorating the tree, and carving paths in the snow between the events.

But Friday is tree lighting day. And I'm over letting the anticipation build. It's worse that Joanie hasn't been around, which is weird because usually, for me, out of sight is out of mind. But I can't stop thinking about her.

So as twilight descends, I do rounds of the town square, checking the strands of white lights strung between lamp posts, making sure Rae's cider stand is adequately covered from the elements, and watching as the townsfolk start to show, gazing up at the massive tree in anticipation.

It looks damn good, even unlit. The towering, fifty-foot monstrosity looms darkly in the square, light from the street lamps and Christmas lights glinting off the hundreds of massive baubles strung around its not inconsiderable girth. Staring up at the neat rows of decorations, nostalgia spreads through me. Alpine Ridge hasn't seen a winter festival in almost thirty years. It brings me back to simpler times.

I shake off the good and bad memories that start to push through. It's almost showtime. The crowd is now thick, and the line for hot cider winds around half the square.

I see Mia setting a tray of something down on Rae's table. And next to her is Joanie.

Since she's not looking at me, I take the opportunity to soak her in. Her tight-fitting fur-lined jacket and snug fleece pants cover her completely, yet she still looks like a wet dream. Sexy as fucking hell. Her dark hair spills around her, and her little bow lips are pursed and a natural peachy color. Her cheeks and nose are red from the cold. An urge to warm her up almost overwhelms me.

Still, I approach casually.

"Hey, city girl."

She turns, and I grin, self-consciously running a hand through my hair. Which I never do. It's that X-ray vision of hers, making me feel turned inside out.

Her brows bunch together, and she tips her head to the side, giving me a confused look.

"Oh, yeah, hey, Gary," she replies evenly.

The smile melts off my face, and I cock an eyebrow. "It's Greg," I correct her.

She gives me the fakest smile I think I've ever seen. "Ah, yes. Sorry, my mistake." She bats her eyelashes and returns to the booth, helping Mia and Rae serve drinks and cinnamon twists. "See you around, Gary."

Rae glances over at Joanie, bemused, just as my douchebag cousin, Ned, steps up to get a drink. And I know Ned. Even without the leering look he's giving Joanie, I knew he'd go straight for her the second I saw him. And he does.

He slicks back his inky hair, which looks like it's been dipped in cooking oil, and gives Joanie a sleazy grin as if she's this year's Christmas treat. "Hello there, beautiful." He sounds just as shady as he looks. And then he leans in and *winks* at her.

Oh, hell no.

But before I can intercede, Joanie does the exact last thing I'd expect, as always.

She leans toward him with an answering wink. "Well, hello," she says huskily. "Cider?"

He slaps a five on the table. "I don't know. Do I get a little sugar with that?"

My fists ball at my sides, but Joanie seems unfazed, throwing her head back and laughing. "I don't know, this might be too much sugar for you to handle, big boy," she teases with a coy smile. "But the cinnamon twists are good, too."

When I almost lose it at her response, it clicks — she's doing it all on purpose: pretending to forget me, calling me Gary, and flirting with Ned.

She's screwing with me.

"Oh, I can handle it. But maybe we can take this someplace more … private?" he asks, not even bothering to keep his voice down.

And that's it. That's my limit. Before I can stop myself, I close the distance and grab Joanie gently yet firmly by the elbow. But my glare is all for Ned.

"Get lost, Edweird," I grind out, using the nickname he earned when we were kids.

Thankfully, he's smart enough to look terrified and scamper away without a word, forgetting to take the food he paid for. I think I see a glint of amusement in Joanie's eyes as she watches him go, but her face is all indignation when she whirls on me.

"Excuse me, but we were talking," she says haughtily.

I snort and lead her by the elbow out of the booth toward the community center.

"I'm not stupid, Joanie."

My long strides have her scrambling to keep up as I pull her by the arm. I push open the heavy door and haul her inside. I'm all reaction now. Logic is out the window. I need to make a few things clear to her.

Darkness envelops us as the door closes behind us. With a flick of my wrist, I turn her and push her up against the back of the door, my arms caging her in.

"I never said you were," she finally replies. Even in the near darkness, I can see her outline, the stubborn set of her jaw, the tension in her body. My head dips down as my eyes take her in. "But I'm also not your property, and I don't appreciate being dragged in here like I am."

"If you think I was going to let my piece of shit cousin lay one disgusting finger on you —"

"That guy is your cousin?" she barks out with a laugh.

"Yes," I reply. "And whatever angle you're working, don't work it with him."

As my eyes adjust to the dimness, our gazes lock. I see fire in her eyes.

"Let me go," she demands, pushing against my chest.

"Not until you admit you were flirting with him to get on my nerves. Just like you pretended to forget my name."

She rolls her eyes. "Someone has a big ego. Maybe I did just forget."

I lean in, my lips parting. "Doubtful. I bet if I fucked you hard against this door, you'd remember whose name to scream when you came all over my dick." The words shock even me. Not because they're not true; they most definitely are. But because I've never spoken to a woman like that. And because they came from such a primal place of need, I can feel them in every inch of my skin. Just as much as I want to own every inch of hers.

Joanie's eyes flash. "Maybe you should —"

But I don't get to hear what she thinks I should do. My mouth claims hers without any forethought. It's pure need on a level so deeply physical I have no control over it. My tongue invades her mouth. My body crushes hers against the doors. My hips press against her, making the erection I didn't even realize I had plain to us both.

And she kisses me back with an intensity that matches mine. Our breaths mingle as we gasp for air between each crush of our mouths, as the palpable heat and need build with every stroke of our tongues. She grinds against my cock, but the lust ruling my body isn't enough to stop me from making her work for it just a little more.

I pull my mouth from hers, keeping her pinned with my hips, my forehead pressed against hers.

"Say my name, Joanie," I demand.

She bites into her lip to suppress a grin. "Gar —"

I growl and twist my hips in an attempt to crush her defiance with my need for her. Her teeth sink deeper into her bottom lip, but her gaze is insolent.

"Say it, city girl," I prompt huskily, more softly this time.

"Make me scream it," she counters. "Like you promised, mountain man."

My balls tighten in answer, and I open my mouth to spew all the filthy things I want to do to her that will make us both scream, but I'm stopped by an attempted shove at

MELANIE A. SMITH

the other side of the door that rattles us both, physically and otherwise.

"What the hell?" Nate's voice comes through the door, muffled.

I pull Joanie into the room, dropping my arms to my sides as the door opens and Nate and Mia appear, framed in light from the nearly full moon and the faint lights around the square behind them.

An awkward silence descends for a few very long moments.

"Uh, it's almost time for the ceremony," Nate finally offers.

I nod and brush past Joanie. "We were just heading out."

Nate snorts. "Sure you were."

I shoulder-check him with a smirk but say nothing as we look back at the girls expectantly.

Mia looks at Joanie, also saying nothing. Well, not with words, anyway. Her knowing look, however, speaks volumes.

"What?" Joanie asks innocently, looping her arm through Mia's.

Mia shakes her head and laughs. "Nothing. Never mind."

Nate and I let the ladies walk out ahead of us, arm in arm. As I make to follow, Nate stops me with a hand on the chest and gives me a hard look.

"Watch yourself with that one," he warns me.

My insides tighten for a different reason this time. It

26

doesn't take me but an instant to recognize the feeling: fear.

"What do you mean?" I ask, playing dumb.

He glances furtively towards the girls. "I know she's Mia's best friend, and I don't want to say anything bad about her. She's just —"

"Nate?" Mia calls, looking back. "Come on, you're going to miss it!"

His eyes dart back to me guiltily. "Never mind, let's just go."

This time, I'm the one to stop him with a hand to the chest. "Short version then," I insist.

"Short version?" he parrots with a sigh. "What's the female version of a player?"

I snort. "You're worried she's going to play me?"

He shrugs. "From what you've told me, you're a relationship kind of guy. I just didn't want you to expect that from her."

I shake my head and laugh. "I mean, sure, I've had a couple of long-term relationships," I allow. "But it's not like I've never had hookups, dude. And here I was worried that she was clingy or crazy."

Nate huffs a laugh. "Clingy? I don't think so. Crazy? Well … if you're okay with kink, probably not in a way that's a deal breaker."

Well, shit, that's got my attention. "I appreciate your looking out for me, man, but you told me what I wanted to know about her."

Nate nods knowingly. "Just … suit up, all right, man? Be safe and all that."

That gets a full belly laugh out of me. "All right, pops," I tease him with a wink. I like to rib him like he's an old man, even though he's only five or six years older than me. But right now, I'm in a pretty good fucking mood. He's acting like a concerned older brother, and I dig that. But what I dig more is that Joanie may be exactly what I've been looking for.

CHAPTER THREE

JOANIE

Unfortunately, there were no screaming orgasms to be had Friday night after the tree-lighting ceremony. Lots of cider? Yes. Eating my weight in cinnamon twists that must have been laced with crack, they were so addictive? Absolutely. But the rest of the night was exactly as Hallmark as I'd pegged this whole event to be. Listening to a quartet that played holiday music. Oohing and aahing over the pretty tree.

Okay, to be fair, the tree was stunning. Then again, I helped decorate it, so naturally, it was beautiful. But at the end of the night, there were no advances. No invitations. And it all broke up so quickly that I didn't have time to make my own before I was in Nate's truck, heading back up the mountain to Mia and Nate's glass palace in the trees.

So, lying in bed on Saturday morning, I decide that today will be different. Starting with a self-provided orgasm. All I have to do is remember how Greg pushed me up against that door, how his woodsy scent alone had me wet. Then there was the kiss. Shit, that was a fantastic kiss. I rub circles over my clit as I think of it. My back arches remembering his taste. How hard his cock was against my stomach. What it might look like. What it might feel like to lick around the crown while he watched, those bright blue eyes challenging me to take it all. The thought starts the low tingle in my core. I remember his breath against my ear as he demanded I say his name. The tingling spreads, and my nipples peak beneath my nightshirt. A few more swirls and presses, and I let myself remember his promise to fuck me against the door until I screamed his name while coming … and then I am. I keep quiet, which intensifies the orgasm, until I slump back down onto the mattress, only partially satisfied.

I try not to think of Nate and Mia in the bedroom upstairs, who I can hear frequently getting much more fully satisfied. I may have even used it as fuel for my own satisfaction once or twice. They do it constantly; I may as well reap the benefits of their ridiculously hot soundtrack. But now? Thoughts of my mountain man are all I need. Gary the Mountain Man. The thought makes me giggle. I really *do* belong on the naughty list.

Once Mia returns from the bakery, we have lunch and head out to the snowshoe obstacle course competition that afternoon. There was fresh snow last night, so the whole town is glistening prettily. And I must admit that small though the town is, it's undeniably beautiful.

As we park near the community center and walk around the building, I notice the ice-skating pond as we head toward the obstacle course. With the rustic building as a backdrop, the whole thing has a very Thomas Kinkade feel.

A feeling that doesn't stop there, permeating practically every corner of the untouched drifts of snow covering every flat space. Well, except for the obstacle course, which looks like it has been dutifully re-dug out of the fresh piles of snow. Greg's work, no doubt. Too bad I wasn't around to watch him. That would've been excellent foreplay.

A staked rope separates the shoveled walkway from the course itself. I can see a crowd gathered at the far end, presumably waiting to start. As we walk the length of the field, the "obstacles" get increasingly weird. The first thing I notice is a group of massive, mismatched tires. All right then. That seems like it would belong on an obstacle course. Then there are a bunch of lengths of rope that I quickly figure out are jump ropes. Normally, I could see that. But in snowshoes? How the hell do they expect people to do that? Since I'm not participating, though, it doesn't worry me. But the bunch of sleds packed with outrageously dressed snowmen gets my attention. The punk rocker snowman with a mohawk, pierced carrot nose, and earphones is good. The police officer snowman with a donut in one hand and a Starbucks cup in the other is pretty funny — because, really, is there even a

Starbucks within an hour of here? But it's the snowman dressed in a Hawaiian shirt, lei, sunglasses, and strapped to what looks like a small surfboard that makes me stop in my tracks.

I pull on Mia's arm, stopping her with me as Nate continues toward Greg, who is standing on the other side of the sleds, presumably at the starting line as the crowd is gathered behind him.

"What?" she asks, giving me a curious look.

I gesture with my chin toward the surfer snowman. "Is that a coincidence, or did you tell Greg about Hawaii?" I ask plainly.

Mia's brows bunch together before a look of horrified understanding crosses her face. "Oh God, no, I didn't," she rushes to reassure me. "I swear I didn't say a word."

"Say a word about what?" Nate asks, appearing behind Mia.

I make to brush it off, but my eyes flick guiltily to the snowman. Nate follows my gaze, then looks back at me with a smirk.

Figures he'd know.

Greg steps up next to Nate.

"Something wrong?" he asks.

The smirk slides off Nate's face, and he claps Greg on the shoulder. "Nope. Are we ready to do this?"

I breathe a sigh of relief at Nate's discretion, and Mia gives me a funny look. I try not to give her a guilty one back. For some reason, I don't want Greg to know about my surfer ménage. When did I start giving a shit what anyone thinks of me? The thought is like a poke on the shoulder that there's something I need to acknowledge here. Instead, I brush it off and follow the guys toward the waiting crowd.

Greg quiets everyone down and explains the drill: The eighteen people signed up will go in six groups of three. Each person must pull a snowman-laden sled — which he assures them are very heavy — from the start to the jump ropes fifty feet away, jump rope ten times, high step through the tires, and sprint approximately two hundred feet to the finish. Nothing *too* crazy, but eyeing the assembled crowd's varying ages and general apparent lack of fitness, that's probably for the best.

Greg explains that the winners of the first three groups will face off, and then the same with the second. The two finalists will then compete to determine the winner.

Greg positions himself at the start, and Nate heads down the field and stands between the ropes and the tires.

"Mia, can you man the finish line?" Greg asks.

"I think you mean *woman* the finish line," I cut in.

The corner of Greg's mouth tips up, but before he can respond, Mia shakes her head and says, "Sorry, can't. I have to meet Rae inside to set up the food for after." She turns to me. "Looks like it's up to you, *woman*." She gives me a wink and walks away, not even waiting for a response.

Greg smiles at me so wide his eyes crinkle at the corners. "You up for it, city girl?"

I contemplate him coolly for a moment. "What the hell, why not?" I reply.

He steps toward me and leans in, his mouth brushing

my earlobe, sending chills down the entire side of my body. "There are two red flags that mark the finish line. Just make sure they're still visible over the snow so you can see who crosses first." He straightens up and walks backward the few feet to the green starting flags.

Refusing to let him see how much he affects me, I head to the opposite end of the field purposefully but without rushing like I'm trying to escape the fact that I'd rather stay there and let him whisper all sorts of other, dirtier, things in my ear.

It's not long before Greg has lined up the first set, and they begin. Right out of the gate, they all struggle with the sleds. I almost laugh, realizing that must mean they formed the snowmen with rocks or something equally heavy because even the biggest dude in the bunch is red and straining the whole way. Alas, that's the funniest part of the course, as the jump ropes, tires, and sprint are all boring to watch. Even in snowshoes, it all looks almost too easy.

And I quickly start to get cold. Thankfully, Mia comes out with a travel mug after the first three batches.

"Thought you might need this," she says, offering me the cup as we watch the next set line up.

"I hope it has booze. Because this will be much more fun if it does," I grumble.

She wraps an arm around me and rubs my shoulder. "Nope. But don't worry, there will be booze later."

I take a deep drink. It's just cocoa. But I'm cold, and it tastes good, so I don't complain. "There better be." I watch as the latest group starts to hit the jump ropes.

"Aren't Nate and Greg going to do this? *That* might be fun to watch. Especially if they did it shirtless." The thought perks me up, and I smile into my mug.

"I'm sure they've already done it to test everything, but Nate said it wouldn't be fair if they competed," she replies with a shrug.

I let out a shriek of laughter as the first competitor of the bunch — a much older man — *trips* the second guy, who is half his age, to get into the tires first. But Nate is right. I haven't seen a single participant who could compete with either him or Greg.

It's not long before the old man is barreling toward me, and Mia takes that as her cue to leave. I try to pay more attention to the race than my cocoa. It's tough. The cocoa is much more interesting, even without the booze.

What feels like a lifetime later, the older man is crowned the overall winner — since all the dirty tricks he pulled to get there somehow weren't against the rules — and is awarded his gift basket, which was no doubt put together by Mia or Rae as it's stuffed with bottled cider, baked goodies, and what appear to be a few gift certificates. Once that's done, the crowd starts to disperse.

Greg starts to head toward Nate, but Nate shouts something, and Greg returns to the starting line. Nate jogs toward me until he's close enough to shout, "We're racing."

I throw up my hands in a gesture of "whatever." And I

may be cold and tired, but I'm lying; I'm not "whatever" about watching these two go at it. I glance guiltily back toward the community center behind me, wondering if I'm betraying Mia by even thinking of ogling her fiancé. But fuck that. I've earned a little show after two-plus hours out here.

As they start, I only wish they were closer. Because while I can see them pulling the sleds, I'm not close enough to see any muscles rippling. It's a travesty. But the jump roping, I can see. Except that they're both so fucking good at it that it's over in *seconds*. And then they're playfully shoving each other as they jockey for position ahead of the tires. Nate wins by sheer bulk and goes barreling through them, with Greg not far behind. But Nate's bulk works against him as Greg emerges from the tires, hot on his heels and much lighter and faster across the snow. While it took the fastest of the earlier competitors a good thirty seconds to cross the distance, I have less than half that before I realize Greg is about to run right into me.

I step out of the way just in time to yell angrily at his passing back, "Watch where you're going!"

He slows to a jog as Nate streaks by me, then slows with him. Laughing, he pats Nate on the back. "Good try, old man."

Nate shakes his head. "At least I can still outlift you." Nate removes the snowshoes and hands them to Greg before heading toward the community center.

I make to follow, but Greg catches my arm.

"Nuh-uh," he protests, still breathing heavily and

holding the snowshoes up. "Let's see what you've got, city girl."

"Oh please, those would never fit me," I scoff.

Yeah. Because that's what's stopping me.

"I've got ones that'll fit you at the starting line," he promises with a sly grin.

I cross my arms over my chest. "I'm freezing. I've been standing out here all afternoon. There's no way I'm doing an obstacle course after that."

He smirks. "You're just afraid I'll kick your ass."

My competitive side yearns to shove his smug mug into a pile of snow. "Of course you'll kick my ass. You're way stronger than I am. Not that I've tried myself, but I just watched a bunch of grown men struggle to pull those sleds. It'd take me as long to move one ten feet as it would for you to do the whole course."

"Then we'll start at the jump ropes," he says with a shrug. "Come on. It'll warm you up."

I shift nervously. I hate admitting I can't do something, especially to a hot guy. But I'm not sure I have a choice.

"I've never worn snowshoes," I confess, looking away from him pointedly.

Greg tips his head back and laughs. I scrunch my face at his enjoyment of my discomfort, but he steps toward me, slipping a gloved hand under my chin and forcing me to look at him.

"Then let me help you. We'll just do it for fun. Promise." He smiles winningly, and it's hard to say no.

I roll my eyes. "Yeah, sounds like a blast." But

secretly, I can't help thinking that for someone with serious alpha male vibes, he's awfully considerate.

He steps forward, his thick jacket now touching mine. Just close enough to command my full attention. "When's the last time you did something out of your comfort zone?"

I keep my face a mask, unwilling to smirk at that question and give any indication that I have no problem being out of my comfort zone.

But then I realize that that's only true sexually. When *was* the last time I did something non-sexual that pushed my limits?

"What do I get if I do?" I ask, just to push back a little.

"How about a kiss?" he teases.

"How about an orgasm?" I counter.

His answering laugh warms the air between us and is so rich and full that I have to smile in return.

"Do I get one too?" he asks teasingly.

I bite into my lip. "I think that can be arranged."

His grin mellows into a small, sexy smile. "Let's just start with a kiss, and we'll see where things go from there, shall we?" He sees the protest forming on my lips because he throws up a hand. "I'm not saying no orgasms. Just trust me. You won't walk away from this unhappy, I promise."

His warm eyes search mine, and while I'd normally balk at not being in control, he's hard to say no to.

"Okay." It slips out more easily than I'd have expected.

So, I let him lead me down the field. I let him pick a

pair of snowshoes and help me into them. I follow him to the jump ropes. And he counts us down.

The rest is pure comedy. I stumble through it like … well, like a lawyer in snowshoes. I'm as awful at it as I feared I would be, and it's way harder than Greg, Nate, and the others made it look. Then again, living in the snowy Cascades, they all probably use snowshoes regularly.

Still, by the time we reach the finish line, we're both laughing uncontrollably, holding on to each other to remain upright. I tip onto my bottom right at the finish line, and he flops beside me.

Only then do I notice that the afternoon has faded into evening. The sun is setting over the mountains, with bright oranges blending toward the deep pink of the horizon, and it's beautiful.

I groan and flop backward, tired but much warmer, as he'd promised.

"What? What's wrong?"

I put my cold, gloved hands to my face. "I've become the Hallmark movie," I moan.

Greg laughs and rolls on top of me, prying my hands away from my face. "If it makes you feel better, I'm having some very un-Hallmark thoughts right now," he says huskily.

I wriggle my hips under him. "Go on."

He grins and touches his lips lightly to mine, making good on his promise. But it's only light at first. Then, like before, he devastates me with his mouth, his teeth pulling at the sensitive skin of my lower lip, followed by his tongue pushing its way between my lips.

A groan breaks through our kiss, and I'm so gone I'm not sure which one of us it came from until Greg says, "God, I can't wait until you make that noise because I'm between your legs."

I arch against him, and his mouth drops to my neck. "With your mouth or your dick?" I ask.

His teeth graze my skin, and his hips dig against me. In any other circumstances, I'd wish I wasn't wearing snow pants so I could feel him.

"With my dick," he promises against my skin. "As much as I want to taste you, I want to fuck you more."

"Then do it," I beg, not really wanting that to happen right here, right now. But I wouldn't say no to the closest warm, dry spot.

His mouth covers mine in a searing kiss that's interrupted by Mia calling from the building behind us.

"I know you guys aren't going to fuck in the snow, so you might as well come in and have dinner," she taunts.

Greg buries his laugh in my neck before he shoves himself off me and stands, offering me a hand. "To be continued," he promises.

I narrow my eyes and take his hand. "Soon?"

He grins. "Very soon."

CHAPTER FOUR

GREG

It takes everything I've got to walk away from Joanie on Saturday night. Am I an asshole because "soon" wasn't that same night? Maybe. But something is telling me to wait. To make *her* wait. That it'll be worth it. And frankly, I'm kind of just enjoying her company.

Nate texts me that morning to let me know he and the girls will be at the skating pond after breakfast. I'm not sure what to make of him informing me of their whereabouts after his warning me off Mia's best friend, but I'll take the help.

I finish off a steaming mug of black coffee as I stare down my snowy driveway, and anxiety settles over me. Not because of skating. That part I'm looking forward to. It's what comes after that.

Yakima. The Tyler clan. And my holiday visit-slash-annual report-in with my parents. Where I get to tell them all about what's happening in Alpine Ridge, and they get to tell me how I'm wasting my life staying here. Good times.

As I throw my suitcase in the backseat of my truck and head out, I realize "soon" will probably have to wait even more. I can't fuck and run with Joanie. Something tells me that I won't want to stop for a while once we start. And I will seriously need my head in the game to survive this week.

I park in my usual spot at the community center, though a few other vehicles dot the small parking lot on the skating pond side of the building, Nate's truck included. I go inside the building and grab my skates from the office.

As I head to the pond, the cold air does a much better job waking me up than the coffee, and I can hear laughter floating in the air. It breaks through the gloomy cloud hanging over my head, and as I get close, I can see that besides Nate and the girls, there isn't anyone else out at the pond yet. It's still early, I guess.

As I get closer, I can see Mia and Joanie spinning in circles, their hands clasped between them as they whirl around, heads tipped back while they laugh. The innocent joy on their faces is something to behold. It probably explains why Nate is stopped, watching them with a grin. Something like I'm doing right now.

I watch the girls break apart, Mia tumbling onto the ice with her momentum, still laughing, while Joanie catapults herself in a wide, graceful arc. She turns, then executes a perfect toe loop jump. And then, with confidence radiating out of her, she follows it with a *double*-toe loop jump.

I grin widely and advance to the pond's edge while clapping, and she skids to a stop, startled at the sight of me.

"Where'd you learn to skate like that?" I say by way of greeting, sitting on one of the nearby benches as I change into my skates.

She glides across the ice and hobbles over the small strip of snowy grass to settle beside me.

"I've had lessons since I was six," she explains, crossing her legs toward me. "So, I'm not shit at *all* winter sports."

I lace up with a smirk. "Just snowshoeing, then?"

She narrows her eyes. "We can't all be good at everything. Surely there's something *you're* bad at."

I finish lacing the other skate, stand, and extend my hand. "I'm sure there is," I agree. She takes my hand and lets me lead her onto the ice. I drop her hand and skate a quick, tight circle around her. "I'll let you know when I figure out what that is."

She rolls her eyes, and I skate away backward, saying hi to Nate as I pass him. Mia rolls her eyes as I glide by her, causing my grin to widen. Okay, so maybe I'm showing off a bit too much. I turn and stop right in front of Joanie.

"Cute," she says. "But can you do any jumps?"

"No," I admit. "I played hockey for years. I can skate, and I can handle a stick."

"I'm not even going to rise to that bait, mountain man," she says with a tilt of her eyebrow.

I tip my head back and laugh. "Then how about a spin around the ice instead?" I offer, holding out my gloved hand once more.

She takes it and lets me lead her around the pond. We do a few laps in perfect, silent sync, and I can't help spinning her into a twirl as we go for our third lap. She laughs as we disconnect and then spins out, using the momentum to execute a loop jump.

I resist teasing her for being a showoff. I'm not exactly one to talk, especially around her. I can't help it; something about this girl makes me want to impress her.

I notice that Nate and Mia have stepped off the skating pond and are putting on their boots.

"Where are you lovebirds off to?" I ask, skating to a stop nearby.

"Oh, noticed we were still here, did you?" Mia replies.

Nate shakes his head with a smile. "We're going to go pick up some lunch. Want us to bring you anything back?"

"What, we're not invited?" I joke.

Nate looks at me and says quietly enough that Joanie, still showing off her skills on the ice, doesn't hear, "I figured we'd give you two some time alone."

"Ah." I nod. Nate knows I'm headed out this afternoon since he'll be covering for me this week at the festival. "Thanks, man."

Mia starts back toward the parking lot, and Nate nods in return. "We'll be back in an hour. Maybe more." He gives me a subtle wink as he follows his woman.

I watch them walk away, climb in the car, and drive off before I return to Joanie. Only to find she's at the bench across the pond, changing back into her boots.

"Going somewhere?" I call across the sheet of ice as I sit back down to change into my own boots.

She smirks and strolls around the edge until she stops before me.

"*We*," she stresses, "are going in there." She tips her head toward the community center. "I'm cold. Want to warm me up?" She looks at me seductively.

I smile at her, then rise, offering my hand again. She takes it, and I lead her through the snow toward the building.

"So, this is your main gig, huh?" she asks, gesturing around her. "Running this place?"

I raise an eyebrow. "The community center? Yeah, something like that."

She peers out over the pond as we make to round the corner. "There are worse jobs," she says, then flashes me a smile to let me know she's not being critical.

"Alpine Ridge growing on you, city girl?" I tease, also realizing I hope it is. I wouldn't mind if she visited more. But I'm getting ahead of myself, I know.

She shrugs, but I can tell it's feigned indifference. "It's all right. So, are you one of the famed locals? Born and raised here?"

I laugh. "God, no. Though my family has had property here for decades," I explain. "But I came back a few years ago and just kind of stuck around."

"Fell in love, huh?" she pokes. Not quite teasing, more … looking for information?

"Not just with the town. I have a lot of good memories of this place, and it's peaceful here," I explain freely. "No pressure. No expectations. I can just … *be* here. Do what I want when I want."

We get to the building, and I push the door open, holding it for her to walk through. I follow her in and let the heavy door close behind us. The sound of it shutting heralds the first time we've been completely alone in private, nobody waiting outside to bust in and bother us. At least not for a while yet.

"What did you do before?" she asks.

I lead her down the hall to the office, the only room with a comfortable seat for us both, while I contemplate how to answer her question without spilling my entire life story.

I open the door into the small room and gesture to the old, maroon loveseat under the window next to the small desk and bookshelves that fill the other side of the room.

She folds herself onto one half and drops her coat, hat, gloves, and skates to the side. I toss mine back in the pile on the other side of the desk before joining her on the couch.

"I was a middle school PE teacher in Ellensburg," I finally admit. "I was 'made redundant' and decided that was as good an excuse as any to focus on something else for a while."

"Did you like it?"

I'm a bit taken aback by her question. "I loved it,

actually. I've always had a passion for fitness, and it was great getting kids excited about it, too."

Joanie's expression softens. "That's sweet," she admits. Then she gives me a wicked smile. "God, I can't imagine if I'd had a PE teacher who looked like you. I bet all those little preteen girls *loved* you."

I chuckle. "Unfortunately, yes, that came with the territory."

"Unfortunately?" she asks shrewdly.

I gaze fixedly into her ice-blue, cutting eyes. I'll never get used to the effect they have on me. Like I want to tell her everything. I'm not sure if it comes with the law degree or if it's just *her*.

"I was dating another teacher. She didn't love it."

Joanie barks a sharp laugh. "Well, good that that's over then. What kind of woman is jealous of a bunch of twelve-year-olds?"

I hesitate, not wanting to badmouth my ex. Or even talk about her right now, not with Joanie.

"We were together a while. I don't think it was a big deal in and of itself, but when you have to deal with that day in and day out for years ..." I shrug.

"How many years?"

"Six." The word drops into the silence like a stone in a still pond. The ripples of emotion on her face come and go, and I give her a minute. "Not one for long-term relationships?"

She tips her head back and forth. "I guess I haven't met someone I wanted to be with for that long."

"How about someone you want to be with for right

now?" I tease, reaching out and running my thumb over her cheek.

She tilts her head into the touch, her long, dark hair spilling over her shoulder. Fuck if I don't want to run my hands through those waves. Gather them in my fist. Pull them hard while I take her from behind.

I shift as my dick rises at the thought. She misinterprets my shift as a move to kiss her, and her mouth meets mine.

Which I can't be mad about at all, as her soft lips open to me, and our tongues meet. I slide my hand to her neck, tilting her head so I can kiss her more deeply, my tongue exploring her mouth. She groans deep in her chest and then moves into my lap.

She straddles me as her face descends on mine, her teeth grazing my lip, the sensation traveling straight to my already too-hard dick. I lock my hands onto her waist, but she beats me to the next move, grinding her hips over mine, her core rubbing across my length through our jeans.

A groan escapes my lips, and she smiles down at me.

"You gonna show me that cock, mountain man? Make me scream with it?" she whispers, circling her hips over me. Electricity zaps down my spine, coiling in my balls. Fucking hell.

"All in good time," I promise, kissing her lightly on the lips. Deceptively. Because my next move is to upend her on her back, which I do in one quick movement, pinning her onto the couch with my hips between her thighs, my dick rubbing her warm center through our clothes. "But I bet I can make you come without ever whipping it out."

She bites into her bottom lip, but it doesn't stop the grin that breaks over her face. "How do you make *not* sticking your dick in me sound so good?" she asks breathily.

"You haven't heard anything yet," I promise, descending on her. I run my lips up her neck, sucking the place where it meets her shoulder, then up the sensitive column to drag my tongue along the shell of her ear. She shudders under me. "I'm going to lick and suck you all over until you're begging for more, city girl."

She nods and turns her head so the other side of her neck is exposed to me. I grin and kiss it gently while simultaneously reaching down and twisting one of her nipples mercilessly. She gasps in surprise and arches into me. I twist it again, and she moans. When I twist it a third time, I bite her neck and suck just as mercilessly. She bucks against me as the pleasure goes through her.

I growl against her skin, the need to dominate, take, pleasure, fuck, own tearing through my veins. I use both hands to squeeze her breasts while my tongue returns to plundering her mouth. She grabs at my ass, desperately grinding against me. I tilt my hips into her, relenting on everything else, letting her focus on the one sensation. I twist and roll circles around her wet heat until her eyes flutter closed, and she stills. Her brows pinch together, and her breathing accelerates. I'd be smug knowing how close I have her already, but the sight is going to make me nut in my undershorts if I'm not careful. So, I slow it down. And her eyes flutter open.

I run my hands down her chest, landing on her hips and pinning her as I lower my mouth to her. As I bite her nipple through her shirt. She fists a hand in my hair in approval. So, I move to the other. She nods and gasps. I move between her breasts slowly, repeating the process as I gradually start to flex my covered cock against her.

I increase my speed leisurely, moving my mouth from her breasts to her neck, then to her mouth, letting my hand tweak her nipple as I speed up. The combined assault has her so worked up that her body undulates to the rhythm I'm squeezing her nipple, which I match to the thrust of my tongue in her hot mouth, the tilt of my hard, denim-covered dick against her warm, damp core, until I can tell she's on the edge.

Drawing my mouth from hers, I lean up and knead both of her breasts with my full hands. Her eyes pop open and stare at me, glazed with lust.

"You like that?" I ask, tilting my hips into her.

She nods.

"Tell me," I push.

"I like it," she breathes. "I need more."

"Like this?" I push myself against her hard, and she groans and nods. I squeeze her nipples hard in tandem, drawing them upward as I push our fully clothed centers together. God, the friction is killing me. I'm not sure I won't come too. But that's not what this is about. "This is just a taste, city girl." I lean in, working her nipples harder, faster as I dry fuck her toward orgasm. "Just a

small preview. When I have the time to get you naked…"
I thrust hard, and one of her legs clamps around my
backside while the other shudders — a good sign. I hold
back my smug grin. "God, Joanie, I'm going to fuck you
so good. So fucking hard. For so long your pussy is going
to —"

"Oh shit, Greg, fuck, fuck, fuck," Joanie screams,
coming apart under me, her hands clamping on my
forearms.

I slow the tilt of my hips and the pressure on her
nipples as she comes down from her climax. I lean into
her, my mouth skating over hers, feeling her sharp, hot
bursts of breath on my lips. I place one soft, sweet kiss on
her mouth, high on hearing her call out my name in
orgasm and so wanting to rub it in her face. But I hold
back. I wait.

Eventually, her eyes open lazily, filled with
satisfaction. A matching smile spreads over her lips.

"So, when will you get me naked? Because if that was
just a preview…"

I laugh and kiss her before hauling us both upright.
"All in good time," I repeat in promise. "But I'm glad it
didn't disappoint."

Joanie levels me with a look so heated my cock almost
finishes what our dry fuck started.

"While it was the best tease I've ever had, I'm going
to need you to fuck me. And soon," she says huskily, not
breaking eye contact.

Her tone, her gaze, the wet spots on her shirt over her
tight nipples make me lose track of everything; whatever I

was about to promise, whatever I'm supposed to be doing today — the beast in my pants wants to do exactly as she demands and fuck her seventeen ways from Sunday.

But just as I'm about to lose control, Nate's voice barks down the hall, "Lunch is here."

Joanie scoots up and pulls her legs out from between my thighs with a grin. She leans in, her breath hot on my ear. "To be continued. Soon, mountain man." And then she licks my earlobe.

I suck in a sharp breath and watch her sashay to the door, flipping her hair over a shoulder and giving me an expectant look.

"I'll be there in a minute," I promise.

She shrugs and waltzes through the opening. I rise to close it behind her. And I waste no time unzipping and gripping my dick hard, stroking it once, twice, and a third time — that's all it takes, and I quietly finish into my waiting palm.

As I tip my head back against the door, breathing hard, I let out a choked laugh. I have a feeling I'm going to be jerking off like a fucking teenager this week because of that woman.

CHAPTER FIVE

JOANIE

While I expected Greg to be an entertaining distraction, what I did not expect was for him to get me off with nothing but some over-the-clothes action. And then I further didn't expect him to disappear completely, leaving me salivating for more. I'm usually the one pulling that move.

I'd be furious with the bastard for flipping the script, but he had a reasonable excuse — it is the week before Christmas, and he'd committed to spend this week with his family out of town. But Bev needs cock. And not just any cock. Mountain man's cock. She's salivating for it. Literally.

Because while there's plenty to do at Mia's bakery, at the daily winter festival events, and just hanging out with Mia and Nate, thoughts of our tryst in that little room on that godawful couch have me wet and distracted all week. I've been masturbating like I haven't since I got my first vibrator.

Not even training for the Freeze Your Buns Run has been enough to cool my libido. I tried to convince Mia to train in underwear since that's what we'll be running in, and it's the only thing I haven't tried to calm Bev the fuck down, but Mia wasn't having it. It's a shame, as she's got a cute little body, and I know Nate wouldn't have minded watching us run the laps in the field behind the community center. I enjoyed watching him run them in only basketball shorts and sneakers. Sue me.

But alas, it was no substitute for what I really wanted. Greg's trouser snake. His cooch cork. His skin flute. His jolly stick. Love plunger. Man meat. Pocket rocket. Third leg. Uterus unicorn. One-eyed snake. Pink torpedo. Taco hammer.

Do I have too many names for a man's dick? Perhaps. But call it what you will, it's not just any dick I want. It is, in fact, his and his alone. The man got my — and Bev's — attention, and I won't be satisfied until I've had the full experience.

So, on Friday afternoon, when I head with Mia and Nate to the community center for the race, I'm full of nervous energy. And not about the race. I may be short, but I'm all legs, and I ran track in college, so I could win this shit in my sleep.

No, my nerves are because Bev and I know Greg is back since he called Nate right before we headed out to ask him to bring some supplies.

Nate parks in his usual spot and unloads the stack of plastic bins Greg requested, crunching behind us in the snow as we head toward the field. I can see people milling about the starting line and that the track has been widened with fresh gravel added to the packed snow, which runs between the drifts that are bound to keep my nipples hard as rocks for the entire four-lap mile-long run.

Just a mile, you say? No big deal, you say? Yeah, you try running a mile in thin air and cold-as-fuck temperatures. And I've only done it clothed so far.

At some point, Nate overtakes us, gets to Greg first, and they line the bins up. It immediately becomes apparent what they're for as a dozen or so men start stripping and putting their clothes in the bins. I shoot Mia a grin, and she rolls her eyes.

"Well, *now* we're talking," I murmur. "Finally, some NSFW, non-Hallmark-y action." I waggle my eyebrows toward the crowd.

Mia snorts. "I'll bet Rae's enjoying this as much as you are," she agrees, jerking her chin toward the starting line flag where Rae stands, overseeing the operation with a grin.

I laugh. "She's been busting her ass these last couple of weeks. I'd say she's earned it."

Mia lifts a shoulder, then heads toward the crowd of remaining men and women in the spectator area while I attempt to follow as my eyes search the sea of skin. Unfortunately, it's not all goodness, as there are plenty of old saggy asses and round, hairy bellies to be had. But what I'm searching for will be worth the mild trauma.

My eyes skip over Nate, as it's nothing I haven't seen practically daily at this point. Nice, but not what I'm after.

And then there it is. Greg's thick, dark hair catches

my eye first. I'd know those waves anywhere. His back is to me, but I remember the feel of those broad shoulders and those strong arms, which are even thicker and more sculpted than I'd expected. And that back ... holy shit. Defined and strong, leading to tight muscles above his perfect globed ass-cheeks, covered only by the dark blue cloth that clings to his beautiful backside. His thick, muscled thighs support his frame, leading to strong calves. I lick my lips, silently begging him to turn around.

But someone fires the starting gun, and he disappears in a sea of moving flesh.

Thankfully, he, Nate, and a third guy pull out of the pack before the first lap is done, and I catch a glimpse of Greg's glorious front as he whips past the crowd. Alas, his perfect ass is gone too quickly to watch for long.

As it comes down to the wire and Greg is clearly in the lead, with Nate not too far behind, I realize I haven't taken my eyes off the race once. Haven't stopped looking for him once. And something about that worries me because I know it's not just wanting to catch glimpses of that body. I'm *rooting* for him. I fucking *care*. Am I getting attached to this sexy, sweet former PE teacher?

I think I am.

Crap.

Finally, he crosses the finish line, arms raised triumphantly to Rae's and everyone else's cheering. He deserved it after stepping aside in all the other events this week. Mia pulls me along to where Greg, now joined by Nate, is fishing around for his clothes. Both men are panting and sweaty. And naturally, I find it insanely hot. I raise my eyebrows and give Mia a look.

"Whatever you're thinking, stop," she remarks drily.

I give her a knowing smile, but she's already on to congratulating her man for making second place.

"Congratulations," I say, stepping into Greg's eye-line as he pulls his sweater on.

He looks up with a smile that doesn't reach his eyes. And it's the first time we've been face-to-face since Sunday. And despite his win, he looks *defeated.*

"Thanks," he murmurs.

I open my mouth to ask him what's up, but Rae calls for the women to get ready to take their marks. In the moments it took me to glance her way and back at Greg, he's disappeared. And now I'm sure something's up.

But whatever it is will have to wait until after I've kicked all these bitches' asses.

I do a few quick stretches before claiming an empty bin and stripping. When I get to the line, I realize there are half as many women as there were men, most of them much older. You've got to respect the grannies out here in their underpants. Hell, I hope that's me someday.

I chuckle at the thought as Rae fires the starting gun … and promptly get elbowed hard just as my left sneaker hits a rock-less, icy patch. My core muscles engage as my body flails, but it's hopeless. My legs fly from under me as I fall backward behind the pack of hos that pay no attention to my plight. Pain registers as the back of my skull meets ice and rock and snow. And everything goes black.

CHAPTER SIX

GREG

I'm standing between the runners and the building, debating whether I should help Rae monitor the race or hide in my office when I hear the collective, horrified gasp of the crowd that can mean nothing good. Thankfully my instincts override my shit mood, and I run the few hundred feet back to the race.

I find Nate, his back to me, dragging someone just off the race's path. Shit.

"Someone get her a blanket," he calls to the unmoving spectators as he kneels to assess the person.

I see Ned spring toward the pile of supplies Rae had on hand, digging for a blanket. But I move faster, removing my coat. Ned is not touching a nearly naked woman on my watch.

But as I skid to a halt, dropping to my knees next to him, my heart drops.

Joanie.

Pale and still, and somehow even more beautiful than

ever. I wiggle my coat under her with Nate's help and button it around her just as Ned arrives with a blanket. I shoot him dagger-eyes and take the blanket for her legs. Thankfully he fucks off right quick.

"What happened?" I ask as Nate delicately examines her head.

"Slipped," he grunts. Then, he fishes a car key out of his pocket with one hand. "Black bag, behind the driver's seat."

I nod and run for the parking lot, trying not to worry myself into a panic.

In the few minutes it takes me to get back, the race has been stopped, and the runners are either crowded around Joanie with the rest of the town or pulling on clothes. As I drop Nate's bag next to him, I note Mia still in her underwear, kneeling on the snow beside her friend, tears spilling down her cheeks.

I shake my head and make for the bins, locating Mia and Joanie's clothes with Rae's help. By the time I get back with them, Joanie's eyes are open, and Nate is asking her questions in a gentle voice. I nudge Mia, then again before she finally looks at me, and I silently hand her the pile of clothes. She nods her thanks and returns her attention to her friend, simply clutching the garments to her chest.

"She's okay," Nate finally declares in a clear, raised voice. Then looks at Mia, "Put your clothes on, babe, so you can help me get her dressed, okay?"

Mia sniffs deeply and nods, fumbling through the pile. With a sigh, I crouch beside her and extract the pieces she needs, handing them to her one at a time until she's dressed. Just as she's zipping her coat, Joanie starts to sit up with Nate's help. He watches her like a hawk as she settles into a seated position.

"Doing okay?" he asks.

"I mean, not really. I feel like I got hit by a truck," she mumbles and glances down at herself. "What the fuck am I wearing?"

Mia lets out a choked laugh. "You're swearing. That's a good sign."

"It's my coat and a blanket," I offer, still crouched near her feet. "But we've got your clothes if you're ready to put them on."

Joanie's eyes meet mine. Her gaze is undecipherable, and I try to give her one in return that reassures her that we're here, that we've got her.

She finally tears her eyes away and looks at the clothes in Mia's arms. "Anything to get off this ice and onto something softer. And warmer."

"I can move her to the couch in the office," I offer to Nate.

"Probably for the best," he agrees, stepping back and deferring to me.

I rise, then position myself back in a crouch next to her. "I'm going to bring you inside, okay, city girl?"

She grimaces and nods faintly — no exuberant agreement to me carrying her while she's mostly naked and only covered by my coat. My eyes flick up to Nate's momentarily, communicating that observation. He dips his chin in acknowledgment.

I slide my arms under her and pull her to me as I rise, cradling her as gently as I can against my chest. Mia performs a few tucks of the coat and blanket dangling around her, and we head away from the dispersing crowd. Nate stays beside us, and Mia gets in front to open the community center door.

I bring Joanie through, and we repeat the process with the office door before I carefully set her down on the small couch.

Rae pokes her head in. "I've got Penny wrapping up the event. I'll find Miss Joanie something hot to drink."

Nate nods. "And something to eat, too, I think, Rae. Thank you."

"Sure thing, Nate." Rae disappears just as quickly as she appeared, and Mia sinks to the floor next to the couch, clasping Joanie's hands in hers.

"Well, that wasn't exactly how I wanted to steal the show," Joanie jokes in a much quieter tone than usual.

Mia huffs a laugh. "I'm just glad you're awake. You freaked me out there, Jo."

Joanie cringes. I'm not sure if it's pain or embarrassment. "How long was I out?"

"Just a few minutes," Nate says. "But you're lucid, the bump isn't big, and you don't have radiating pain, so it's probably a concussion at most. Though given the fact that you were unconscious at all, and you did hit your head, I think it's best if we take you into the emergency room just in case."

Joanie grimaces again. "What, no ambulance?" she remarks drily.

Nate's eyebrows jump up, and he holds up a hand with three fingers raised. "How many fingers?" he asks abruptly.

Joanie rolls her eyes. "Three. And it was sarcasm. I'm fine."

Nate continues to eye her skeptically. "First of all, you don't fuck around with head injuries. Second, it'll be far quicker if we take you. I'm not sure emergency services will come here unless someone needs to be airlifted."

"That's barbaric," Joanie scoffs.

Mia nods in agreement. "I know. When I started the bakery, I tried to push to incorporate the town so we'd get basic services out here. No dice."

Well, that's news. I've attempted it myself, but now isn't the time or place to swap stories.

"We can discuss town politics another time," I inject pointedly. "Joanie should get to the hospital as soon as possible."

Nate nods his agreement and gestures for Mia to grab Joanie's clothes.

I move next to Nate. "Let me know how it goes, okay?" I say in a low voice.

But apparently, it was not low enough because Joanie turns her gaze from Mia, who is starting to help dress her, and gives me the biggest puppy dog eyes I've ever seen. "You're not coming?"

If the look didn't do it, the soft, sad tone does. I hesitate for only a heartbeat.

"Of course I am, city girl."

Nearly five hours later, we arrive at the community center parking lot so Nate can drop me off at my truck before heading back up the mountain. Thankfully, the doctor's exam came to the exact conclusion as Nate had: just a concussion and a mild one at that.

Joanie is leaning into me, my arm around her. The thought of leaving her is giving me a pit in my stomach.

She looks up at me with a vulnerability I've never seen her display, and the knot in my gut tightens.

"Come home with me," I murmur. "Let me take care of you."

She goes to respond, but Nate turns his head toward us. "I don't think that's the best idea."

I raise my eyebrows, looking around at the dark sky and deep snow. "Why not? She's tired. She's already been dragged all over hell and back, and my place is five minutes away. In these conditions, it'll take you guys another forty minutes to get up the mountain. Plus, it's not like I have anything else to do."

Mia turns fully around in her seat. "She's my best friend. There's nothing more important I have to do than take care of her," she insists sharply.

Joanie sits up, ramrod straight. "Um, hi, hey," she cuts in, waving a hand between us. "Adult here. I'm not dead. Just a bump on the head. Pretty sure I get to decide for myself."

Nate frowns. "I'm glad you're okay, Joanie," he says, then turns and looks at me. "But I'm going to say this flat out. Can you tell me if you take her home, you won't fool around? Because sexual activity is off the table —" Joanie opens her mouth to interject "—sexual activity of *any kind*," he stresses, and she sinks back with a grimace, deflated, "for at least twenty-four hours. Ideally, more. She needs to rest. Physical stuff aside, even getting too worked up isn't good right now."

I huff a wry laugh. "Believe it or not, I am capable of putting her needs before mine, or I wouldn't have offered," I respond matter-of-factly.

Mia arches a brow. "You may be, but her —" she tips her chin at Joanie "— I'm not so sure about."

Joanie rolls her eyes. "I'd rather stay with him and keep it Hallmark than go home and listen to you two fucking," she retorts. "So going with you is practically a guarantee that I'll get all hot and bothered with that soundtrack playing all night."

Nate turns bright red, and I hold back a laugh. "City girl has a point. She might get more rest with me since your ... nightly activities won't keep her up."

"First of all, I had no idea you could hear us —" Mia starts, clearly mortified.

Joanie cuts her off with a sharp laugh. "Mia, you're both so loud in bed, even *I* know the exact noises you both make right before you —"

"Okay, okay, we get it," Nate interjects. "But I think Mia's 'second of all' was going to be that we can ... not do that while you rest — no big deal. Then I'll be around if you need medical care. I'd feel better that way."

"And you'd do what?" I counter. "It's not like there's

much you could do that I couldn't. I'm first-aid and CPR certified. Plus, if she needed a hospital, she'd get to one much faster from my place. And I won't be in another room not fucking my fiancée."

Nate presses his lips together as he realizes I'm right. Confirmed when he gives Mia a look. She throws her hands up. "Fine. But text me regularly."

Joanie scoffs. "Okay, Mom. Jesus Christ, why do I feel like a teenage girl whose parents don't want her to be alone with her first boyfriend instead of a grown-ass woman who can do what and who she pleases? I promise I'll be good." She shakes her head and gives me a small nudge. "Let's go."

Mia follows us out of the truck, and the girls embrace despite their tension, murmuring words that I can only assume mean they're making peace. Then I help Joanie get into the passenger side of my truck.

As I climb into the driver's seat and close the door, she sighs in relief. "Their kids are going to be so fucking neurotic."

I laugh. "But well-loved," I point out.

She shrugs, but I can see a small smile on her lips. And exhaustion written all over her face.

"Come on, city girl. Let's get you to bed." I give her a wink.

CHAPTER SEVEN

JOANIE

Greg's bed, as it turns out, is the stuff of legend, humongous and the exact right balance between soft and firm, with silken pillowcases that make me feel like I've died and gone to heaven, and the highest thread count sheets I've ever felt outside of a hotel.

And between his sheets is exactly where I am now, wearing only one of his shirts and panties as he puts together some food in the kitchen. The gorgeous kitchen of his modestly sized yet beautifully appointed home just outside of "downtown" Alpine Ridge. Nothing about it says "bachelor" from the stylish yet functional furniture to the Pottery-Barn-esque décor.

"Dinner for the lady," Greg announces as he walks in, carrying a laden tray.

"What, you're not going to eat with me?" I tease as he sets it down in front of me.

"Oh, I am," he assures me with a wink. "I'll be back with my tray."

When he turns and leaves, I look at the spread before me. And I burst out laughing. I'm still laughing a minute later when he returns.

"What?" he asks, clearly a little affronted as he settles beside me. "You don't like it?"

I wipe the tears of laughter from my eyes. "No, I love it," I declare. "Really. Tomato soup with grilled cheese sandwiches takes me right back to third grade."

He shrugs. "It's what my mom always made me when I wasn't feeling well. It's my go-to comfort meal."

I tilt my head, an unfamiliar sensation washing through me. "Greg, I'm … touched," I say, naming the feeling. "You wanted to comfort me."

He blushes and takes a bite of his grilled cheese with another shrug but says nothing. So, I go ahead and start eating. And it tastes every bit as nostalgic as I'd expected it would.

We eat in companionable silence until another unfamiliar feeling starts gnawing at me, and I stop eating.

"Is something wrong with the soup?" he asks. I look up to find him gazing at me in concern.

"Not at all. I was just … thinking," I respond.

"About?"

I push the tray away, agitated in a way I'm ashamed to admit. "Nobody has ever cooked for me before. I mean, my mom has. And lord knows Mia has, but …"

"Ah," he says, pushing away his own now-empty tray. "You've never had a *man* cook for you before."

I press my lips together and shake my head. "Can't say I have."

Greg reaches up and brushes his thumb over my cheek. "I'm honored to be your first," he teases, leaning in and placing a chaste, grilled-cheese-flavored kiss on my lips.

I scrunch my nose and make a face at him. "Well, I'm willing to bet I'm not the first girl you've fed in this bed. No man chooses sheets this nice by himself." I try not to think too hard about the fact that I care about being another notch on his seriously luxurious bedpost.

"Well, that's presumptuous," he scoffs.

I raise an eyebrow. "You're telling me you picked these out?" I ask, running a hand over the luxuriously thick and smooth material.

He rises and carefully sets the trays on the dresser opposite the bed before climbing back in until he's right in my face. "No. I'm telling you that you're the first girl I've fed in this bed." And then his mouth is on mine, gentle but firm. Unbidden relief washes over me, and I open my lips to welcome him in, but he pulls back. "And that's all we're doing in this bed tonight, city girl. No taking advantage of me." He winks and pulls me back on the pillows, cradling me against his chest.

"So, a woman did pick out these sheets," I say, but since it's against the hard plane of his pecs, it comes out garbled. He laughs, the sound rumbling through where my lips and cheek meet his shirt. And it makes me smile.

"Yes, but it was my Aunt Margaret, so you have nothing to worry about. I haven't fucked anyone in this bed."

I pull my head back to look at him. Hating that I'm not

up for all the things I want to do to him after that declaration. "Yet," I reply, batting my eyelashes.

He smirks and shakes his head. "I'm glad you like the sheets."

"And I liked the dinner." Greg gives me a deeply skeptical look. "Really. Thank you," I add, running my hand down his chest, once again struck by this softer side to him.

"You're welcome," he replies. And then, as if out of nowhere, "What are you still doing here, Joanie? I didn't expect you to stay in Alpine Ridge this long."

I'm a little startled, but it's a fair question. "I didn't either," I admit with a small shrug. Then, with a sly grin, "Maybe there's just been enough worth sticking around for."

Now he looks surprised. "Me?" he asks incredulously.

"Full of yourself much? I was talking about the macarons. And the spectacular array of winter sports. Concussions and all."

He narrows his eyes at me, my humor fooling nobody.

"You like me." It almost sounds like an accusation.

I roll my eyes, playing it off. He's not wrong, though admitting things like that out loud isn't my style. "I'd like your cock in me, but since that's not an option, I'm happy to lay here and feel you up."

Greg grasps my chin and looks into my eyes. "Well, I like you, Joanie — a lot. You're smart, honest, and sarcastic. Oh, and way too sexy for your own good. Especially tonight."

I lick my lips. How does this man always know the

right things to say? And how can he turn me on so much while barely touching me?

"You know, maybe we could just …" I slide my hand lower, down his tight abdomen, but don't get far before he laces his fingers with mine.

"Is intimacy without sex that terrifying for you?" he asks bluntly.

A sarcastic remark hangs on the tip of my tongue, but something about his expression seals it behind my lips. His pupils are dilated, his expression open and searching.

I take a deep breath. In through my nose. Out through my mouth.

"Yes. If a guy isn't looking to just fuck me, he's looking to get something by fucking me. Ergo, I don't do real intimacy. It's asking for trouble. I like my life how it is. I don't need intimacy, just sex. Relationships complicate things."

He shakes his head sadly. "Are you telling me there's not a single man who has successfully broken through your bullshit?"

"Excuse me? My bullshit?"

"Yes, Joanie. Your bullshit. Your 'I don't need men for anything but sex' attitude. Are you telling me you honestly don't want more? A life partner?"

"Not a priority for me," I reply flippantly.

"Maybe not, but isn't everyone looking for someone who gets them? Who wants to be with them for who they are? For more than just sex?" he presses.

I close my eyes and realize I'm too tired for this shit.

And the pain is creeping back out from under the drugs they gave me at the hospital.

"If you're looking to uncover some trauma that's made me afraid to love, you're wasting your time," I say flatly, then open my eyes and stare hard into his. "I guess I just haven't found anyone worth sharing … *more* with. Which is fine by me. I like my independence." I scooch up into a sitting position, and he scrambles to follow. "Can we just … not talk about this anymore? I need more acetaminophen and some rest."

His eyes search mine for a long moment. "Yeah, okay, of course," he finally accedes, rising from the bed. He stacks the contents of both trays onto one and takes them out of the room with him. He returns a few minutes later with a glass of water and two pills. "Here."

I take them without looking at him, swallowing the pills and chugging the water. "Thanks."

Greg draws the blackout curtains, sealing the room in semi-darkness, the only light from the lamp on my side of the bed.

I slip under the covers and lay on my back, watching Greg round the bed to his side. He kicks off his slippers and removes his sweatpants, revealing boxers underneath. Despite the tension of our conversation, I'm disappointed when he leaves his T-shirt on and climbs into bed.

After all, he is ridiculously attractive. But then, I've been with plenty of attractive men. With Greg, though, it's … more than that. I mean, the physical attraction is clearly strong for both of us, but he's the first guy possibly ever to want to stick around when sex was off the table. On top of that, he's taken care of me. And even though he doesn't seem to get that I don't need a man to feel complete, he respectfully dropped the subject when I asked him to.

I think he's what most women would call a keeper.

Shit, do I want to keep him?

I realize … maybe.

Maybe I do.

The realization makes emotions drum quietly but steadily against my insides. So, against my better judgment, I decide to let him in. Just a little. Just enough to reassure him that I'm not *totally* opposed to the idea. That I've just never trusted someone enough for things to get even close to needing them. That maybe I've just been looking in the wrong places all this time. Places that weren't here.

"When a man wants to focus on his career to the exclusion of an intimate relationship, he's seen as ambitious and hard-working. But when a woman does it, she's closed off and frigid and clearly messed up somehow," I begin. I feel rather than see Greg stiffen beside me. "I love being a lawyer. I loved the challenge of getting ahead at my firm. Even though I don't work there anymore, I still need that kind of challenge. And I intend to find it again." I turn, and we lock eyes. "What I didn't intend was you."

Greg considers that before sitting up and stroking a hand down my back. "I'm not trying to distract you from getting your career back on track. I did a shit job of saying it, but what I was trying to tell you is that … well, I don't just want you for sex, Joanie. If you want more, I'm up for it. That's all."

A smile pulls at the corners of my lips. There he goes, saying exactly the right thing again. "And if I just want sex?"

Greg's eyes darken, and he goes still. "Christ, I wish you didn't have a concussion right now."

A laugh slips through my lips, and he chuckles. "I'll take that as you're up for that, too," I tease.

Greg closes his eyes briefly, shakes his head, then reaches for my hand and places it over his boxers. Letting me feel the hard length of him underneath. "Definitely." My breath catches, and I look up to find his eyes open again and fixed on my face. "But I'm not going anywhere, city girl," he says in a deep, warm voice that washes through me like a balm.

I take a subtle deep breath. I'm too tired and in too much pain to deal with what I'm feeling and how that fits in the picture I had for my life. I'm not sure what excuse I'll have once I'm feeling better, but one problem at a time.

"Good. Because tonight we're going to have to settle for spooning," I tease, trying to lighten the mood as I slip down so my ass is right over his hard cock.

He groans and rests his forehead on my back. "You're killing me here."

I laugh and pull his arm around me. "Well, if you're not up for the challenge ..." I wiggle my ass, and he laughs, thrusting his hardness into me.

"I am if you are," he says huskily in my ear.

I bite into my bottom lip, even though I know he couldn't see me if I did smile.

Well, when he puts it like that …

"Weren't you listening? I'm always up for a challenge."

CHAPTER EIGHT

GREG

I wake on Saturday morning with Joanie's sweet ass still planted firmly over my hard dick. It makes me wonder if it ever calmed down. But feeling her in my arms right now? Worth a hundred cases of blue balls.

I also realize that since her fall, I haven't thought about the fiasco that was the visit to see my family this past week. Not that I'm glad she was hurt, but it has distracted me from my pity party. But then, Joanie has been the distraction I didn't know I needed from the moment we met.

I love Alpine Ridge. I didn't come here to hide like Nate. I came here out of duty. Though like Nate, I stayed because I found peace here. But Joanie has blown that all apart. Because now? I want to be wherever she is. Maybe it's just infatuation, but it's certainly something I want to explore. Though to do that, I need her to see this as more than just sex.

Having to delay fucking until she's recovered will

help. Today, we'll spend all kinds of non-sex time together, cookie decorating, sampling at the chili cookoff, and watching the orchestral Christmas Eve show. All low-key enough that they've been Nate-approved during Joanie's recovery. And I will use every minute to convince her there's something here. It's a feeling that burrows deeper the more I'm around her, and I know she feels something, too. Or she would if she'd let herself.

Today's mission: Give Joanie enough space and opportunity to connect with those feelings. With no pressure.

Easier said than done. Thankfully, I've already realized I'll take whatever she's willing to give.

"Are you sure you're up for the show?" Mia asks Joanie for the third time in as many minutes. "You've already done so much today."

Joanie rolls her eyes. "I ate my weight in cookies and chili, Mia, I didn't run a freaking marathon. A little Christmas music will probably just put me to sleep."

Mia looks pleadingly at Nate, but he shrugs. "I was worried last night, but she's fine. Just let her enjoy the show, babe." Mia grimaces but finally seems to accept it as we take our seats: Nate, then Mia, then Joanie, then me.

Joanie leans toward me and whispers, "On second thought, if Nate thinks I'm good as new, maybe we leave now and go back to your place." She gives me a meaningful look.

And I'm so fucking tempted.

"No can do, city girl. Trust me; you'll want to stick around for this." I nod toward the stage where a jazz quartet has taken the low stage, along with Rae. Joanie quirks a brow at Rae's appearance and gives me a look. I simply gesture to the stage with a smile as the musicians tune their instruments.

And then the show begins. Alpine Ridge may be a small town, but the people who own homes here are as cultured and varied as you'll find anywhere. Three of the four were professional musicians at some point. And Rae ...

"*Oh my God,*" Joanie gasps as Rae sings the first few notes of *Let it Snow*. She looks over at me with wide eyes, and I shrug. It surprises everyone when sweet, unassuming Rae busts out her sultry, smooth singing voice.

As Joanie watches the performance, I watch her. Her pure, simple joy. She's been like this all day. Icing cookies like it wasn't something mostly kids were doing. Tasting the various chilis like they were all gourmet. Experiencing everything in an un-sarcastic or cynical manner. Enjoying all the things that I enjoy about this small but tight-knit community. I'm not sure if it was the bump on the head or what, but she seems happier.

When the final notes of the last song fade, she looks over at me, her eyes filled with emotion. But then her brows bunch together.

"Why are you looking at me like that?" she asks.

I laugh. "I'm just in awe. What's gotten into you today?"

She shrugs and rises from her chair. "I don't know what you mean."

I purse my lips but keep my thoughts to myself. Either she knows she's bald-faced lying and doesn't want to talk about it, or she doesn't and nothing good will come from me pointing it out.

"All right guys, we're headed to Portland early tomorrow for Christmas morning with Nate's parents," Mia declares, opening her arms to Joanie.

"Better get home so you can fuck *and* sleep before then," Joanie teases, hugging her friend. "I'll see you guys for dinner tomorrow."

We finish a round of goodbyes, and I look to Joanie. "So, I guess that means you're coming home with me?"

She smirks, the first sign of the naughty girl I've seen all day. "Was that ever even a question?" She bats her eyelashes at me, and I laugh.

"Guess not. What if I had plans for Christmas?"

She cocks her head. "Do you?"

"Nope. Got enough of my family last week. You're not spending Christmas with yours?"

Joanie shrugs and loops her arm through mine as we return to my truck. "Mia *is* family. But no, my parents are in Australia. Christmas tradition. They despise the cold."

"And they're fine leaving their only child alone at the holidays?"

"Oh, they used to offer to bring me out there to join them. But I've always worked through the holidays, so at some point, they just stopped asking."

I frown. "Do they know you lost your job?" I ask curiously.

She gives me a sharp look. "Not yet, no," she responds, her tone as sharp as her gaze.

I nod, reading between the lines that it's not something she wants to discuss.

She stops so abruptly that I end up a few steps ahead of her before I can react. I turn back, and she's frowning.

"Do you *want* me to come home with you?" she asks, seemingly equally irritated and disappointed.

I quickly close the gap between us, choosing the language she speaks best to answer first. My mouth is on hers, my tongue pushing between her lips, and my arms pulling her to me. I'm afraid at first when she doesn't respond, but after a few long moments, she opens her mouth for me.

When we finally break apart, I rest my forehead against hers. "More than anything," I swear. "I want you more than anything."

I lace my fingers with hers, and we silently walk the rest of the distance. We finish the short ride to my place in silence. We make it to the bedroom in silence.

Joanie sits on the edge of the bed, patting the spot next to her seductively. Rather than take it, I drop to my knees before her, looking up into her ice-blue eyes. Her gaze is filled with heat and lust. But all I see is her.

"Time to make me scream, mountain man," she purrs.

I shake my head. "Another time. Tonight, I'm going to worship you." We stare at each other for a moment. I'm waiting for her to protest at the intimacy of that request.

She's ... well, I can't tell if she's more confused or excited. I hope she's both. I want to turn everything she thinks she knows about me on its head.

I start by slowly slipping off her shoes and socks. She watches, allowing it, somewhat amused by the process. When I'm done, I lift her sweater up and over her head, revealing a red, lacy bra through which I can see her peaked nipples.

"Fuck, city girl," I breathe, leaning in and closing my mouth over her left nipple. I suck at it through the fabric, and she winds her fingers into my hair, tugging with approval, so I do it to her other nipple, too. Then I move to her mouth, using a kiss to press her back onto the bed.

I pull away, unbuttoning her jeans and shimmying them over her pert ass and down her long legs. Unsurprisingly, her panties match the bra perfectly, and dark curls are visible underneath, into which I promptly bury my face and inhale. The scent of her arousal has me hard in an instant.

"You smell like heaven," I murmur. She giggles, presumably at the sensation of my voice reverberating through her core.

But we can't have laughing. Not while I'm between her legs. So, I move aside her panties and plunge my tongue into her, lifting her knees to widen her slit, diving deeper. She groans and arches and squirms, so I press a hand on her hips, stilling her for my mouth.

"Look at me, Joanie," I demand.

She presses onto her elbows, drawing her head up until

our eyes meet. I flick my tongue from ass to clit and she hisses in a breath but maintains eye contact.

Next, I use a thumb to press into her, slowly fucking her. Her breaths come heavier. So, I use the other thumb to circle her nub. Her eyes drop closed as she moans. So, I stop. And her eyes spring open. It takes a couple of rounds of that for her to realize she has to watch for me to keep going.

Her eyes on me, as I pleasure her, have me so wound up, it's all I can do not to pounce on her. But I don't. I keep fucking her with my thumb, fingers, tongue. Alternating each at various speeds and forces. Until I find what makes her grip the comforter, pant, groan, and struggle to keep watching. And I do that faster, harder, until her pussy convulses around my hand. I reach in deep and twist, throwing her higher, so high that she falls back, grabbing at her tits, tweaking her nipples to keep it going. It's so fucking sexy I have to stop before I come on the spot.

My absence goes unnoticed until she rides the wave down. I'm still gritting my teeth against the image of her coming when I hear, "Greg?"

I suck a breath in sharply. God, I need to hear her say that when she orgasms with me inside of her.

I climb onto the bed, over her, and hold myself above her. "I'm here." I give her my mouth and let her taste her juices on me. She moans as our tongues tangle.

"I need more," she demands.

I lick up the column of her neck, stopping with my mouth at her ear. "Tell me what you need."

"I need you inside me. On top of me. Behind me. In my mouth. I need you everywhere."

I shiver hard and let my hips fall between her legs, my hardness rubbing into her slick cunt. "You need that?"

She nods, and I push harder. The front of my jeans will be soaked, but I don't care. I use the friction to tease her, grinding in circles until she can't take it anymore.

"Jeans off," she demands. "Now."

I rise, unzipping and pulling my dick out while I head to the nightstand drawer, where I fish out a condom. She turns her head and licks her lips at the sight of my engorged cock.

"You like that?" I ask.

She nods.

"You want to suck my dick, Joanie?"

She bites into her lower lip and nods again.

I grin, kicking the jeans off. Then I rip the foil and roll the condom down my dick, climbing over her and settling between her legs. "Another time, beautiful." And without warning, I bury myself in her in one smooth stroke.

It was stupid. It's been too long since I've been with anyone, much less someone who turned me on as much as Joanie does. My dick has swelled to epic proportions. And she's so tight and wet from her first orgasm. The hot clench of her pussy makes me see stars.

I lean over her onto my arms, catching my breath and mastering myself before I nut in one.

"Fuck," I groan, sliding back out. Joanie shivers under me. And then I plunge back into the abyss. Over and over. Slowly. Deliberately. Until my body cooperates with my need to keep it together. So I can feel her for as long as possible. Watch her arch under me for as long as possible. Make her come harder than she thought possible.

I lean up, hauling her hips into my lap as I continue to pump into her. She's almost a rag doll, clearly surrendered to the pleasure. I hold her in place with one hand and use the other to knead her covered breast. God, I should've taken her underthings off, too. Because frankly the friction of her panties on the side of my cock may ruin my plans.

I pull out and rip them off. Then I roll her over and undo her bra before hauling her hips up and plunging back in. She groans into the bed. But I can't hear it like I want to. So I pull out again and roll her onto her side, positioning myself behind her.

Lifting her leg, I slide back in. And fuck, she's tight from this angle. It also allows me to hear her moan as I take her. Still slow and steady. I'm a little surprised she hasn't demanded fast and hard. She seems like the kind to want it rough.

"You like that?" I ask as I flex my hips and bury myself deep in her.

"God, yes," she moans.

"You know what I'd like?" I ask, kissing her neck. "I'd like you on top of me. So I can kiss you." I kiss her neck again. "Suck on those gorgeous tits." I squeeze one for effect. "Watch my dick going in and out of your beautiful pussy." Her back arches, and she nods.

I pull out, leaning back into the pillows. I expect it'll take her a minute to gather herself, so I'm more than a little surprised when she immediately climbs on top of me, and her mouth devours mine as her wet cunt devours my cock. I groan into her mouth now, helpless against her as she controls the speed and depth.

She leans back, bracing herself with her hands, using the arch of her back to fuck me. Watching her is hands-down the hottest thing I've ever witnessed. I grip her thighs, watching as my dick repeatedly disappears into her dark, wet curls. As her peaked nipples point to the ceiling. Her mouth goes slack while her legs tremble, and her pace stutters.

I take the cue and thrust up into her, dropping a thumb to circle her clit. She falls backward, which would've separated us if I weren't ready for it. I switch my grip to her hips and pull her toward me so I can keep thrusting up into her. So I can watch her shatter.

"You are so sexy, Joanie," I groan as I pick up my pace, feeling her walls start to clench harder. "Come for me, baby. Say my name."

And I unleash. Hard and fast. Pounding her pussy until she clenches so tightly it's all I can do to keep fucking her through her orgasm.

"Oh … oh … oh," Joanie cries. "Yes, God, yes, Greg, oh my God, yes!"

When my name falls from her lips, I'm done. My cock explodes, release whipping through me like a firebrand as I empty into the condom. As she quivers around me. As my world shifts.

I may have gotten her to scream my name. I may have owned her orgasm. But the truth is, Joanie Morris owns me.

CHAPTER NINE

JOANIE

Even though I've never been big on holidays, Christmas morning holds the echoes of the joy of all my childhood Christmases. But this Christmas morning holds the echoes of the joy of all my orgasms of the past twelve hours. And there have been a lot.

With that thought, I wake fully, suppressing my giggle in case Greg's not up yet. Because there's one thing we *didn't* do last night that I will make sure we do this morning.

Unfortunately, the blackout curtains make the room so dark that all I can see is his outline. I listen quietly and hear only his deep breaths. He's still asleep. But not for long.

With a sly grin, I slip under the covers. And then I close my lips over his cock. Already semi-hard with morning wood, he nearly fills my mouth. And a few good sucks leave me with not much more than a crown and Greg groaning.

"Shit, Joanie," he says. "That's ..." More groans.

I slip my hand around him, grinning and pumping his shaft as I emerge to find he's turned on the lamp. The low light casts a golden glow over his gorgeous face.

His head is thrown back, his eyes closed as his muscles tighten against the sensation of me working him.

"Look at me, Greg," I demand, just like he did when he went down on me yesterday. And I intend to make this every bit as epic as what he did to me, if that's possible. It was the best oral I've ever received, after all, but I'm confident I can give it as good as I got.

His eyes are dark and filled with need, but he watches. And I watch back as I lick around the tip of him, the fantasies of doing this to him coming to life even better than I'd imagined. He grits his teeth, and I smirk, pumping him with sure, wet strokes before closing my mouth over him again, opening my throat, and releasing my hand. One of the few ways I'll surrender to a man.

With a sharp groan of approval that shows he understood the invitation, Greg pumps into my mouth, bracing himself against the bed to get as deep as he can. Moisture streams from my eyes and down my cheeks as I take it all, sucking around his thrusts as he fucks my mouth until my clit is throbbing, my nipples are hard, and my throat is raw. With a roar, he spills down my throat. I smile around his cock, then lick gently to clean him as he withdraws. But then his dick is replaced by his lips as he pulls me in for a claiming kiss, his tongue plundering my mouth.

Once he lets me go, he drops back to the bed, panting.

"Fucking hell, Joanie," he groans. "Give me a minute and then I'm going to make you come so hard you —"

The sound of a door closing outside the bedroom makes us both sit up abruptly.

"Gregory?" a man's voice calls.

I look over at Greg, wide-eyed. His expression is sour.

"Fucking hell," he mutters. "It's my father." He rises and goes to the door, sticking his head around the gap where it was open. "I'll be out in a minute." His tone is terse, unfriendly. I don't miss that there's no "*Merry Christmas, Dad*" or "*Hey, Dad, what a nice surprise.*"

Greg closes the door, then walks to the window and opens the drapes, presumably so he can see better. He pulls on his jeans and a sweater before ducking out of the room and pulling the door almost closed behind him … but not quite all the way closed. And seeing as how I have no shame, I slink out of bed and retrieve my sweater from where it'd landed on the floor last night, slipping it on. Since it hits below my ass, it covers everything that matters in case I get caught, so I don't bother with anything else. Instead, I creep to the door to listen.

"—and I told you that your mother and I expected you to come home. We've had enough, son."

"First; I'm a fucking adult, and you may not like that I decided your plans to turn Alpine Ridge into the next tourist trap in the Cascades would destroy everything I love about this place —"

"It's not your decision to make," Greg's father interrupts, his voice icy.

"Not *just* mine, maybe. But I came here to look after

our investments this side of the mountains. I was happy to do that until you wanted to change what that meant. I never agreed —"

"I thought you'd care more about what's in the family's best interests, Gregory. But since you don't, you have no right —"

"I have *every* right. Your father left me half of that land, plus *all* of the property you're standing on. Clearly, you didn't get that Grandpa Tyler was trying to get us to learn how to work together, Dad. But it's all about what you want, isn't it?" The harsh, commanding note in Greg's voice sends shivers down my spine.

Greg's dad scoffs. "So, what, you want to waste your life with no career, no wife, no *family*, and now without thought for the real estate empire you've been part of since birth? You're abandoning your duties to yourself and your mother and me. If you won't see sense, at least come home for your mother. You have no idea how devastated she is by your behavior."

Now it's Greg's turn to scoff. "You're peas in a pod. Do you care at all that being here is what makes me happy? That I'd rather leave *no* legacy than one built on greed?" My heart clenches at the plea in his words, the obvious desire for his father's approval. While my own parents weren't the most hands on, all they've ever wanted was my happiness. It hurts knowing Greg's clearly never had that, and I find my anger rising against his father.

"Those are interesting words, considering you've lived large on the legacy that your grandfather and his brother started. That your trust fund has allowed you luxuries that —"

Greg's laughter cuts off his father. "Shows what you know. I haven't touched a fucking dime of that money. I've lived only off the fruits of my own labor." My eyebrows fly up at the information spilling out of this argument.

"From being a *PE teacher*?" His father practically spits the words. "You truly expect me to believe that?"

"Just because I haven't sold or developed our joint land doesn't mean I haven't done anything, *Dad*," Greg throws the last word back at him with as much disdain as his dad had with his former title. "You need me because, unlike you, I learned from Grandpa Tyler. And I've made my own money with other investments. So, I have absolutely nothing to gain from destroying this place so you can make money. And using Christmas and Mom to guilt me into coming home and being a good boy? That's low, even for you." I bite my lip, pride and respect flowing through me that Greg isn't taking a lick of shit from this tyrant.

"Fine," his dad seethes. "Stay here. Miserable and alone."

And I can't help it, my anger boils over. I didn't even grow up with this dickwad and I've had enough. I swing open the door and sashay out, delighting in the surprise on both men's faces as I tuck myself against Greg's side. He wraps his arm around me reflexively, but I don't meet the questioning gaze I know is pointed my way.

No, my eyes are on Papa Tyler right now.

"Oh, he won't be alone," I greet him with my favorite intimidate-the-prosecutor glare.

Papa Tyler's eyes narrow on me. "Great, now you're bringing prostitutes home?" His eyes flick to his son's.

Greg steps forward menacingly, tucking me behind him. The gesture makes my heart race and I place a hand on his back in solidarity.

"You're going to apologize for that remark, and then you're going to leave," Greg says in a calm, dangerous voice.

"Or what? You'll make me?" his dad asks flippantly.

Tense silence hangs in the air. Knowing nothing good will happen if things don't calm the fuck down, I step forward, placing myself in front of Greg, resting my hands on his chest. "Don't rise to the bait, darling," I purr. "He's not worth it." And then I turn to face the old man. "For the record, I'm a lawyer, though I guess some might say that isn't much better than a prostitute. But I sure as fuck know how to make your son a whole lot happier than you seem to be able to. So, I highly suggest you take your self-righteous bullshit and shove it up your guilt-tripping, delusional ass."

His father's mouth opens and closes in shock. And when the vein on his forehead starts pulsing, I almost laugh.

"I won't be spoken to like that by some gold-digging trollop who —"

"Oh, I'm most definitely a trollop and proud of it. But I had no idea Greg came from money or even had any of his own to speak of. Not that I would care because, as it happens, I'm also a trust fund baby who doesn't need her family's money since I'm more than capable of making piles of my own. And if you don't like how we talk to you, you know where the door is. That you dared to walk through it in the first place is beyond me. In case it wasn't clear: whatever power you think you had here? You don't. Now run along like a good boy, and please, don't have a Merry Christmas. Because you're a fucking asshole who doesn't deserve it." I turn back to Greg, who is grinning from ear to ear. "Now. Ready to make me come like you promised, baby?"

Greg shakes his head and laughs. Then, he looks up at his father.

"Well. I couldn't have put it better myself. You know where the door is. Bye, Dad."

His father starts spluttering threats, but Greg ignores him and lifts me up. The near-joyful look on his face sends warm tingles through my whole body. I wrap my legs around his waist, and he turns his back to his dad as he carries me to the bedroom, clearly paying him no attention.

He kicks the bedroom door closed behind us and tosses me on the bed.

I watch him carefully as he stalks the length of the bed until he's hovered over me.

"I hope I didn't go too overboard out there. I couldn't listen to his bullshit anymore," I offer. Even though I'm not sorry, I know if I emasculated Greg, the whole orgasm promise might be out the window.

"Are you kidding?" he asks, looking down at me with

dark eyes. "That was the hottest fucking thing I've ever seen." He grinds his pelvis into mine, demonstrating his excitement.

I make to return the sentiment, but out in the main room, the front door slams. We give each other a triumphant grin.

"So, you're rich, huh?" I raise an eyebrow.

He smirks. "Guess the cat's out of the bag. I wasn't trying to hide it or anything." He shrugs lightly.

"I meant what I said. I honestly don't care if you had nothing. But …"

"But?" he asks, his brows jumping.

"It did make me realize that there's a lot I don't know about you," I reply.

Now his brows bunch together. "There's *nothing* I'm trying to hide. I swear to you; you don't have anything to worry about from me."

I chew my lip. "I know. It's not that. I just … it also made me realize …"

I cover my face with my hands, unsure I can admit this to myself. I feel his weight settle and his fingers close around my wrists, pulling my hands from my face.

"Talk to me, city girl." The look he gives me is all lust and longing. And it makes me realize that's what I'm feeling. Longing. For more.

"I want to know you," I admit in a whisper. "I want more than sex, too, Greg."

He goes perfectly still, and I worry that he'd changed his mind about wanting that, too, based on my little performance with his dad. I guess even I get insecure putting myself out there.

It's weird that I'm waiting for his answer with bated breath. But … good weird. I think. Though just when I think I may not be cut out for going beyond sex, that he may have truly realized I am as bat-shit crazy as … well, I am, his lips are on mine. His hand freeing his cock. His tip nudging me for permission to enter bare.

I don't even have to think about it. I use my heels to pull him in, joining my mouth to his as he slides in deep. I groan into his mouth when I feel the silky hardness of him thrusting into me.

It feels *so* good. And a man who answers my vulnerability with his dick? I'm so screwed in every way.

"I take it," I say, panting, "that means you're okay with that?" I give him a teasing smile as he rears back, continuing to slide in and out of me.

He smiles back, running his hands down my tits to my hips, holding tight. "More than okay," he agrees, then leans forward. "Because all I wanted for Christmas was you."

I tilt my hips to meet his thrusts. "Oh, but I'm on the naughty list. I'm nobody's present, baby."

He slams into me, and my head drops back. "Fuck, Joanie. Keep calling me that, and I'll show you just how much it pays to be naughty."

"Calling you what?" I ask innocently, wiggling my hips against him. "Baby?"

His jaw tightens, and he unleashes, pounding into me. "Fuck yes," he agrees in a husky, gritty whisper in my ear as his thrusts turn frenzied. "Scream it for me, naughty girl."

I tip my head back, surrendering to how much he owns me. How much I want him to own me. No man has ever brought that feeling out of me during sex, much less outside of it.

"Make me yours, mountain man," I groan in agreement.

Even though deep down, I'm pretty sure he already has.

CHAPTER TEN

JOANIE

By the time Greg and I arrive at Mia and Nate's Christmas evening, Bev's insatiable appetite has been quelled many times over, but my stomach is rumbling and ready for the feast I know Mia's likely whipped up, even with having traveled hours to and from Portland.

As Mia opens the door, the wall of heavenly aromas that hits me confirms my assumption.

"Hey guys," Mia greets us, her eyes falling on our linked hands. She quirks an eyebrow and smirks at me.

"Merry Christmas," I respond, holding up my other hand with the bottle of wine Greg thoughtfully suggested we bring.

"Merry Christmas, indeed." She grins and takes the bottle, stepping back to allow us over the threshold, and I'm stunned by the complete lack of decoration inside. Especially considering how much Mia loves Christmas.

Mia rolls her eyes, interpreting my shock as Greg

shrugs out of his jacket. "It's been busy. We didn't have time to decorate," she explains with a shrug.

"Well, as long as you had time to cook, you know I'm a happy camper," I respond.

Greg helps me out of my coat, his fingers skating over my collarbone, sending pleasant shivers down my arm. I give him a suggestive grin, which he returns. Mia narrows her eyes at the exchange but says nothing.

I'm distracted by a brush against my legs, and I look down to see Simba, Mia's cat, once her Gran's, begging for pets. I reach down and scratch him between the ears as he purrs against my palm.

"Aw, did you miss me, buddy?" I croon.

Apparently, not that much because he quickly abandons my affections to explore Greg's legs. Much to my surprise, Greg picks him up, and Simba nuzzles Greg's chin.

"Okay, he'll tolerate me petting him, but he never lets me do *that*," I grouse.

Greg smiles at me beatifically. "Stick around a while, and he will, city girl." He leans in and gently kisses my lips, then winks and heads down the hall.

Mia's eyebrows rise so high that they're threatening to merge with her hairline. I purse my lips and push her down the hall toward the dining room.

We enter the room to find Nate pouring drinks — red wine for us ladies and whisky for the guys, apparently. Nate looks at Mia expectantly.

"Dinner will be ready soon," Mia assures him. "Joanie, want to help me in the kitchen for a minute?"

I raise an eyebrow since we both know I'm not the help in the kitchen type, but I nod, following her out of the dining room. As soon as we're out of earshot, Mia turns on me.

"Okay, spill. What is going on with you two? You've obviously had sex already. But why do I get the feeling there's more going on here?" she demands.

I shrug nonchalantly. "You're right. We're together."

Mia's brows jump to her hairline. "Together? Like *together* together?" I shrug again but can't contain my grin. "Jo! This is huge! I assumed you'd have fucked him out of your system by now, given your history. But *together* ... like for real? I never would've predicted that."

I can't help my goofy grin. "It's new, so we haven't exactly labeled anything. But it's good, Mia. Really good. Like ... not just the sex," I admit. Then I close my eyes briefly and shudder, remembering exactly how good the sex is. And how much it means to admit that it's more.

She takes me by the shoulders and looks me dead in the eye. "This is a big deal for you, I know."

I inhale, slow and deep. "It is. But I'm happy. So fucking happy, Mia. It's crazy, right?"

She shakes her head slowly. "Like I can't even process it, crazy. Yes."

I laugh. "Well, process it, sister. Because I may be sticking around for a while to see where things go."

Mia's eyes fill with tears, and she puts a hand to her mouth. "My little girl's all grown up," she teases. I scoff and shove her shoulder playfully. "Well, he better treat you right. Ooh, do I need to give him the best friend talk?" she adds sternly.

I laugh. "Stand down, tiger mama. I'm a big girl. I can handle myself. And him. *All* of him." I wink salaciously.

Mia grimaces playfully. "Ugh. Forget I asked."

"Forget you asked what?" Nate asks, popping his head into the kitchen.

"Nothing," we reply in unison.

Nate looks between us skeptically and shakes his head. "Oookay then. Well, the table is set if dinner is ready ..."

"Five more minutes," Mia tells him.

He nods and disappears.

"I mean it, Jo," Mia says quietly, leaning in close. "I know how much you've avoided relationships. I just want to make sure you're ready for this and that Greg is on the same page. I don't want you to get hurt."

I clasp Mia's hands in mine. "I promise. We're both grownups, and we both want this. The rest ... well, it will be what it will be. You don't need to worry. But thank you. I'm glad I have you in my corner."

Mia smiles gently. "Always, bitch."

We laugh and turn to finish getting dinner on the table.

As we all sit down to eat Mia's famous prime rib feast, Greg rests his hand on my thigh under the table, his thumb rubbing possessive circles close to my core. I shoot him a heated look as the warmth of his touch seeps through my leggings and my resolve to act like I wouldn't have rather stayed in bed with him all night. Thankfully, with all that sex, Bev needs a break anyway, so I manage to overcome the urge to tear his clothes off right here.

"Well, Merry Christmas, everyone. And since it's Christmas, Alpine Ridge's first winter festival in years is over. And it seems like it was a huge success," Nate says, raising his glass. "Here's to doing it all again next year."

We clink glasses and drink deeply. Mia makes an insanely good prime rib, and the wine Nate picked pairs with it perfectly. However, I wouldn't say no to a glass of whisky later.

"I'll say," Mia agrees. "The bakery has never been busier. I'll need to hire more staff next year to keep up if it's like that again. My property manager said the B&B was full all week for the first time since we converted it. Gran would be pleased that so many people are staying in her house and learning to love this town."

"I know you remodeled, but I haven't had a chance to see it," I remind her. "It was pretty dated. I bet you had to use a good chunk of the cash Gran left to convert it."

Mia nods. "Yes, but not nearly all of it. Though the rest will probably go into maintenance and the bakery. Business isn't always so good, after all."

Mia smiles in a way I know she thinks is reassuring, but I'm her best friend. And I see the exhaustion under that smile.

As if reading my thoughts, Greg says, "I know I've been here for it all, but I never thought about how hard it must've been this past year converting your grandmother's house into a bed and breakfast while starting up your bakery at the same time. How are you doing with all this, Mia?"

Mia smiles sadly. "Honestly? I miss Gran every single

day. Sometimes, I swear I can feel her around me. But I think she'd be happy with the changes, and business is better than I expected, in no small part thanks to her." She lifts her glass again. "To Gran."

"To Dorothy," Nate and Greg chime in as I echo Mia's words, swallowing around the lump in my throat. She was like a grandma to me, too, after all. I shake myself. All this emotion lately is a lot.

"What about you, mountain man?" I ask lightly, turning to Greg. "How's business at the community center?" The seemingly superficial question is a disguise for my curiosity over what his official day job is really like.

Greg gives me a quizzical look. "How'd you know I own it?"

I raise a brow. "I didn't; Mia just told me you ran the place. Though I guess I know now. Except, aren't community centers usually public property?"

"Alpine Ridge is unincorporated," Greg reminds me. "The only public property is owned by the county, which doesn't include any actual buildings. Just land, some utility access points, main roads, that sort of thing."

"Huh," I reply, wheels turning.

"Anyway, I definitely saw a lot more activity during the festival. Some of our residents live pretty far out, so it was good visibility for the center. I'm hoping we got enough traffic to make an impression so more folks will use the facilities regularly now that they know what's there."

I nod and turn to Nate, now curious about how this

tiny town works. "And the wellness center? I bet you all are regular business moguls by now with all the festival traffic."

Nate huffs a laugh. "I wish. I mean, it definitely drives more people looking to get fit after gorging themselves on sweets —" he cuts a playful glance at Mia, who feigns indignation in response, "— but I'm getting more and more folks with actual medical problems that I'm not equipped to deal with."

I frown. "What do you mean?"

He sighs. "I have people coming in with undiagnosed conditions looking for help since the nearest medical facility is anywhere from half an hour to an hour away, depending on where in town they live, and as you know, there's no urgent care here. Or medical care of any kind, as it were. It kills me to turn them away, knowing I probably *could* help with my medical background, but I can't risk the liability, and I sure don't have everything I'd need to treat patients."

I'm confused. "But you helped me when I fell during the race. What was different about that?"

Nate shakes his head. "I didn't do anything any other bystander with first aid training wouldn't do. I checked you out, then got you to a hospital for scans since you'd lost consciousness. I wasn't diagnosing or treating you in any formal capacity."

"Okay, I guess that makes sense," I allow. "But surely, with the older population base, the town council would prioritize having emergency medical services available? There have to be hundreds of people who live here."

Mia sighs heavily. "You'd think. And it's actually a few thousand. But we're unincorporated, so there's no established tax base for that kind of thing. No local ambulances, police, fire department, or any other municipal services. It's crazy. And not helping the town any."

"Didn't you say you tried to get the town incorporated?" I ask, recalling an earlier conversation.

Mia nods. "Yep. I went to the town council and everything. They shot me down immediately. They said it would drive up costs, that people choose to live here precisely to avoid those things."

"Same thing happened to me when I tried," Greg commiserates.

"Sounds like the town council needs some new blood," I muse.

Greg shakes his head. "They'll never go for it, Joanie. We've tried everything."

"If you say so," I murmur, ideas already taking root.

The conversation moves on as Nate asks Greg about equipment sharing between the wellness practice and the community center, but I don't miss Mia giving me an assessing look. Like she knows what I'm thinking about doing.

I give her an innocent smile even though I know it won't fool her. It doesn't matter. Either way, the town council won't see me coming. Because if I'm going to stick around and see where things go with my mountain man, I might as well make myself useful. And what better way than to help my friends out? With that thought, I decide that making Alpine Ridge an official town, with all the bells and whistles, just became my new mission.

Thankfully, the conversation soon turns to other topics I can engage in so nobody else catches on to my scheming. For example, Nate and Mia's wedding plans, when Greg jokingly asks if they wouldn't rather elope than deal with the hot mess that is the situation with Mia's parents.

"How do you even know about that?" Mia asks sharply, casting a suspicious gaze at Nate.

"Oh, don't blame him; this town *talks*," Greg responds. "You probably didn't notice, but there were a good number of townies at Dorothy's funeral."

Mia's face falls. "Ah."

Ugh. I wasn't able to go to Gran's funeral due to work commitments, but Mia told me about the epic bout of awfulness that was her parents that day. I reach over the table and cover her hand with mine.

"Still nothing on that front?" I ask gently.

Mia shakes her head but sniffs briefly and collects herself. "Nope. But Carrie and I are talking a lot more these days. She graduates this summer. She's making noise about trying to break away from them. I'm trying to be as supportive as I can without saying anything bad about our parents."

I snort. "Because they're giving you the same courtesy, I'm sure," I reply sarcastically, shaking my head. "You're a better person than I would be in your shoes."

Mia gives me a shaky smile. "Honestly, I could probably use your take-no-shit attitude when it comes to them. I may yet have to. Weddings bring out the worst, it seems."

"Hey," I protest. "Not yours. Yours will be the fucking *best*. Even if I have to fight some bitches."

Mia laughs heartily and wipes away her tears. Greg chimes in that he's ready to throw down for her and Nate, too. Soon, Mia's happy again, and we're back to joking and laughing.

As we all tease and chatter over the remnants of a fantastic meal, I realize how seamlessly we fit together. And for a moment, I can see life as part of a couple. Life in this town, with close friends, good food, and beautiful vistas. And even though I'd never admit it? Well, it makes my heart swell a little.

Under the table, I lace my fingers with Greg's where they still rest on my leg. He looks at me with such open affection that I lose my breath for a moment. Whatever is happening between us, I know Mia is right — it's a big deal for me. I hope I'm ready for it. But as Greg squeezes my hand, I know one thing: I'm willing to try.

CHAPTER ELEVEN

GREG

The crisp mountain air fills my lungs as Joanie and I hike the trail to my favorite lake. I've wanted to share this place with her, and today seemed like the perfect opportunity.

"Ugh, why did I agree to hike to a fucking lake in the mountains the day after Christmas? I'm going to be picking ice out of my ass for a week," Joanie grumbles from behind me as she picks herself up from her third slip.

I snicker and shoot her a look over my shoulder. "Can't handle a little snow, city girl?" I tease.

She stops and plants her pole-filled hands on her hips. "Last I checked, two feet of snow is not a little."

"I guess that depends on where you're talking about. Though last I checked, Seattle gets its fair share of snow from time to time," I respond. "And it's not like you aren't wearing snowshoes and using poles."

"I'm a runner, mountain man, not a snowshoer, remember? I live in one of the hilliest neighborhoods in north Seattle, but I do not go gallivanting about in these conditions. These are stay inside and fuck conditions."

"We'll get there, but you've got to earn it first," I tease her. She shoots me a deeply unsatisfied look, and I can't help but laugh. "All right, fine. Climb on." I shift my pack to my front and crouch down for her to get on my back.

"Seriously?" she asks incredulously.

I smirk at her over my shoulder. "Seriously, city girl. Come on, I'll carry you. Part of the mountain man boyfriend privileges."

The small rosy circles on her cheeks expand, presumably due to the B-word. I had to try it out to see how she'd react. When she climbs on my back, I decide she must've liked it.

"You know I could whisper all sorts of dirty things in your ear right now," she murmurs, her hot breath fanning over my ear and cheek.

I smile but don't respond. Well, at least not in words. My hardening dick sure has an opinion. She must've *really* liked my using the B-word.

I push forward, and as we crest the final hill, the lake comes into view, its still surface reflecting the surrounding snow-capped evergreens like a mirror. The flat expanse of the serene water is surrounded by snowy rocks, dense white-flocked evergreen forest, and dramatically tall, snow-covered mountains against a clear blue sky. I hear and feel Joanie's small gasp, an excited puff of hot air on my neck. I turn my head to see her jaw drop and her eyes widen.

"It's beautiful," she murmurs.

I slide her gently back to the ground and slip my arm around her waist, pulling her close. "Not as beautiful as you."

She rolls her eyes but leans into me. "Cheesy much?"

I chuckle and press a kiss to her temple. "Only for you, baby," I murmur in her ear. I feel her shiver, and I smile against her cheek. "Remember what you asked me about my mountain man life?"

I see the moment she remembers as she slowly turns her head and looks at me like I'm crazy. "We are not swimming in *that* naked. It's freezing!"

A mischievous grin spreads across my face. "Just for a minute. I dare you."

Her eyes spark with challenge. "How about we have sex on that rock instead?" She gestures with her chin toward a large, flat rock that's bare of snow. Presumably, that melted off under the midday sunlight that's hitting it. "That'll warm us up."

I raise an eyebrow. "I thought you said it was too cold?"

She shrugs, already pulling off her pink gloves. "In the water, sure. And skinny dipping is so cliché. I bet you've never fucked by a lake, mountain man."

"And you have, city girl?" I taunt back.

She reaches down and feels the front of my dark blue snow pants. "Not yet. Worried someone will catch us?"

A thrill shoots through me at the idea of someone happening along while I've got this woman panting under me, screaming my name. "Nope. Just worried I can't get my dick out of my pants fast enough."

She grins and pulls me along before unbuttoning her snow pants and pulling them down with her leggings. With both around her ankles, she bends over, planting her hands firmly on the rock, her sex glistening in the sunlight like the gates to heaven.

I drop my pack, and I've never pulled my pants down faster. Within seconds I've shoved my now rock-hard cock into her soft, slick waiting flesh. The way she's bent causes me to slide all the way home with no effort at all, and her wet heat around me sends a surge of blood to my dick that nearly knocks me unconscious.

She groans at our joining, and the sound brings me back to earth. And then she starts to move, and my senses snap into focus as I watch my cock disappear into her pussy over and over.

Fuck, this woman.

I stand there for another moment longer while she fucks me before I grab her by the hips and take control.

I slam into her hard, pounding and fucking and taking until she's limp in my arms, until I'm holding her up by her hips as I unleash myself on her, driving into her over and over as indecipherable noises tumble out of her mouth, as my balls tighten and heat spreads through me.

I feel her walls flutter around my dick, and I sink in deep, wrapping an arm around her to tease her clit while I tilt my hips over her to rub her deep inner wall. It triggers her climax, and her inner muscles strangle my cock, wringing my orgasm out of me all at once as I empty into her, hot and hard.

As she convulses in my arms, as I come inside her, I

walk through the gates to heaven, and the feeling of bliss spreads through every cell in my body.

Our knees give way simultaneously, pitching us into a crouched heap on the ice-cold rock. The frigid surface is a welcome contrast to the heat radiating from our still-joined bodies.

"I think they call this position 'make a child pose'," Joanie jokes from under me in a sultry, sex-saturated voice.

I stroke a hand down her side and laugh because she's not wrong. With her head resting on the rock and her arms splayed in front of her while I'm still buried in her from behind … it's like the bastard Kama Sutra-Yoga baby of doggy style and child's pose.

And when Joanie lets her chest sink down, her ass tilts up ever so slightly, causing my slippery cock to slide in deeper.

"Fuck," I grunt at the unexpected friction. "That's … holy shit."

Joanie giggles and flexes her hips. And holy. Fucking. Shit. My flagging cock starts to harden again.

"You like that?" she asks sensually. But I know she can feel me getting hard again, so I don't answer.

Instead, I press my chest into her back, letting my dick slide through her folds, teasing her sensitive labia. She groans under me. "As much as you like that," I finally murmur in her ear. "God, I love fucking you, Joanie." She trembles beneath me, and it eggs me on. "I love feeling you surrender that pussy to me." Her breaths turn short and sharp, and she tilts her pelvis frantically.

"You want me to keep fucking that beautiful, tight pussy?"

"Fuck yes," she breathes. "Fuck it, baby."

A bolt of lust shoots through me, and I'm fully hard once more. So I do exactly as she asks, fucking her with sharp, shallow tilts of my hips that I know are hitting her G-spot based on her rapid breathing and hungry cunt that sucks me in with every thrust. Something about the position, about her clear surrender, undoes me on a level more primal than I've ever felt.

And I unleash. Hard then deep, soft then shallow, fast then slow; I lose myself to how she feels, how my body responds to hers, to the dirty words she inspires me to growl in her ear as our bodies realign on a level I didn't even know existed until all that I am is hers, and all that she is is mine. Until my world shrinks to one woman, this woman, and my heart expands with the understanding that she has offered herself to me in a way I don't think she's ever offered herself to anyone; a way beyond sex, even though it's the language our bodies seem to understand each other best.

So I say everything I'm feeling by worshipping her with pleasure. I offer myself as a partner who can speak the language she understands. The language of her body. Of our bodies, entwined. And as she convulses underneath me, gasping my name over and over, as I explode once more inside her, I know when all the pieces of me come back together, they'll be rearranged.

And they will all be hers.

They all are hers.

I'm hers.

The thought has gravity, and it settles deep in my chest as we both come down from orgasm.

I pull away slowly, retrieving a towel from my discarded pack and using it to gently clean Joanie and myself. She rolls over on the rock and lifts her hips to shimmy back into her pants while I put my own to rights.

I've caught my breath by the time I sink down beside her. Mostly. I lose it a little again when I look at her. Her alabaster skin is flushed, her ice-blue eyes bright, and her dark hair spilled out from under her cap and splayed over her shoulders and neck. She's just-fucked beautiful, and with the snow-covered trees and mountains behind her, she's this mountain man's dream girl.

That feeling in my chest burrows deep, and words escape me. At least all the ones that mean anything. I know she doesn't usually do deep, and the last thing I want to do is scare her off so soon.

So I settle for asking, "Hungry?"

She grins, and her face lighting up outshines the bright winter sun above us. "Starving."

I unpack the lunch I brought, and we settle on the rock, side by side.

Joanie lifts her sandwich with a laugh. "First grilled cheese, now PB&J? You sure you weren't a mother hen in another life?" she teases, taking a big bite of her sandwich.

"Hey, I'm no Mia, but I'll have you know I make a mean PB&J," I tease back.

She chews, a thoughtful expression on her face before finally giving a slow nod. "That you do." She looks like she wants to say something else. Eventually, she asks about my work at the community center.

Even though I'm pretty sure that's not what she wanted to say, I go with it.

"It's rewarding," I tell her. "I get to help people, whether it's seniors staying active or kids learning new skills. Plus, it gives me plenty of time for my own hobbies, like fishing and hiking."

She nods. "Sounds idyllic. Very different from my old life."

"What kind of law did you practice?" I ask, realizing I don't know much about her career.

She sighs. "I was a corporate defense attorney. Basically, I helped big companies get away with shady shit." She shakes her head. "And the higher-ups never took me seriously no matter how good I was. I was too 'aggressive', apparently. A man with my style would've made partner years ago."

I frown. "That's bullshit."

"Tell me about it." She takes another bite of her sandwich. "Anyway, enough about my past. Tell me more about this town. Who runs what around here?"

I'm surprised by how little she wants to discuss herself, but I don't push it. So, I give her the rundown.

"My Uncle Henry owns the grocery store where he handles the second half of business hours, with my cousin Ned, who you've met —" Joanie smirks "— handling the first half of the day. My Uncle's wife, Margaret, runs a small mail shop with the world's tiniest post office inside. My father and uncle co-own the gas station and convenience store-slash-tackle shop. Jerry owns the tavern and the sad excuse for a coffee stand. Then, of course, there are Nate and Mia's businesses. And as you know, I own the community center, though I also own the land with the pond, my house, and a good amount of acreage besides. Oh, and I co-own a shit ton of land in and around the town with my father."

"Hm," she murmurs. "So what's with the whole Old West vibe? The wagon wheels and stuff?"

I explain the town's gold rush history and the shuttered museum.

Joanie mulls on that for a minute before asking, "Who owns the museum?"

I stop, realizing I'd never thought about that. "I don't know," I admit.

"So no one in your family then?" she presses.

I shrug. "Guess not. Anyway, my dad had all these grand plans to turn Alpine Ridge into a Wild West tourist trap, which sounds great, in theory, since that's the town's roots. But all of his ideas were so over the top that they'd make a mockery of it. Themed campgrounds, boardwalks, the works. He even wanted to put in an amusement park. But he couldn't get approval for any of it, thank fuck."

Her eyes narrow. "So he's not on the town council?"

I laugh. "God, no. He only inherited land here a few years ago. He hasn't spent much time in Alpine Ridge, but he's sure got opinions on what to do with it." I shake my head. "His pushiness has made things harder for me with the council. They're all old-timers who resist change, and now they don't trust me much either." I pause, debating whether to ask her something.

"What's that look?" she asks, furrowing her brow.

"I'm just not sure why you'd care about any of this," I say, not technically asking while asking.

The corner of her mouth lifts in a half-smile. "I guess I just wanted to know more about this town. Because it's important to people I care about. Including you."

I reach over and tuck a strand of hair behind her ear. "I care about you too, Joanie," I say, my voice thick with more emotion than I've felt in a long time.

We stare into each other's eyes, a thread of understanding weaving between us. Her eyes soften, and she leans in to kiss me deeply.

When she pulls back, there's a glint in her eye that I'm coming to recognize. "Take me home, mountain man. I'm not done with you yet."

I grin and start packing up. "Yes, ma'am."

Later, as Joanie sleeps curled against my chest, I think about what she said to me. She's right — Alpine Ridge is important to me. And the idea that Joanie might be warming to it makes me feel even more protective of it. And of her.

My last thought before drifting off is that maybe, just maybe, I've finally found a place worth fighting for ... and someone worth fighting for.

CHAPTER TWELVE

JOANIE

I've been in Alpine Ridge for about three weeks now, and the more I learn about this town with its character and unique beauty, the more I realize how much potential it has and how much the people here, especially my beautiful best friend, are missing out on because the town has not been incorporated.

With only a few thousand residents, there isn't enough traffic to sustain her business long-term, even alongside the folks ambling through from Ellensburg looking to head to Wenatchee or Leavenworth. Or any of the businesses. And then there's the other thing my research turned up: Alpine Ridge's population is aging *and* dwindling. In short, the town needs fresh blood if it's even going to survive, much less thrive.

So, given my new mission to breathe official township life into this place, armed with more knowledge thanks to Mia and Greg, I do what any good lawyer would do and spend the day researching. And what I find is pretty damn shocking.

It turns out, by definition, that there shouldn't even *be* a town council in an unincorporated town. Which means this supposed "council" that denied Greg and Mia's requests to incorporate? They had no right.

Since Mia isn't around to hold my earrings while I make to throw down, I do the only logical thing I can: I go find her. Greg took off way too fucking early this morning, so that leaves me to drive in my car, which Mia thoughtfully drove down the hill yesterday while Greg and I were hiking. Thankfully, my Subaru has all-wheel drive, and it's not that far.

Still, with ice and an uneven road, it takes way longer than I expected to get here, with a good heap more sliding around and nearly losing control of the car than I was prepared for. By the time I arrive, it feels like it's been ages since I made myself a light lunch, so I'm less ready to fight some old farts and more ready for a hot cup of coffee and some pastries.

"Jo," Mia greets me with surprise. "I wasn't expecting to see you emerge from the sex cocoon anytime soon."

I shoot her a mock dirty look, and she smirks.

"Coffee," I grunt jokingly, collapsing into a chair across from the pastry display case. "Sugar," I add. Mia crosses her arms over her chest and gives me an expectant look. "Please?"

She grins. "You got it. And you're lucky because Rae just pulled a fresh huckleberry pie out of the oven a few minutes ago."

"Ooh, I haven't tried the famous huckleberry pie yet," I say excitedly. To hear Nate and Mia talk it's life-changing, but Mia and Rae have been so focused on holiday treats lately.

A couple of minutes later, Mia sets a large, steaming cup of Joe down on the table in front of me, then a delicate round plate decorated with pink flowers and topped with a huge slice of gooey purple-blue filled pie crust covered in an artfully swirled pile of whipped cream. And my whole mouth fills with saliva.

As Mia sits across from me, I don't even pretend to have manners; I grab the fork and shovel a scoop of the warm, fragrant sugary goodness into my mouth. The sweet, tart taste of the filling spreads over my tongue, and I'm a goner.

"Ohmygawd," I mumble around the pie. "Dish is uhmashing."

Mia shakes her head and laughs. "Oh, I know. But geez, Jo, for the love of God, swallow before you speak."

I shrug, then down another huge bite, causing Mia to chuckle as she sips her coffee. After that bite, I take a drink from my cup and sigh contentedly.

"Rae, you're fucking awesome," I call to the back of the bakery.

"Glad you like the pie," she calls back.

I smile at Mia. "You're never going to believe what I just figured out." I take another bite of pie as I watch her eyes light up with curiosity.

"Well?" she demands after I don't cough up the info immediately.

117

I take another sip of coffee and slowly set my cup down before leaning forward on my elbows. "The town council?" She nods encouragingly. "Total bullshit. Unincorporated towns don't have town councils, Mia. Those old fuckers are frauds."

Mia gasps. "No way!"

"Way," I respond before eating more pie.

Mia slams a fist on the table. "Assholes! Holy fucking shit!"

I can't help but laugh a little. She must be *really* pissed. She rarely curses this much.

Rae steps out of the back, drying her hands on a dishtowel. "Is everything okay out here?" she asks, her brows bunched together in concern.

"No," Mia says vehemently. "Did you know the supposed town council isn't legitimate?"

Rae's brow furrows farther in confusion. "I don't understand," she replies.

"Alpine Ridge isn't technically a town, right?" I offer, babystepping her through the information. Rae nods, though she still looks confused. "If it's not a town, it can't have a council."

Rae's mouth pops open. "Well fuck me sideways," she murmurs. "I never thought about that." She shakes her head slowly as her features pinch together in anger. "Those old bastards sure have some explaining to do."

I nod smugly. "They sure do. Any idea where we can find them?" I look between Mia and Rae.

Rae lifts her chin. "Now that I'm working for Mia, Jerry has to handle my old afternoon shift at the tavern.

He's been lording his town council member status over everyone for as long as I can remember. How about we close up a bit early and go have a little chat with him?"

Mia and I exchange a look. "Let's do it," Mia agrees.

After a quick clean-up, Mia shepherds us out, flips the sign on the door to "closed," and locks up. Mia peeks into the wellness center but comes back shaking her head.

"Nate's working with someone. We'll tell him later," she says.

"I'll drive," Rae offers, gesturing to a well-kept older Bronco.

We pile in, and Rae guns the engine a little more than is necessary.

"Easy there," I tease. "Maybe we should pick one of us to take point so we don't all rip his throat out at once."

"I vote for you, Jo," Mia says immediately. "Not only did you make this discovery, but I've seen you go after someone on the witness stand."

I smirk but wait for Rae's response. She nods in confirmation. "If I open my mouth, nothing good will come out of it," she mutters.

She navigates down the road and into the tavern's parking lot, pulling smoothly into a spot and cutting the engine.

"All right, let's do this," Mia says darkly.

The three of us march into the tavern, and Rae jerks her chin toward an old guy behind the bar. Jerry.

I zero in on him, prowling forward with Mia and Rae flanking me.

He looks to be in his mid-sixties, with dark grey hair

neatly clipped short. He's wearing a faded blue and grey plaid shirt tucked into old Wranglers. His light brown eyes scan me from head to toe as I approach, but not in a skeevy way—more like assessing. Given my company and manner of approach, I can tell he senses something is up, not to mention the fact that I wore a starched blue button-up blouse and black slacks to at least look like I meant business.

"Hello, Rae," he says, addressing her first. Then he looks at Mia and dips his chin. "Mia." His eyes flick back over me. "Who's your friend?"

I slide a business card out of my pocket and deposit it on the bar. "I'm Joanie Morris, a corporate law attorney. I have some questions for you about the town council," I begin, not bothering with small talk.

He shifts uncomfortably. "What about it?"

"Is it true that you and your fellow 'council members' —" I throw heavy sarcasm into the words and add air quotes to give a nice, bitchy edge to it "— have been purporting to legally represent Alpine Ridge?"

Jerry's neck turns red, and he stops toweling off the beer mug he'd been drying. "Well, I … that is to say …" he splutters.

"I'll take that as a yes," I press on with a dangerous smile. Aware that the tavern has quieted around us, I raise my voice and continue, "I presume you're aware that since Alpine Ridge is, in fact, an unincorporated area of Kittitas County, it is not legally recognized as a town and, as such, there is also no legally recognized town council or governing body of any kind?"

"Listen here —" Jerry starts, seeming to find his voice.

I don't let him finish. "And given that, you had no right to deny Gregory Tyler and Mia Anderson's requests to pursue incorporation for the town, likewise denying necessary services, including emergency responders, utilities, infrastructure, and more to the residents of this area?"

"You've got this all wrong, we just —"

"And surely you know that misrepresenting yourself as legally capable of denying such requests is a violation of county and state ordinances —"

"Now, wait just a minute!" Jerry bellows.

The silence that follows his outburst is deep. I fight back my smirk, knowing everyone in the place is waiting for Jerry to dig himself out of or deeper into this hole.

Jerry, for his part, is breathing hard, his eyes angry and wild. "The people here needed someone to look to for help, for answers. They like it quiet and simple, but sometimes someone has to make decisions to keep everything from going off the rails."

"So you and your friends —" I pull a sheet of paper from my pocket and read the short list of names while Jerry becomes increasingly pale at the depth of my knowledge "— decided it was your job to take that on? Even knowing you had no legal right to do so? And denying residents and business owners of the area the resources they need?"

"Nobody here wants to pay more taxes so some stupid bakery can keep making cookies," Jerry says bitterly. Mia scoffs, and Jerry's eyes narrow on her, delivering his next words as if only for her. "It died years ago for a reason, and it should've stayed dead."

Mia pushes forward angrily, but I lift an arm to stop her.

"What about this tavern, then? And the grocery store? The gas station? There are necessary services here that are dying too, and you're putting the nails in their coffin all in the name of your property taxes not increasing a few dollars a year," I point out calmly. "Awfully short-sighted considering that statistically incorporation causes a boost in property values and business revenue that *vastly* outweighs property tax increases." I pause, tilting my head and returning the assessing look he gave me when I entered.

"Did you consider that, or simply your own wishes for things not to change, despite the steady decline in population in this area over the last thirty years? By my calculations, based on those rates, your businesses here will all die within ten years, with your population dropping to nearly zero within another ten years. Were you banking on not living long enough for that to be your problem?"

Rae chuckles beside me, and Mia's hand squeezes mine, communicating her approval.

But the real success comes with Jerry's silence, which stretches long enough for one of the guys in the tavern to stand up and ask in a demanding voice, "Jerry, is this all true?"

Jerry splutters, the redness having crept from his neck to his face, and he's unable to form a coherent response.

I finally allow Mia to step forward. "She's right. The bed and breakfast, the bakery, and the wellness center aren't doing as well as they could be, and they won't last more than another few years with the way things are. I pushed for incorporation to give the town the resources to draw more people in, which would be good for *all* of the businesses in town." She turns to face the room. "My Gran lived here for decades, and I spent a lot of time here over the years, even before I became a permanent resident. Through her love for this town, I came to love it too. And I can't watch it die. Not when we have the power to do something about it."

Jerry's face turns an alarming shade of purple. "You're all ungrateful," he spits out. "You're going to ruin what makes this town worth living in."

The crowd, whose faces had shone with empathy after Mia's speech, turns angry. But it's Rae who scoffs and says, "Jerry, your own wife died because an ambulance couldn't get to her in time. Is that what you want for everyone else?"

The tavern erupts in murmurs.

Rae continues, undeterred. "Joanie's research is right. The town is shrinking. I knew that without research and numbers. We need new families if we want Alpine Ridge to survive. And how will we attract them when we have no schools? When residents have to drive nearly an hour to get to the dump, and at best, have to live with satellite internet and TV service that only work half the time? Not to mention all the other services Miss Joanie listed."

Her speech is met with vocal agreement from most of

the patrons. Outnumbered and outmatched, Jerry angrily throws his towel down and stomps through the swinging door behind the bar.

The patrons continue talking, though, sharing stories about how great the town used to be and the audacity of Jerry and his cronies to pretend like they ran the place.

As the ideas we planted catch fire, Mia pulls me aside. "This was your plan all along. To publicly humiliate Jerry and get the town talking?"

"Damn straight. But this was just the beginning. Let them stew on it for the week. We can't do anything until after the New Year anyway."

"And then?" Rae prompts.

I wink at them both. "Then we start working with the county on incorporation documents. Because we don't need anyone's fucking permission."

Mia and Rae exchange an excited glance.

"I should go back and tell Nate what's going on," Mia responds. "Plus, he'll expect to head home for dinner soon."

I nod, and we follow Rae back out to the Bronco.

Once she drops us off, Mia keeps me from heading into the wellness center.

"Have you told Greg yet?" she asks.

I shake my head. "He's at the community center today, so I came straight to you. Besides, I figured once we tracked down one of the council members, I'd have more to share anyway, so I wanted to wait until I had more to tell."

Mia nods distractedly, and I can tell her mind is racing through what this means for her and Nate.

"Hey," I say softly. "Is this okay? I'm mostly doing it for you. But if this causes too many waves, I don't have to go all Hurricane Joanie on Alpine Ridge."

Mia huffs a laugh. "It's more than okay. If I had the time and energy, I'd be going after this too. Which has been tearing me up because I knew if it didn't happen, all the time and energy I'm using on the bakery instead would be a waste."

"Honestly, you're right, it would be. While I haven't seen your financials, even my generous calculations for the businesses here weren't pretty," I admit. "I don't want to see you put your heart into this only to have it die, babe. The world deserves your pastries, after all." I wink at her playfully, trying to lighten the heaviness of the conversation.

"Is that all this is?" she asks.

My brows dip together. "What do you mean?"

"I mean … are you maybe doing this because you can see yourself spending more time here with a certain mountain man?" she clarifies with a mischievous smile.

I press my lips together. "Okay, maybe a little?" I admit cautiously. Mia gets a look on her face, and I hold up a hand. "Let's not make it a thing, okay?"

"I mean, I'm not, I just …" she trails off, chewing her lip nervously.

I sigh heavily and cross my arms. "Okay, fine. Get whatever it is you need to say off your chest," I say, gesturing for her to continue.

She rolls her eyes. "You know you'd give me the talk, too," she points out. I nod resignedly and gesture again for her to continue. "Just ... don't move too fast with Greg, okay? Keep your options open. Maybe even start looking for jobs back in Seattle?"

I narrow my eyes at her. "Are you trying to get rid of me?"

"No, of course not," she rushes to assure me. "I just can't see you being happy staying in a small town long-term. And it won't hurt to keep your options open," she reiterates.

I take a deep breath and try to focus on where I know this is coming from. "I hear you. I know you're trying to look out for me. And that's good advice."

"But?"

I let out a breath and laugh. "God, you know me a little too well, Mia." I shake my head. "But I don't know any other way than all in," I say with a shrug.

Mia steps forward and wraps her arms around me. "I know. It's one of the things I love most about you."

I hear her unspoken concern that it's also the thing that might get me burned.

I want to dismiss it from my thoughts as easily as I did in our conversation, but her words niggle at the back of my mind as we say our goodbyes and I head back to Greg's.

Will I be happy here? I'd been so caught up in my budding relationship with Greg and the thrill of taking on the town council that I hadn't thought too hard about the future.

Maybe she's right. Maybe I'm not cut out for small-town life. Maybe I'm not cut out for a relationship and the thrill of being with Greg will wear off. Hell, maybe Greg will get sick of me.

That thought makes me laugh. Because based on my history, I'm far more likely to get sick of him first. And he seems like a relationship kind of guy.

When he returns from the community center, I'm still stewing on it an hour later, curled up on his couch that faces the expanse of forest behind the house.

"There's my girl," he says with a smirk, settling beside me.

"Hey," I reply. And then I look closer at his face. "What's with the smirk?"

"A little birdie told me you and the girls visited the tavern this afternoon."

I huff a laugh. "Jesus H. Fucking Christ, news travels fast in this town," I grumble. And then, to cover my ass, "I was going to tell you."

He grins and nods. "I know. I'm not mad. In fact …" he leans forward and hauls my legs up so I'm lying flat on the couch under him. "I think you deserve something for what was evidently a fantastic performance."

I bite into my lip. "Yeah? Like what?"

He smiles and dips down to run his nose down my neck and between my breasts, stopping to place a kiss on my now-exposed navel. "I don't know, what do you want?"

I take a deep breath. And I let the dirty thoughts pass through my head because those are fleeting desires.

"I want to know what we're doing here," I say honestly.

He sits up, brows raised. "Seriously?"

I scoot back up to a sitting position, wrapping my arms around my legs. While I'm not usually self-conscious, I've never had a conversation like this. With anyone. Ever.

"Seriously," I confirm with a trace of irritation. "Obviously, we're enjoying ourselves, but what is this? I know we said it's more than sex. But how much more?"

"How much more do you want it to be?" he parries.

I flinch at his response. "I don't know," I reply honestly. "I mean, I have a condo in Seattle. I could go back there and start looking for a job."

"Or?" he asks, sensing the implied choice.

"Or I could stay here for a while and use my time to pursue making Alpine Ridge official and handling all the legalities that come with that. From my preliminary research, that's no small task, and it would require someone with my knowledge and contacts to pull it off."

"Are we going to pretend like that's not exactly what you're planning to do?" he asks with a smirk.

I scrunch my nose and press my lips together to keep from smiling. Shit, he already knows me too well. "No. But even if I do, that doesn't mean I have to keep staying with you. I mean, this is your sacred space. It occurred to me that I might already be intruding on that."

"Occurred to you, or Mia told you we're going too fast?" he asks bluntly.

Fuck, he clearly also knows Mia too well.

When I don't answer, he slides close to me and takes

my face in his hands. "You don't have to stay with me if you don't want to, Joanie, but I fucking love having you in my bed. In my life. And I loved coming home to you today. I don't see that changing anytime soon. I'm not saying I want you to live here permanently yet ... but I also don't want you to go. Beyond that?" He strokes his thumb over my cheek and looks deeply into my eyes. "While I've never cared much about getting married, I'll admit that I want someone to share this life with."

His eyes continue to search mine, and I feel the words he's not saying. *I want to share this life with you.*

A knot forms in my throat. I can't tell if it's fear or love. This is new territory for me, but I realize I'm falling for Greg. And he's clearly falling for me.

I should find it comforting that we both seem to have a healthy fear of it because love isn't something to be taken lightly. Nor is commitment. I've never been good at either. But with Greg, I want to try.

I nod softly and let him make love to me on the couch. Everything feels so much ... *more.* By the time we curl up in bed that night, Greg's warm body wrapped around mine, I'm no less concerned about whether this is the life for me or a pitstop.

But as Greg pulls me closer in his sleep, I can't ignore how my heart clenches at the thought of leaving him.

Shit. When did this get so complicated?

I close my eyes, pushing the doubts away. I'll figure it out. I always do.

But for now, I'm exactly where I want to be.

CHAPTER THIRTEEN

JOANIE

The community center is a flurry of activity as we all pitch in to decorate for the New Year's Eve party Greg decided to have earlier this week. Mia, Nate, Rae, and I have been here for hours, hanging streamers, setting up tables, and generally helping Greg make the place look festive.

Since I didn't think there would be any time to change, I did it all in my halter-necked champagne sequined bodycon dress. But if I can litigate in four-inch heels, I can sure as hell decorate in a tight outfit. I also got to watch Greg working in his own tailored black dress shirt and tight black pants. It was worth it.

Looking around, I'm pretty satisfied with what we've accomplished. Nate made a trip to Costco, and you can tell by looking at the two joined long, loaded buffet tables. We're not lacking food or alcohol. And with Mia around, we're never lacking for sweet treats. Positioned at one end of the tables are cupcakes with sparklers waiting to be lit; at the other end, round sugar cookies decorated to look like clocks striking midnight, and toward the middle, a large tray with two types of macarons, white chocolate ones arranged in the new year's numbers and dark pink raspberry ones arranged around the numbers to make them pop.

Small bar-height tables with pairs of matched chairs dot the edge of the room, their plain black utilitarian look disguised by sparkly slip-on covers.

As I arrange a centerpiece with white flowers in a tall, blinged-out vase for the main tables, I hear the door open and turn to see Mia's sister, Carrie, walking in. It was a pleasant surprise to hear that Mia invited her. I thought it meant both women were working past the bullshit their parents thrust upon them.

But instead of the excited smile I expected, her face is pinched. The obvious trauma on her features starkly contrasts the playful beaded blue sweetheart-neckline dress with a flared skirt she's wearing, which offsets the long, wavy brown hair and blue eyes that run in the family. But as she approaches, I see those dark blues are red-rimmed.

Mia notices Carrie's distress too and rushes over to her sister, enveloping her in a hug, careful not to snag the fringe of her silver sheath dress on the beads of her sister's. "Oh no, Care-bear, what's wrong?"

Carrie sniffs and wipes at her eyes. "When I told Mom and Dad I was coming here for New Year's, they tried to guilt me into staying home. They said I was choosing you over them."

Mia's face hardens. "That's not fair. Seeing me doesn't mean you're choosing sides."

Carrie nods. "I know. Still. I hate being in the middle of this." She gives Mia an apologetic smile. "Not that I'm blaming you."

Rae and I exchange a look and move to join them.

"They're just being assholes," I offer by way of greeting, rubbing Carrie's back. "Trust me, we've had our share of drama this week with the old farts in town."

Carrie looks up, her curiosity obviously piqued. "Really? Drama in sleepy little Alpine Ridge? I've got to hear about this."

So we fill her in on our confrontation with Jerry and the whole town council debacle. By the end, she's laughing.

"Serves them right," she says with a grin. "I can't believe they thought they could get away with pretending to be in charge."

"Yes, well, there are certainly enough power players in this town to be getting on with. Turns out my new boyfriend's family owns most of it, and they're as wackadoo as your parents," I offer.

Carrie gives me a sympathetic smile.

"Hey, not all the landowners here are assholes," Mia interjects.

I smirk. "Of course not. You, Nate, and Greg are all gems. And I'm sure whoever owns the old gold-mining museum is sane because they don't seem to be making a fuss," I add thoughtfully.

Rae's eyebrows jump in surprise. "You didn't know?" she asks.

Mia's brow furrows in confusion. "Know what?"

Rae looks between us almost guiltily. "I own it. Well, now I do. It was passed down through my daddy's family. He used to run it when I was a kid. But when he left my mom ... well, you get the idea." She shrugs sheepishly.

My jaw drops. "Seriously? Well, I guess it *used* to be owned by an asshole, anyway. Yeesh. I'm so sorry, Rae." I pause, wondering if I should even ask my next question. But then again, why start holding back now? "Why haven't you done anything with it?"

Rae shrugs. "Never had the time or money. But maybe now, with the town incorporating, we can figure out how it fits into the new Alpine Ridge."

The wheels start turning in my head, but people arrive for the party before I can voice my ideas. Rae rushes off to change out of the T-shirt and jeans she'd showed up in and returns in a gorgeous mint-colored wrap dress that sets off her short, golden blond locks and brings out the green in her hazel eyes. I give her a thumbs up, and she grins at me across the room.

Nate also reappears, looking like hot business in grey slacks that look painted on his huge, muscled legs and a starched white button-front shirt.

Still, he's got nothing on Greg, I decide as I watch the two men talk. Greg's back is turned to me, and his gorgeous backside is calling my name.

But the community center begins to fill quickly with what seems like half the town before I can make it to him.

133

However, it doesn't take long before Greg weaves through the crowd to me, grinning from ear to ear.

"It looks like the festival got people excited about community events after all," I comment as he approaches.

He slips an arm around my waist and pulls me close. "Seems that way. I'm glad we're keeping the momentum going. Save me a dance?"

I nod, and he kisses me before disappearing into the crowd, presumably to ensure everything is running smoothly. I watch him flit around the room before sampling the food and getting myself a drink.

As the party kicks into high gear, the music is loud enough to dance to but soft enough to hold a conversation, and I lose track of Greg completely. I'm chatting with Mia and Rae when I spot Carrie across the room, looking uncomfortable as Greg's cousin Ned corners her.

I remember the first time he approached me. He's as sketchy-looking now as he was then. Wrung out, greasy, and sporting a leer that would make a prostitute turn tail and run in the opposite direction. The guy is bad news. And Carrie looks like she wants to bolt, but he's got her trapped near the drinks. And I know Carrie. She's too polite for her own good.

I'm about to intervene when I see Ned turn away and slip something into a cup, then try to hand it to her. He's not subtle about it, but I can tell it was just out of Carrie's eye-line, and the crowd around them is thick enough that she likely didn't notice. But before I can react, Nate is there, snatching the drink away and grabbing Ned by the collar.

Mia catches the look on my face. "What is it?" she asks, turning toward where I'm looking just in time to see Nate drag Ned toward the door, fury etched on every line of his face.

"Oh shit," Mia curses.

Rae's eyes finally catch up, and she puts a hand to her mouth. Having lived here longer than us, I'm sure she's more than familiar with Ned and his way of creeping on the ladies.

We watch as Nate tosses Ned out the door, pulling it closed behind him. Greg appears and, after a tense conversation with Nate, storms outside after Ned.

"I'm going to go check on Carrie," Mia tells us.

"I'm coming with you," I insist, following her through the crowd.

When we get to Carrie, she looks beyond confused.

"Are you okay?" Mia asks, checking her over like she's looking for injuries.

Carrie nods, looking shaken. "I think so. What the hell was that?"

"Nate saw Ned put something in your drink," I explain.

Both Carrie and Mia's eyes widen. "He tried to drug me?" Carrie asks incredulously.

"He tried to drug her?!" Mia echoes, outraged.

Nate joins us, still seething and clearly having heard Mia. "Yes, but I took the drink before he could hand it to her. Fuck, I hope Greg is beating the shit out of that psychopath." My eyes widen at how hard he grinds his teeth in anger. "Fucking hell. We don't even have a damn police force to report it to."

We all stew momentarily, the gravity of the situation sinking in. Then, raised voices draw our attention outside. Yes, from outside. That's how loud they are. Murmurs start to ripple through the crowd, so Mia and I follow Nate to the door to help get things back under control so the whole town doesn't know about this in the next two minutes. As we pass Rae, I ask her to go look after Carrie. She nods, and we continue.

Once outside, we find Greg in a heated argument with an older couple.

"... refused to believe all the other reports of his bad behavior, and now this!" Greg is shouting.

"He's a good boy; he wouldn't do something like that," the woman insists. Ah. This must be his aunt and uncle.

Greg laughs harshly. "A good boy? He's a predator. But you two are so far up Dad's ass, you can't see what's right in front of you."

"How dare you speak to us like that!" his uncle bellows. "You're a disgrace to this family, turning your back on us, on the business. You're nothing but a disappointment. Our Ned is twice the man you'll ever be."

I scoff loudly, but they've already turned and stormed off. Greg stands there, chest heaving, hands clenched into fists.

We all let out a collective breath. I'm relieved it seems to be over, but I'm worried about Greg.

I start to go to him, but Mia catches my arm. "Give

Nate a minute," she murmurs as her fiancé heads over to him.

We watch as Nate says something to Greg that is too low for us to hear. Greg nods, and they head back inside together.

Mia turns to me with a rueful smile. "Well, this isn't quite how I expected to ring in the new year."

I snort. "At least it's not boring. Remember our last New Year's together?"

"God, don't remind me. My apartment. That sad little cake and cheap champagne ..."

"And the kiss at midnight since neither of us had anyone else," I finish with a smile.

Mia chuckles. "We've come a long way since then, haven't we? I mean, even with all this drama tonight, look at us. Look at where we are."

I pause, unsure I want to unpack that with Mia right now. "Where we are is outside of the party. Let's go back in, shall we?" I deflect.

She nods and leads the way, but as we head back inside, I privately consider her words.

She's right. Two years ago, Mia was miserable at her job, and I was burning the candle at both ends and trying to find fulfillment in all the wrong places. And by places, I mean dicks.

And now? Mia is engaged to the love of her life, running a successful business she's passionate about. She's happier than I've ever seen her, even if she's not exactly more relaxed these days. But that's Mia. Like me, she needs a challenge, and now she's got one that she actually enjoys.

As for me, I walked away from a going-nowhere career which gave me the opportunity to take a chance on something that matters. This incorporation project has meaning. Purpose. And in Greg, I may have found a partner who will support me and give me room to do my thing. That's always been my biggest reason for not getting into relationships: losing myself. And on some level, I know that if this relationship goes the distance, that won't happen with Greg.

The realization hits me like a freight train. I want that. I want him. Not just for now but for … no, I can't think the F-word. I may have come far, but there are still things I'm not ready for, and forever is definitely on that list. Only time will prove whether we work together on that level.

As if summoned by my thoughts, Greg appears at my side. "Hey," he says softly. "Sorry about all that."

I shake my head and lean into him. "Don't apologize. You were standing up for what's right. I'm just pissed that that little weasel of a cousin of yours isn't going to face any consequences for trying to drug Carrie."

He presses a kiss to my temple. "He'll get his, don't worry. But I'm sorry because that is not how I wanted this night to go."

"It's not your fault," I assure him. "And it's totally last year, baby. Let's start the new year how we want it to be." I give him a suggestive grin as I slide my hand up his chest and sink my fingers into his dark curls.

As if on cue, the crowd around us starts chanting. "Ten, nine, eight..."

Greg smiles slyly and pulls me against him, his hands wrapping around my backside possessively.

"Seven, six, five..."

I run my nose along his.

"Four, three, two, one ... Happy New Year!"

As cheers erupt around us, Greg lowers his mouth to mine. He nibbles gently at my bottom lip, then swipes his tongue over it. I open to him, and he slips inside, meeting me in gentle strokes that get harder as his cock does against my stomach. His hands pull me tighter, sliding up my back and tugging at my hair. Still, he's gentle and thorough, clearly devoted to making me feel the passion behind the kiss. But given the timing, it also feels like a promise for the coming year of the passion waiting for me. For us.

When we break apart, he rests his forehead against mine. "Is it too soon to tell you I love you?" he whispers.

My heart races in my chest at his question-slash-confession. "It's never too soon to tell someone how you feel," I reply honestly. "But I'm not sure I can say it back yet."

He pulls back slightly, disappointment flickering in his eyes before it's replaced with understanding. "That's okay. I can wait."

I smirk at his clear confidence that I will say it back when I'm not even sure I will. But then, as he pulls me back into his arms, I breathe him in, feeling the rightness of this, of us, settle into my bones.

I may not be ready to say the words, but I know, without a doubt, that I'm falling head over heels for this man.

And I'm not running from it for the first time in my life. So maybe he's right after all, and I will say it someday. Perhaps even someday soon.

"Is it too late to tell you I want to be fucked thoroughly in your office for New Year's?" I tease, deflecting the seriousness of the moment.

His pupils dilate as his cock twitches against me, and I bite my lip.

"It's never too late for that," he replies before his mouth crushes mine. But only briefly before he breaks off and pulls me through the room and to his office, where we ring in the new year properly. Twice. And if the crazy hot sex shoved up against his door is any indication, it's going to be a good year.

CHAPTER FOURTEEN

GREG

I wake up on New Year's Day with Joanie curled against my side, her soft breaths tickling my chest. Last night was incredible, both the party and the private celebration with Joanie afterward. I should be feeling great and ready to start the year strong.

Instead, my mind is consumed with thoughts of Ned and the stunt he tried to pull with Carrie. I spin through all the times he's crossed the line by propositioning women who come through his checkout. And that's not even the worst of it. I knew it had escalated lately, hearing through the town's grapevine that he'd recently put his hands on at least two women. Unfortunately, he's always careful to stay in line when Nate or I are around, even if he does mutter insults under his breath that he thinks we can't hear. That shit is nothing. But groping … I should've realized it was a progression toward something even worse.

I'm sick to my stomach, not just over his behavior, but

that I haven't found a way to put a stop to it sooner. Based on the discussion Nate and I had last night, he feels the same way. Surely, between us, we should've seen this coming and been able to stop it before he got as far as he did.

And yet, we weren't. My biggest fear is that he'll succeed sooner rather than later because one of us won't always be there to stop him.

Restless and agitated, I slip out of bed, careful not to wake Joanie, pulling the bedroom door closed behind me. I walk through the living room and head to the kitchen to make coffee. I'll think better with caffeine, though I feel pretty fucking defeated on the idea front right now.

I suddenly wish I'd thought to put socks on. The tiled floors are cold, and though I'd gone with all the bells and whistles for my bachelor pad, the heated floors take longer than I've got to start working their magic.

With a sigh, I drag the coffee maker across the granite countertop and pull the supplies out for my usual brew. The rich aroma fills the air, soothing me a bit. I lean against the counter and rub a hand over my face as I stare out the living room window at the quiet, snow-covered forest surrounding the house.

Despite the calmness I'd purposely designed for myself here, this whole thing with Ned has me shaking and doubting myself in other ways, too.

Really, how can I be of any use to Joanie with the town's incorporation when I can't even keep my own family in check? What kind of person does that make me?

And then there's the reaction from my aunt and uncle.

Their blind defense of Ned, their anger at me for calling out his behavior — it's disheartening. They've always been my dad's little soldiers, but this? This is a new low.

I pour myself a cup of coffee and wander to the living room, sinking onto the soft, brown leather couch. The worst part is that I know this will get back to my father. And that's sure to stir up even more drama. As evidenced by his Christmas morning tirade, he's never approved of my "abandonment" of the family business, and this will be one more thing for him to hold against me.

I'm so lost in my thoughts that I don't hear Joanie approach until she's beside me, with a concerned look, wearing only one of my T-shirts. It just goes to show how pissed off I am that it barely stirs me to see so much of her creamy skin on display and the outline of her soft, perky tits through the thin fabric.

"Hey," she says softly, sitting down next to me. "I was surprised to wake up alone. You okay?"

I force a smile. "Yeah, just thinking about everything that needs to be done at the community center," I lie.

She studies me for a moment, clearly not buying it, but for the first time possibly ever, she doesn't push. I'm partly relieved and partly disappointed.

"Okay. Um. Are you going in today, then?" she asks tentatively.

Something's off about her tone, but I'm too distracted by my bullshit to pull at the thread of whatever hers might be.

I shrug, rising from the couch. "Yeah, actually. I

should put everything back so the center's ready for tomorrow."

"All right … well, I'll dive into more research today. Don't forget, Mia's making dinner tonight," she replies.

I grunt my understanding and dump the dregs of my coffee in the sink before heading upstairs for a shower. I'm just not capable of talking about this right now, which I know is making me an asshole. Which, in turn, makes me feel like even more of a failure. Definitely not how I saw the new year starting.

It only gets worse over the next few days. I spend every day at the community center, thankful for New Year's resolutions and the influx of people who want to get fit. It's exactly the distraction I need.

Joanie buries herself in her work and doesn't even stop when I get home. She's always polite and asks how my day was, but there's a wall between us that wasn't there before. As the week rolls by, she becomes more and more distant.

It's not until the end of the week, when I'm showering at the center before heading home, that the massive erection I get soaping myself makes me realize we haven't had sex since New Year's Eve.

Every night, I've been going to sleep early, physically exhausted from the day, assuming she'd wake me up when she came to bed. But she never did. By morning, my dreams had chased me from sleep and dragged me deeper into my pit of self-flagellation.

How could I be so distracted not to realize we'd drifted so far? And why hasn't she said anything?

I resist the urge to jerk off, intent on fixing this between us. Whatever it is that needs fixing.

And then, as I'm dressing, it hits me like a sledgehammer why Joanie wouldn't seek me out for sex, why she'd be burying herself in research and not demanding to know what the hell my problem was this week.

She thinks I'm pulling away because she didn't say "I love you" back. And like an idiot, I didn't even realize it.

I hurry through the rest of my tasks for the day and am just about to head out when there's a knock on the community center door.

Confused, I open it to find a stern-faced man in a suit.

"Gregory Tyler?" he asks.

"Yes?" I reply suspiciously.

He thrusts a packet of papers at me. "You've been served. Have a nice day."

Well, shit. This can't be anything good.

My heart sinks as I close the door and look down at the documents in my hand. As I read, my confusion turns to anger and disbelief.

It's a lawsuit from my father to start a partition action on the property we co-own. On the surface, it's baffling because I thought a partition action was when one property co-owner doesn't want to sell, and the other does. While my father has asked me to agree to development, he's never said a word about selling the property. But clearly, I don't understand all the ins and outs of partition actions because this paperwork flat out says that the motherfucker is claiming rights to *all* the land, citing mishandling of the original trust from my grandfather.

While I know fuck all about the legalities of trusts and how someone could challenge one this long after the fact, or what that has anything to do with a partition action, luckily, I know someone who almost certainly does.

With shaking hands, I pull out my phone and call my second cousin, Sera. She inherited my grandfather's brother's investments and owns a real estate business in Seattle. If anyone can make sense of this, it's her.

"Greg!" she answers warmly. "It's been a while. To what do I owe the pleasure?"

"Hey, Sera. I wish I were calling under better circumstances. Unfortunately, I just got served with some papers from my dad, and I could use your help figuring out if what he's trying to do is even legal and, if it is, how I can stop him. He's trying to claim full ownership of the properties we co-inherited from my grandfather."

There's a pause on the other end of the line. "Shit, Greg, I'm sorry. Your dad's a real piece of work, isn't he? My mother was talking about doing something similar when my grandfather died. Luckily for you, that means I'm pretty familiar with this kind of scenario. Send me the paperwork. I'll take a look and see what your options are, okay?"

I let out a massive sigh of relief. "Thanks, Sera. You

have no idea how much I appreciate it. Or, actually, maybe you do," I reply.

She chuckles empathetically. "Family legacies, eh?"

"Indeed," I murmur, realizing that Sera, on top of being smart as a whip, has gone through a lot in the last few years and probably understands where I'm at better than anyone. "Maybe we can meet for lunch to talk when you've got something?"

"I'd love that," she replies sincerely.

"Great. Talk to you soon, then."

We say our goodbyes, and I hang up, feeling marginally better. At least I have someone in my corner who knows their shit. Now it's time to head home and make things right with Joanie.

I find Joanie hunched over her laptop in my home office, which I'd encouraged her to use. She looks up as I enter, her expression guarded. Her long, dark brown hair is piled haphazardly on her head, and she's wearing another one of my T-shirts. I resist smiling at her adorably disheveled appearance. She's obviously buried herself in her task to the exclusion of all else.

My throat constricts, knowing it's because she's avoiding me.

"Can we talk?" I ask.

Her wary, ice-blue eyes thaw a bit, and she nods, closing her laptop. "Of course. What's up?" She pulls her legs up to her chest and wraps her arms around them.

The move is so defensive it makes my chest hurt.

I settle on the loveseat next to the window on the opposite wall from the desk and gesture for her to join me.

It takes her a minute, but she eventually unwraps herself and rises, revealing pink plaid lounge pants and purple fuzzy slippers that make her look even more adorable. She settles tentatively on the other seat but still draws her legs up in front of her, though her hands rest on the cushion.

I reach out and offer a hand. She slips hers in it, and the tightness in my chest eases a bit.

"First of all, I'm sorry. I know I've been distant this week, and I didn't realize until today that you probably think it was because of what happened on New Year's. What you didn't say, I mean. But that's not it at all."

Her expression softens. "It's not?" she asks so tentatively that I want to punch myself in the fucking face for not realizing it and reassuring her sooner.

"No," I reply adamantly. "The truth is, I've been stressed about Ned. And about what he might do next. I'm frustrated that my family can't see him for what he is. That I haven't been able to stop his escalating behavior somehow."

Joanie shocks me by climbing onto my lap and cupping my face in her hands. "Well, now I feel like the asshole for assuming it had anything to do with me. I can see why it would bother you, but listen to me," she says, gripping my face tighter and looking deep into my eyes. "It's not your fault that your piece-of-shit cousin is a walking felony waiting to happen. It is, however, my fault for letting you deal with this alone. I should've asked what was happening with you instead of conceitedly assuming it was all about me." She tips her head back and groans.

"Okay, fine, we're both assholes," I murmur teasingly. Still, I can only be mildly amused because I haven't told her the worst part. I want to kiss her so badly, but I don't want to get distracted from the rest of the conversation we need to have. I sigh heavily and lean my forehead against hers. "There's more. My aunt and uncle clearly ran and tattled on me because my dad just served me with papers. He's trying to claim full ownership of the property we inherited."

She pulls back abruptly, shock written all over her face. "Are you fucking kidding me? Can he even do that?"

I huff out a breath and shake my head. "I don't know. I've got my cousin Sera looking into it. She's in real estate and has dealt with this kind of thing before, so hopefully, she can help me figure out my next steps."

Joanie chews on her lower lip. "How can I help?" she asks softly.

I look up into her eyes. Concern and something more is written there. To me? It looks like love. It's not the first time she's looked at me this way, and it's why I was so confident she'd say "I love you" back. But the rawness I'm feeling right now makes her obvious feelings hit differently. I want to beg her to say it. But I know I can't. She needs to say it when she's ready.

"Just knowing you're not upset anymore is all I need," I promise.

She gives me a faint smile. "I'm not. I was never upset

with you. I was upset with myself, which was silly. And so not me," she says with a shake of her head.

I tug on an escaped lock of her hair. "I wasn't exactly myself this week either," I offer. "But I'm glad we finally talked. Forgive me?"

She smirks. "I'd say there's nothing to forgive, but you were pretty moody all week. And apparently extremely oblivious to how that came off," she teases, poking me in the stomach.

I wrap my hand around her finger and lift it to my mouth, placing a gentle kiss on the tip. "How can I make it up to you?"

Her smirk turns into a salacious grin. "Oh, I can think of many, many ways," she murmurs, giving me a searing look as her hands trace my chest.

"So can I, city girl," I murmur, running a finger down her cheek. "Starting with eating that pussy while you ride my face."

Her pupils dilate, and a small, breathy gasp slips between her lips.

"Dirty boy," she says mock-accusingly.

I can't help but unleash a predatory smile. "Are you going to punish me?" I reply teasingly.

In answer, she lifts her shirt and tosses it aside. Her creamy breasts are a sight for sore eyes, and her nipples are tight. She brushes a hand down her chest, over one rosy peak invitingly.

"No, I'm going to reward you, silly. So. Do you want me to fuck you here or in bed, mountain man?" she asks sultrily.

My balls tighten in anticipation. "There's not enough room here for you to ride me like I want, baby."

Her back arches, and she inhales sharply, and I can tell she feels those words down to her core — a core I want wrapped around me as soon as possible.

I shift her off my lap and turn her toward the door with a playful smack on the ass.

And as she leads me to the bedroom, stripping off her pants as she goes, giving me a gorgeous view of her perfect ass, I feel a weight lift off my shoulders.

Yes, there are challenges ahead. But if we can end a week this epically awful with understanding and amazing sex? Well, it makes me realize that I can face anything with Joanie by my side.

I also realize she probably needs this as much as I do, though in a different way. So, I will also focus on reassuring her of how much she means to me and that it doesn't matter if she's not ready to leap. But that when she is, I'm here to catch her. With lots and lots of orgasms. And killer grilled cheese sandwiches, of course. What woman could resist that combo?

CHAPTER FIFTEEN

JOANIE

Sunday, two days after Greg's bombshell about his father's legal action, I gather him, Nate, Mia, and Rae at Greg's house for a strategy session. I've done enough research. It's time to get this incorporation ball rolling. And maybe it'll be a good distraction for Greg.

"Okay, folks," I begin, spreading a stack of papers on the coffee table. "I've reviewed the codes and procedures for incorporating a town in Washington state and consulted with some lawyer friends who specialize in this area. Here's what we're looking at."

I look up to make sure everyone's with me. Greg slides his hand over my thigh encouragingly, and I look at Mia and Nate on the other corner of the sectional, then at Rae, who is sitting on a floor pillow by the window. They all nod that they're listening, so I begin by outlining the key steps.

"All right. We have to propose town boundaries and then determine the population within those boundaries, which I can do using census data since it doesn't have to be precise; that'll come later.

"We also have to decide whether Alpine Ridge will have a mayor, which is an elected position, or a town manager, which is similar in function but is appointed by the town council members.

"Once we have those, we can file the incorporation proposal. I'll handle the paperwork portion since it's mostly legalese," I assure them. "But we'll need a surveyor or someone like that to help with the boundary map. Does anyone know someone?"

Nate raises his hand. "I've got one that did my property before we built. I know he's worked with the county plenty, so I'll call him and see if he can do that."

I nod. "Great. Now. Should we ask the town for input on the mayor versus manager question or pick an option ourselves?"

Rae leans forward. "I think we should involve the community as much as possible. Builds trust and buy-in."

"I agree," Mia chimes in. "What if we go even further and hold a series of meetings? Give people a chance to learn about the options and voice their opinions?"

We all agree it's a good idea, so we plan to hold three meetings next weekend at the community center: one Saturday morning, another that afternoon, and a final one Sunday afternoon. Not Sunday morning, less due to potential church conflicts, and more because Saturday night is apparently a big night for folks to hit the tavern.

In any case, Nate offers to make a flyer, which Mia will take to the mail shop post office to distribute to every resident of the area. Finally, Rae will post the flyers in all the local businesses she can. Though we all agree Jerry probably won't let her put them up at the tavern or coffee stand.

"Hopefully, this will help generate some early support," Greg muses after we draft the flyer's wording. "We're going to need it."

I nod my head in agreement. "Especially since after the initial filing, the county's boundary review board will hold a meeting to give everyone a chance to say their piece for or against the incorporation. Best to have as many people behind us as possible by then."

"When will that happen?" Mia asks.

"Code says within thirty days, but I did some preliminary poking around, and it seems like Kittitas County is pretty good at getting things done quickly," I respond. "But we'll see. I'll let you know as soon as I know. Either way, that's just a bitch fest, and I doubt it's going to sway anyone one way or another. The biggest hurdle comes after that. We'll have about six months to get signatures from at least ten percent of the population, which will mean a lot of answering questions and hand-holding. I'm hoping to get that done as quickly as possible to get it over with. And, the sooner, the better anyway."

Mia's eyes light up. "What if we throw a big St. Patrick's Day event? Food, drinks, games, and a petition signing booth. We could get a huge chunk of signatures in one fell swoop while people are in a good mood and a little liquored up."

Rae snickers, though we all agree it's actually a

brilliant idea. The timing is perfect, and we've already established that the folks here can't resist pastries, drinks, and holiday-themed events.

"All right. Good plan, guys," I say encouragingly. "After that, we file the paperwork, and the county auditor reviews — and hopefully approves — the petition in about a month. Then, there's one final boundary review board meeting to formally approve the incorporation plan. Which is, incidentally, where my role in this hootenanny ends."

Mia's brow furrows. "That's it, then Alpine Ridge is a town?"

I huff a laugh. "Um. No. Not even close. After that is the voting phase. First, a vote of the affected residents to approve the incorporation. Assuming a forty percent or higher approval, it goes on to a vote to nominate town officials. Then, finally, a vote to elect those officials. Those'll all be pretty spread out. And even once that's done, it's up to the new town council and mayor or manager to finish the incorporation and start setting up town services. Which could take years."

"Shit," Nate mutters.

"Yup. We're just getting started here, kiddos. Strap in for a long, hard ride. And probably not the fun kind," I tease.

Greg laces his fingers through mine, and I glance over at him. "You said 'we'," he murmurs. I suppress a smile, but I do lean in and kiss him. Because he's not wrong. I'm already thinking of myself as part of this kooky town. When the hell did that happen?

I look up to find everyone watching us with doe eyes, and I roll my own. "All right, back to business," I snip jokingly. "So, as I was saying, the actual election process will need to be handled by someone else, alongside the county. You'll need someone who understands the electoral system, or can at least figure it out, and can support and organize the candidates."

Mia perks up. "Carrie's getting her master's in political science in June. Maybe she could take that on?"

Rae hesitates. "The townsfolk might not take kindly to an outsider running things, even if she is your sister. We should look for volunteers locally first."

Mia concedes the point, and we agree to start recruiting election volunteers once the incorporation is approved. There's no rush, considering that it will be anywhere from four to six months from now.

With the plan laid out, a sense of excitement and purpose settles over the room. We're really doing this.

As the conversation shifts to more casual topics, I turn to Rae. "Hey, have you thought about what you want to do with the museum?"

She leans back against the wall, considering. "It's a great space with a lot of history. Maybe we could turn it into a community center annex? Offer classes, workshops, events that Greg can't accommodate?"

Greg nods thoughtfully. "That could work. Or what about keeping it a tourist attraction, at least partly? Play up the gold rush angle and give people a reason to stop and spend money in town. Keeping it low-key, of course, nothing too flashy, so it's in keeping with the feel of the town."

We discuss a few more ideas but agree to decide later — one step at a time.

But as I think we're wrapping up, Nate's expression turns serious. "Guys, what will we do about Ned in the meantime? It could be a year or more before we have a police force."

A heavy silence falls over the room. And it may be just that I'm more tuned into him, but I can feel Greg's unease. Yet Rae is the first to speak.

"We can't just let him keep preying on women," she says firmly, her usual friendly smile notably absent. "But we also can't take the law into our own hands."

"What if we encourage anyone who's had a run-in with him to file a complaint with the county sheriff?" Mia suggests quietly, twisting her fingers together. "Establish a pattern of behavior, even if they can't act on it immediately."

"That's a good start," I agree. "And we should spread the word for women to be cautious around him and report anything immediately."

Nate snorts. "Oh, believe me, everyone here knows. It's outsiders I'm most worried about. Like Carrie." He grimaces and slips his hand around Mia's.

Mia nods her head in solemn agreement. "Especially if this whole plan to draw more people to town works. But what can we do?"

Greg runs a hand through his hair, his frustration boiling over. "I hate feeling so powerless. Not that I want him to do something so awful again, but I wish there were a way to catch him red-handed if and when he does, so there'd be no question of his guilt."

"Except, we kind of already did," I point out. "I saw him put something in Carrie's drink."

"So did I," Nate agrees, his tone laced with anger and frustration.

Mia nods again, slowly, sadly. "I'll talk to Carrie about filing a report. If she doesn't, maybe you two still can?"

Nate squeezes her hand, and I nod somberly. Carrie's something of a little sister to me, too, after all these years. I don't know why I didn't think of it sooner.

A dangerous idea starts to form in my mind, but I keep quiet. I know they'd never agree to me putting myself at risk, no matter how noble the cause. But if we can't catch him red-handed accidentally … maybe we can on purpose. There's a fine legal line to walk there, though, and I'd have to be smart about it, so they can't call it entrapment.

Still, someone needs to do something about this guy before he gets away with something horrible when we're not there to do anything about it. The exact scenario I know Greg is tearing himself up over these days.

As everyone starts to leave, I watch Greg as I hug Mia and Rae goodbye. He's talking lowly with Nate, looking defeated again. It makes me want to wrap myself around him, and not even in a sexy way, which is big. My chest aches for his obvious struggle, and I wish we hadn't ended on such a sad note.

I sigh internally as the door closes behind our friends, and Greg turns to me.

"Thank you for doing all this," he says softly, slipping his arms around my waist and burying his face in my hair. My arms circle his neck almost automatically. "I know it's a lot of work, but it means the world to me. To all of us."

"That's just how I am. Point me at a problem, and I'll fix it," I murmur, still struggling with how to fix Greg's feelings of failure. Even though I know that's not my burden. It's his. Still, I don't want him to carry it alone.

God, I feel *protective* of him, I realize. That's a first for me with a man.

I pull back a bit and look into his bright blue eyes. And in another first, I feel *those* three words catch in my throat. No, not "fuck me now." The serious ones that show how far gone I am for this man. I shake my head, refusing even to think them. It still feels too soon, like we haven't been together long enough, gotten to know each other well enough, for the urge to say those words to be coming from a real place. It could be just lust and the intensity of it all.

"I know," he replies. "It's one of the many things I love about you." He leans in and presses a tender kiss to my temple. Between his words and his actions, I melt inside. The backs of my eyes prickle with tears.

Despite myself, I feel so much I can barely stand it.

I just need time. We need time.

And orgasms. Lots of orgasms. Yes, that's always the answer.

So I push up and cover his lips with mine. He groans into my mouth as he responds, his hands sliding over my ass.

"Let's go to bed, and I'll remind you of everything

else you love about me, mountain man," I murmur against his lips.

I feel his grin on my mouth and his hardness on my stomach. "Fuck yeah, city girl."

Greg lifts me, and I wrap my legs around him as he carries me to his room.

Greg's dad? Ned? They'll get theirs. I'll make damn sure of it. But right now, all I care about is getting mine. And Greg damn well gives it to me all night.

When we finally come together, when he whispers dirty sweet words in the dark, I realize I can't fuck my feelings away. Because it's all I can do to swallow *those* three words down when they climb from my throat to the tip of my tongue as he holds me while we drift to sleep.

CHAPTER SIXTEEN

JOANIE

The week leading up to the town meetings is a whirlwind of activity and not the fun, sexy kind. No, it's me helping Greg plan the agenda and pull out what feels like a million chairs from storage while he constructs a new podium since the old one had apparently bit the dust. Definitely not sexy … well, unless you count watching Greg work with his hands.

But I'm neck deep in my own world, thinking through how this will go, and as we're setting up the great room, I eye the sea of metal folding chairs skeptically. "Is two hundred chairs going to be enough?" I ask.

Greg shrugs. "There will still be room for people to stand. And we've done this kind of thing before — at best, a quarter of the town will show up total."

I'm unsure if that's encouraging, but I trust his judgment. He knows this town better than I do. Still, doing that math in my head, assuming a few thousand residents, we're likely to be over capacity for all three sessions.

Unfortunately, at this point, it is what it is.

On the bright side, while we're working, Nate drops by with a progress update. "So good news and bad news," he hedges, arms crossed over his massive chest.

I raise a brow. "Well, out with it, muscles."

Nate smirks. "The bad news is that my surveyor doesn't handle town-level boundary definition. The good news is he put me in touch with someone in Seattle who's handled multiple cases like that in the Pacific Northwest. He books up quickly, but he just had a cancellation for next week. Unfortunately, I don't have time to meet with him, and I didn't want to volunteer your time without checking with you first." He hands me a small square of paper with a name and phone number scribbled on it. "I'd advise you to call him ASAP."

"Thanks, Nate. I'll reach out to him," I promise, taking the slip.

He nods, then turns to go but stops short. "One more thing. I tried to talk Mia out of it, but she's insisting on making cookies for the meetings. Like thousands of cookies. And she plans to set up a coffee and water station."

I laugh. "That's Mia for you. Always trying to feed everyone."

"We'll put some tables in the entryway," Greg assures him. "Fuck knows I'll need plenty of coffee and a cookie or ten by the time this is all done. Let her know I'll pay her for it too."

Nate huffs a laugh. "You know she won't let you do

that. At least I convinced her not to do pastries, hot chocolate, or anything else too fancy."

"Cookies are fancy enough, in my book," Greg returns. "Tell her thanks."

I hold up the slip of paper Nate gave me. "And thanks for this, hot stuff." I give him a wink as he heads back out, and he waves as he goes.

I turn to find Greg giving me a look.

My brows pinch together. "What?"

He cocks an eyebrow and approaches slowly, slinging the hammer he's holding through his belt loop before putting his hands on my hips and drawing me close.

"Do I have something to worry about?" he murmurs, looking down at me.

My brow furrows deeper until I realize he means me calling Nate "muscles" and "hot stuff," and I burst out laughing. "Of course not. Nate just has a habit of being shirtless around the house. The nicknames came from me teasing him about it." I leave off how much I enjoyed the sight and Nate's reactions to my taunting. What can I say? I love making a grown man blush.

Greg looks understandably skeptical. "Yeah, I've seen him without a shirt plenty of times," he says drily.

"Oh, baby, are you *jealous*?" I tease, running my hands down his dusty shirt. I lean in and lightly touch my lips to his. "I hope not because he's got *nothing* on my mountain man."

Greg narrows his eyes, but a grin pulls at his lips. "Still. I think I might need to find a way to wipe that image from your mind forever," he murmurs, teasing his lips along the shell of my ear, sending shivers down that entire side of my body.

"Mmmm, you definitely need to do that," I groan, my hand slipping over the front of his pants before I press him away. "Tonight. Because right now, I need to call the boundary definition guy."

I step back and pull out my cell phone, waving teasingly at Greg as I head outside to make the call. He shakes his head and laughs before heading back to podium construction.

Chuckling, I place the call. A few minutes later, I've scheduled an in-person meeting for the following week, which is one more item checked off the to-do list.

By Saturday morning, the great room is stuffed with chairs, an elevated podium sits at the front, and the foyer is set up with Mia's promised refreshments. Greg and I are ready to take the stage, with Rae, Mia, and Nate on hand to help field questions. It's go time.

And before I know it, the first session is in swing. I'm not sure if it's because it's the first or due to the early hour, but it's nowhere close to full, with only about a hundred and fifty people in attendance. There are very few questions, which I'm unsure whether to be grateful for or nervous about. It's hard to get a feel for whether they'll support the incorporation if they don't speak up. And just as I feared, when we ask for a show of hands on the mayor versus manager issue, only a smattering of people vote, all for mayor.

But then, as we're about to wind down, an older woman with a short grey bob and a purple pantsuit stands up. She identifies herself as Betty McDonald, then asks, "Why are we even bothering with this? Nobody here wants to pay more taxes to make a few small business owners feel important when the town was just fine before they showed up." She lifts her chin, and her too-familiar words have me seeing red. And I know, based on Nate throwing a hand up to hold Mia back, that I'm not the only one.

Greg shoots me a sympathetic look that still clearly tells me to stand down. He's far more diplomatic than I would've been as he calmly reiterates the benefits of incorporation: improved infrastructure, essential services, increased property values, protection for local businesses, etc.

And the more Betty parrots what are obviously Jerry's words, the more advantages Greg is able to highlight. It's annoying that Jerry has influenced some of the other townspeople. But by the end, the rest of the attendees seem more convinced of our position, given the questions they finally start to ask. There's more curiousness and openness than there was at the beginning of the session, that's for damn sure. And when Betty finally retakes her seat with a "harumph," I can feel the smugness rolling off my bestie. Me? I'm ready to rip Greg's clothes off right here. His calm and masterful handling of the situation was *hot*.

"Ever thought about being a lawyer?" I murmur to him as the crowd breaks up.

He turns to face me with a smirk. "Not really."

I slide up to him and lean in, lowering my voice so only he can hear what I'm about to say. "You'd make a good one. You owned this room, baby. And later, I'm going to own that dick." I reach around and squeeze his ass for effect.

"I'd say get a room, but we only have an hour for lunch," Nate points out drolly from behind me, herding us toward the hallway. I smile up at him innocently, but before I can respond, Mia interjects.

"Thank you for handling that so well," Mia says to Greg as we pass the last of the folks leaving. I don't miss Mia watching Betty McDonald snatch three cookies from the table before scampering out. Mia shakes her head. "Gran hated that bitch, and I'm starting to see why."

My eyebrows jump. "Dorothy Lewis, the sweetest and most patient woman to ever grace this earth, *hated* someone? Wow. Betty McDonald must be a bigger pain in the ass than I realized."

Nate grimaces. "Unfortunately, Alpine Ridge isn't short on gossipy, controlling busybodies. She was the first disruption, but I guarantee she won't be the last."

I shrug lightly. "Honestly, I'm just surprised there was someone Gran couldn't melt. But I think Betty speaking up turned the tide. Before she said anything, everyone seemed really ..." I tap my lips, trying to think of the word.

"Unsure," Rae offers. "They don't know what to think

at this point." She pauses. "They were waiting for someone to speak up and lead them one way or another."

"I wish it were someone other than Betty McDonald. Even if we managed to convince them otherwise, if she keeps that up outside this room where we can't refute her, she's bound to sway them back," Mia grumbles.

Rae smiles patiently and shakes her head as we sit down at a table Mia set up in another room with our lunch. "Oh, honey, don't you worry. I didn't mean Batty Betty. I meant Greg."

Surprise flashes across Greg's face, stopping him with a half-filled plate in hand. "Me? They can't possibly look to me as a leader. I've only lived here a few years."

Rae shrugs as she loads up her own plate with a sandwich and chips. "I think they might. You've given yourself a lot of positive visibility lately between the winter festival and New Year's Eve. You reminded them that you built someplace for them to come together. And those who have come to you for help over the years will likely vouch for you as this all plays out. I think you're in just about the best position of all of us to make them see sense."

Greg blows out what I think is a nervous breath. I look at him appraisingly. Hoping he's up for it. Because Rae is right, people are sheep. Better one of us takes the reins in leading them than someone like Batty Betty. I snag a pre-packed chicken salad and a bag of chips and sit beside Greg.

"While I agree that Greg is a great person to lead this charge," Nate interjects from across the table, speaking to Rae. "Why not you? You've lived here the longest."

Rae's eyes go wide as saucers, and she tips her head back and laughs. "I have, but that means I've got history with this town and its people. Unfortunately, to them, I'll always be Chet's little girl who was just as much trouble as her daddy." She shakes her head. "Besides, I'm no leader. But you, Greg? You're a natural."

The tips of Greg's ears turn pink as he eats, and he is pointedly staying silent.

"Well, here's hoping for an even better turnout this afternoon. And maybe another Betty McDonald or two to give my man room to shine," I tease, nudging Greg with my elbow.

Greg glances at me skeptically, then gives Nate a long-suffering look. Both Nate and Mia bust up laughing. Mia lifts her styrofoam cup of coffee.

"Here's to round two with the old busybodies of Alpine Ridge," she teases.

I hoped for a better turnout, and boy, do we get it. The afternoon meeting is standing room only, with nearly three hundred people crammed into the space. Like word has gotten around about all the questions asked at the first session, the questions in the afternoon session build on them, coming fast and furious, mostly about timelines and money.

When will incorporation be complete? How soon can we get trash service? How high will taxes go? We answer most of the queries, though not always to the asker's satisfaction. But the fact that almost every question assumes the incorporation is going forward makes me want to run a victory lap around the town.

Even more interestingly, almost everyone votes when asked, and nearly all for mayor as well.

The final session on Sunday is full but not quite as packed. The discussion flows more smoothly and less contentiously than yesterday, with more fundamental questions about what it means to incorporate and what will be expected of them through the process. I can see that Greg is worried, presumably because it means that people are talking about the incorporation with each other. And that it might not all be positive. I try to reassure him with my presence and a few subtle touches that their engagement is a good sign. The vote, once again, goes for mayor.

Greg concludes the meeting, and people rise from their seats, talking in small clusters and grabbing what's left of the cookies and coffee.

"I like how not even one of them asked what a town manager is," Mia says quietly.

I snort.

"I doubt anyone wanted to look stupid by asking," Rae comments in a low voice.

"So they all voted for a mayor to save face?" Nate asks, screwing his lips to the side.

"It's as stupid and plausible as it sounds," I murmur. Greg snickers. I shoot him a look. "We all agreed you should lead this charge, remember? What are you waiting for? Go mingle and win over the doubters." I shove him jokingly toward the crowds.

He swoops in and kisses me. "Yes, ma'am," he replies, trotting off to do what I suggested like the good boy he is. I giggle to myself at the fantasies that thought brings to mind.

"We should all probably do that," Mia points out. I nod my agreement and pretend like I wasn't imagining role-play kink while the rest of our group breaks up to work the room. Still, my eyes follow Greg for a few moments as I watch him settle into a conversation with a group of older ladies who look a hell of a lot nicer than Betty McDonald.

Then my gaze drifts toward the foyer, and I notice Ned lurking by the snack table. My inner sneak lifts her head. I watch him stand there awkwardly for a few minutes until his gaze meets mine. And like I'd cast a fishing line and started reeling him in, he moves toward me. I can't help the satisfied grin that settles over my face.

Instead of seeing the cunning behind it, he takes it as encouragement, his leering grin answering mine.

"Looking good today, Joanie," he says, his beady dark eyes scanning me from tits to ass before landing on the former. "Can I get you a drink?"

I paste on a flirty smile. "Oh, I'd just love that. I'm so thirsty after that long meeting." I lay my hand on his arm and bat my eyelashes at him invitingly. "Thank you, Ned, you're so thoughtful."

Ned dutifully scampers off, and I watch him approach the table. But his back is facing me, I hope strategically, as he prepares my drink. He returns a few minutes later, handing me a styrofoam cup of black coffee.

I carefully accept it with my fingertips holding the rim, but I don't take a sip.

"Thank you," I purr.

"I hope you like your coffee black," he responds. "I love the taste of straight-up coffee, don't you?"

I nod agreeably. "Oh, absolutely. I like my men *and* my coffee tall, dark, and delicious," I say, pointedly scanning him from head to toe.

He misses the innuendo, his eyes flicking between me and the cup, and I work to school my expression — time to distract him from the fact that I'm not drinking it.

"So tell me more about yourself, Ned." I run my free hand down his arm. "What do you do for fun?" I give him a meaningful look from under my eyelashes.

His grin stretches even wider. "I could tell you," he says in what I'm sure he thinks is a sexy voice. He leans in, and it's all I can do not to wince at the foul odor of his rancid breath. "Or I could show you."

"Oh Ned, you're so funny," I titter, stepping back. Not getting the hint at all, he presses forward.

"And you're —" I don't get to find out what I am because a growl rips through the air between us, and suddenly Greg is there.

All I see is thick, dark hair, broad shoulders, and a

tapered waist as he shoves in front of me. He pushes Ned, and though Ned's a touch taller, his skinny ass stumbles back several feet.

"Touch her, and you die," Greg snarls.

The hair on the back of my neck stands up, and a unique mixture of fear and arousal courses through me. Ned, for his part, scurries away like the rat he is.

And Greg whirls in place to face me, fury written all over his face. "Come with me." His hand closes over mine, pulling me through the thinning crowd and into his office. I struggle to keep the coffee from spilling as he slams the door behind us.

"What the hell was that?" Greg demands, barely containing his anger.

I sigh and shake my head, pulling a folded plastic zipper bag from my back pocket. I set the cup on Greg's desk, open the bag, slip it in, and carefully seal it shut. Greg's eyes track every movement as his chest heaves. With that done, I step into him, placing my hands gently on his chest. But I can see in his eyes he already has a pretty damn good idea of what I just did. And that it was, at least in part, premeditated.

"Tell me you didn't bait him into trying to drug you." Greg's tone is as hard as his expression. His hands are clenched into fists, and his eyes are wild.

I can't help it; my hands find my hips as I glare back at him. "I didn't bait him to do anything. He offered me a drink, and I accepted, but I didn't drink it. That's all."

"That's all?" Greg explodes. "You had a fucking evidence bag ready, Joanie! Even if you were just waiting for him to make a move, he could have tried to lure you away, or injected you with something when Plan A failed, or —"

"We were in public. And I can take care of myself," I cut in calmly.

He scoffs. "Oh really? So if he grabbed you, you'd be fine?"

I raise an eyebrow. "You think I couldn't handle that?" I challenge. "I'd like to see you try to grab me against my will."

Greg smirks, but it quickly fades at my stony expression.

"Don't mess around, Joanie," he replies, irritated.

"I'm not messing around. Go ahead. Try to grab me," I grit out through my teeth.

His brow furrows. "I'm a lot stronger than you. I don't want to hurt you, even by accident."

I roll my eyes. "Quit treating me like a china doll and fucking grab me, wimp," I goad him.

Greg gives me the "Oh no, you didn't" look, and I almost laugh. Almost.

"Fine," he says in a clipped tone. And then he lunges.

In a flash, I have Greg pinned to the ground, my knee at his throat. He tries to shove my knee off, but I twist, cutting off his air. His face turns red, and he taps out.

"Third-degree black belt in taekwondo," I explain, releasing him. "I'm not as helpless as I look." I bat my eyelashes at him in the most menacing way I can manage.

"Holy shit." He sits up, gasping and rubbing at his neck. As he climbs to his feet, I see a mix of emotions on his face: surprise, relief, and ... arousal? "Still ... what you did was reckless," he says, but his voice has lost its edge, and he won't meet my eyes now. "You shouldn't take unnecessary risks. I couldn't handle it if anything happened to you."

And now I feel like a complete asshole. Greg wasn't saying he didn't think I could handle myself. He was saying he couldn't handle knowing I'd have to. I soften, touched by his concern. "I'm sorry. If I knew you'd be this upset ..." I trail off, chewing at my bottom lip.

He huffs a dry laugh. "You would've what? Not done it?" He shakes his head. "I think we both know that's not true."

I scrunch my nose and reach out, lacing my fingers through his. "Still. I am sorry."

He nods and pulls me into his arms. "I know," he murmurs into my hair. "And it helps that you're even more capable of handling yourself than I knew. But that doesn't stop me from wanting to tear Ned's head off at the thought of him even looking at you wrong. So maybe just ... be more careful? Please?"

I melt into his embrace at the earnestness in his voice. And even though I despise being told what to do, especially by a man ... well, I'm finding I can't deny Greg anything. And the idea that I mean enough for him to threaten his own family member like he did ... it makes those three little words dance on my lips again.

But I bite them back. Though I do say, "I will, I promise." I blink hard as the feelings Greg stirs in me bring tears to my eyes. It's still all too much. So I do the only thing I know how to do to distract myself with a man. "And to show you I'm sorry, and I mean it ..."

I press him away and unbuckle his belt, dropping to my knees.

Greg's eyes darken. "You don't have to do that, Joanie." He makes to tug me up, but I can't handle looking him in the eyes right now because my name on his lips sends a fresh wave of things I'm not ready to feel coursing through my body.

So instead, I withdraw his cock from his boxers and shove it down my throat. His head tips back, and I let those three words melt back into my mouth as he does. I let his moans fill the space in my head where my swirling emotions were. I let his gentle touch on the back of my head soothe the turmoil inside me. But nothing, not the taste or smell of him, the way he feels thrusting in and out of my mouth, or the hot spill of his seed down my throat can distract me from the realization that my heart is his.

Or the knowledge that this visit, this project has become more than a pitstop between what was and whatever comes next. Deep down, I know it's now my path. And ready or not, I'm walking it with this man. He's what comes next — no pun intended, for once.

I'm shaken out of my thoughts by Greg hauling me to my feet and kissing me with such passion that it nearly knocks me back off them. When he stops, he's breathing hard, our foreheads pressed together. "Goddamnit, you drive me so fucking crazy," he groans against my lips. And I know by his tone and body language that he doesn't mean sexually. He means that a stellar blowjob wasn't enough to distract him from what I did and how that made him feel.

"I know," I murmur back. "I'm sorry for making you worry today."

He nods, his nose grazing mine with the motion. "I know. But if anything happened to you ..." He pulls back to look into my eyes, and I see fear at the idea in them. He shakes his head, and his hand reaches up to cup the back of my neck. His thumb swipes tenderly over my cheek. "I love you, Joanie."

My heart nearly stops in my chest at his words. I reach for something, anything to say. Except "I know." Because I'm not going to Han Solo him after that heartfelt confession, after what I did today.

Instead, I nod. "I'm ..." I swallow hard. His thumb swipes over my cheek again, making my thoughts go haywire.

"I know you're not ready to say it yet."

I look up into his dark eyes with surprise. But I shouldn't be. He gets me like no one has in a very long time. Possibly ever. And again, the knowledge that he will never ask me to be anyone but who I am nudges me toward giving in.

And yet, I can't. Not yet.

"I'm not," I agree. "But take me home, mountain man, and I'll show you how I feel about that." I bite into my bottom lip, willing my arousal to show through more than my feelings. Though I'm pretty sure he gets the message: I may not be ready to say it, but that doesn't mean I don't feel it.

CHAPTER SEVENTEEN

GREG

As much as I've enjoyed burying myself in Joanie in every way possible these last few days, I'm glad to be driving out of Alpine Ridge and into Seattle to meet with Sera while Joanie meets with the boundary map expert.

After talking to my lawyer, I better understand what my father can and can't do. However, he's also waiting for me to speak with Sera before responding to my father's suit. Since she left a voicemail letting me know she'd finished her research, I suggested we meet for lunch to discuss it and catch up.

The two-hour drive out of the mountains and through the Eastside is like descending into a different world. Busier. More packed. Businesses, homes, roads, people — more of them than even the last time I was here a few months ago — and the hundred miles feels like light years from the quiet isolation of Alpine Ridge.

Despite the gorgeous drive past Lake Sammamish, over Lake Washington, and toward the striking downtown

Seattle skyline, I'm not excited to be back. I'm a small-town guy through and through, and this is all ... well, a lot. Or maybe I'm already on edge from the looming conflict with my father.

Given that, as I park and walk to the café where I'm meeting Sera in Belltown, I'm not surprised that I find the amount of traffic and noise overwhelming. Then again, it could just be from growing up in Yakima, a small city in the middle of Washington state, far from the bustle of Seattle, and then having moved to an even smaller one, even though Ellensburg barely counts as a city with just under twenty thousand residents. And then again to an even smaller town ... well, *almost* a town. In any case, I'm just not equipped to be in the city anymore.

I sigh in relief as I spot Sera at a small table in the back corner. I wave and head over. She stands to greet me, her long and wavy light brown hair shifting with the movement. She's wearing a long-sleeved purple shirtdress that's somewhere between business and casual. She hasn't changed a bit since I last saw her, save the happy grin she's giving me. I remember her being more serious. It's a good change, and I smile at her as I approach.

"Hey, you," I greet her, pulling her in for a hug.

She squeezes me hard. "Hey, hermit, long time no see," she teases.

I release her and shake my head, laughing. "Don't knock the hermit life. It's pretty nice. I don't know how you live in all this chaos," I respond as I sit across from her. "Though I gotta say, you look pretty happy."

Her grin widens. "I am. And I'm sorry we're not

getting together under better circumstances," she responds, her smile fading.

I nod and grab a menu from between the napkin holder and the ketchup bottle. "We'll get to that. First, food. What's good here?"

She makes some suggestions, and we order. "So, shall we get the worst of it over with?" she asks bluntly.

I give her a wry smile. "Let's." It's one of the things I love about Sera and why she's one of the only family members on my dad's side, or at all for that matter, that I get along with. Well, that, and she doesn't get along with most of our family either. Neither of us suffers fools or sugarcoats things. Two traits that have always kept my circle small.

She folds her hands together and leans on the table. "All right. I imagine it will come as no surprise that the window to challenge your grandfather's will has been closed for a long time. So he's got no legal basis for challenging your ownership from that angle," she begins.

"But?" I ask suspiciously.

"But he's clearly up to something. However, I can't figure out what. A partition action can only do one of three things: force a partition in kind, which is a physical partition of the property that divides the land equally and assigns you each a wholly-owned parcel; a partition by sale, which is exactly what it sounds like — the property is sold, and the proceeds are split equally between you; or a partition by appraisal, where, in this case, your father buys you out by paying you your share of the appraised value of the land. So the only way he could claim complete ownership is the partition by appraisal."

"But he'd have to buy me out to do that?" I clarify.

Sera nods. "Yes. By bringing in the trust, I believe he's trying to prove he shouldn't *have* to buy you out. But no judge in Washington state is going to buy that. Trust laws are clear on challenge periods, and you're well past those."

"So why try? Why not just offer to buy me out?"

Sera's eyebrows raise. "He hasn't?"

I shake my head. "Not once. He's always only pressured me to go ahead with development I didn't support."

A look of understanding passes over Sera's face. "Have you considered that your father may not have the money to buy you out?"

My jaw drops. "No, I haven't." But I kick myself because I should've. "But I think you might be onto something."

"It would explain his attempts to drive you out without a payout. And his grasping at legal straws," she muses.

"It's also consistent with his complete inability to have ever run Grandpa's empire to begin with," I murmur, my mind spinning on the possibility that my parents might be that broke.

Our waiter delivers our food right then, and we eat silently while I process this. After a few minutes, Sera gently says, "If it's true, you hold all the cards, you know."

I set my burger down and wipe my mouth. "How so?"

"If he doesn't have the cash to buy you out, he sure as hell doesn't have enough to go forward with development."

"And?"

Sera smirks. "He must be planning to finance it. Which he's obviously figured out he can't do without your approval."

"Fuck."

Sera smiles wryly. "Precisely," she replies, going back to her sandwich. After she chews and swallows a bite, she adds, "But unless you get really lucky with a judge who's willing to dismiss the case, you're likely to be offered the choice between the three options."

"You mean I'd be *forced* to choose."

"That's exactly what I mean. If one owner initiates a partition action, most judges will require the other owner to choose between the three options unless there's a procedural or other issue that stops them from doing so. So you need to ask yourself which you think *he'll* want and which is most advantageous for *you.*"

My appetite is gone; I think about that as she eats. If it's the first option, he'll own his part of the land and can finance development. But at least it would be limited, and perhaps there's a way to control how much development and what he can do. If we both have to sell … well, who the hell knows what the next owner would want to do with the land? It could be worse than what my father has planned. And we've already established that he doesn't have the money for the last option.

The kernel of an idea forms in my mind.

"So, how are things going at Sutton Developments, by the way?" I ask, referring to the company that bought out the real estate business she'd built.

Sera narrows her eyes at me. "Things are great. The owner, who is my boss and mentor, plans to retire in another five years, at which point I'll take over." She tilts her head. "You have that look Grandpa Tyler used to get."

I can't help the grin that escapes me because I know exactly what she means. My Grandpa Tyler, her grandfather's brother, got the same look when he smelled a good deal.

"How would Sutton Developments like to get in on the ground floor of a newly forming town in the Cascades? One that can be a rustic yet luxury second-home location for hikers, skiers, and other outdoor enthusiasts?"

"You're going to turn Alpine Ridge into a destination vacation home spot for the rich and snobby?" Sera asks drily.

I press my lips together. "Okay, I just came up with the idea. Because my dad wants to turn it into the next Leavenworth, and I've been fighting that pretty much since we inherited the land. But if we turn it into something else ... something that preserves what makes it special ..."

"Then you could cut him off at the knees and kick him out of your hidey-hole," Sera surmises. She huffs a laugh. Then she levels me with a look. "This is a stretch, you know that."

I nod. "I know. If you have a better idea, I'm all ears."

Sera stares at me evenly for a minute. "My husband

runs a corporate security firm. Are you sure you don't want me to have him see what he can dig up on your father?"

I bark a laugh. "You want me to *blackmail* Everett Tyler?" I scoff.

She shrugs lightly. "You said it, not me," she responds with a twinkle in her eye. "Couldn't hurt to try it."

I shake my head, still chuckling. "Even the thought of having to talk to him enough to pull that off has me 'noping' out of that one. But I admire your boldness." I take a deep breath and let it out slowly. "I'll do my own research, run some numbers, and get you a proposal. Either way, I think pushing for an outright sale is the best path. I don't want this to end with any of that land solely in my father's hands. And I want him out of Alpine Ridge." And my life. But I don't add that out loud, even though I'm pretty sure she picks up on it. "Thanks for looking into this for me. I appreciate your help."

Sera smiles and nods. "What's family for?" she replies.

We both pause and look at each other before we burst out laughing. Because our families? Yeah, no. They're for driving us crazy, apparently. But it's nice that we still have each other anyway.

We finish our lunch and chat for a few more minutes before saying our goodbyes. As I walk out of the café, my mind is already churning on this new idea and how we could pull it off. But first, research. Lots and lots of research.

No, actually, first, I need to check on my house in

North Queen Anne before I head back to Alpine Ridge. It's another property I inherited from Grandpa Tyler, and it's where I usually stay when I'm in Seattle for more than a day. I've got a property manager who generally looks after it for me, but I like to see it for myself occasionally.

Since it's only about fifteen minutes north, I make it through the packed streets to the 1920s remodeled craftsman that's one of the only things I love about this town. The inside has wood detailing, and the back has a huge outdoor porch and sprawling views going down the hill to the ship canal into Lake Union. It's about as nature-oriented as it gets in Seattle, but it's enough to make me feel a little less caged in when I visit.

I park in the narrow driveaway and note that the maple tree branches, still bare for the winter, have grown over the walkway to the porch. I tilt my head, realizing I haven't been here in longer than I thought ... probably closer to a year.

I shake my head and let myself into the house, noting that the blue paint on the front door could use touching up. I make a mental note to tell the property manager. Per our agreement, a stack of whatever mail comes to the house is on the table inside the foyer. I toss my keys next to it, deciding to do a lap through the house before I go through what is likely all junk mail.

Three bedrooms, three bathrooms, and all two thousand square feet later, and I'm satisfied that the place has been well cared for. It has the musty smell of dust, but the sheer curtains let enough light in to keep the house from looking too dark and disused.

Satisfied, I grab the stack of mail and take it through the entryway, past the stairs, the kitchen, and out onto the back patio. I brush some old, dried-out leaves off one of the wicker patio chairs and settle on it, flipping through the envelopes and glossy advertisements. Halfway through, I find a folded piece of paper.

I open it to find a handwritten note. My heart stops in my chest at handwriting I remember all too well.

> Greg,
> I know this seems out of the blue, but I've just moved to Fremont and thought I'd look you up since I knew you had a house here, though I don't know how often you get out this way. I hope that's not too creepy. But since you've seen me naked more times than I can count, I figured it might be okay, and I have something I'd like to tell you. Call me?
> Hailey

I sigh heavily, debating whether to ignore it. Then I debate whether to call my property manager and ask if he remembers when and where he found this note because it was clearly not mailed. I nix that idea since, ultimately, it doesn't matter anyway.

Unfortunately, I know myself. And if I don't call, I'll always wonder why the woman who dumped me after six years together suddenly wants to talk to me. It could be as simple as her wanting to get together for old times' sake. But it could also be a secret child she's been hiding from me. Doubtful, since we were way more careful than I've been with Joanie, which should tell me how I felt about Hailey all along. Still, the possibilities are endless.

So, in the end, my curiosity gets the better of me, and I dial her number.

"Hello?" Her voice stirs the dusty corners of my mind, and not so much in a good way.

"Hey, Hailey, it's Greg," I say awkwardly. "I just found your note."

"Greg, oh my God, hi," Hailey replies, sounding surprised and pleased. "Thanks for calling."

"Yeah, no problem," I respond, trying to keep my tone neutral. "What's up?"

"I was hoping we could talk in person. I have something important I want to discuss with you. Are you in Seattle?"

"I am, but I'm heading out in a bit," I respond.

"Oh. I see. I mean … I can come over now if you have a few minutes?"

I hesitate; I'm not sure I want to open that can of worms. But I find myself agreeing anyway. Curiosity and all. "Sure, I guess that'd be okay."

"Awesome. I'll head over now. See you soon."

I barely have time to register what the fuck I just agreed to before Hailey is knocking on the door less than fifteen minutes later.

I open it expecting to feel something. But even though

her blond hair is the same cascade of golden waves, and she wears the same tight T-shirt, a light blue this time, and jeans she's always favored that show off her huge chest and tiny waist, all I feel is wary.

"Hey," I greet her.

She grins and launches herself at me, wrapping her arms around my neck and squeezing me tight. "I missed you," she breathes against my ear. Her heavily perfumed smell wraps around me, and I shake off all the sense memories that go with that as I gently press her away.

"Why don't you come in and tell me what's up," I offer, stepping back and gesturing toward the living room.

She nods and heads in, sitting on one end of the light grey three-seater couch. She looks up at me earnestly as I settle on the other end.

"I'm just going to cut right to the chase because seeing you makes me feel even more like no time has passed, and I know you need to get going soon," she begins, then takes a deep breath. "Letting you go was a mistake. I want us to get back together."

I blink in surprise; this is a huge shock. "Wow, that's … unexpected. But we haven't spoken in years, Hailey. We can't just … get back together," I reply slowly. "I'm not who I was back then. And I have no idea who you are now or where you're at." I take a deep breath, gentling my voice. "But most importantly, I'm with someone else now. I've moved on. Haven't you?"

"I've tried. But I can't stop thinking about you," she admits, twisting her fingers in the long strands of hair that flow over her shoulder.

I shake my head. "I can't say the same. I'm sorry."

"But … we were together for six years, Greg." She slides closer, dropping her hand on my knee. "And we were so good together. Don't you remember?"

I wrap my fingers over hers and gently remove them from my leg. "I remember. I also remember you leaving me."

"I know. And I'm so sorry. You have no idea how sorry. Surely that means something to you?"

I close my eyes and take a deep breath. "It does," I admit. "I'm glad you realize it was a mistake, at least." I don't say it, but it hurt me a lot more than I wanted to admit for a long time that I was so easy to leave after giving her all those years. After thinking we might be headed toward marriage. "But that doesn't change anything."

Hailey grabs my retreating hand and squeezes. "But it does. It changes everything. How long have you been seeing the person you're with?"

I shrug lightly, not sure I like where she's going with this. And then I pause, realizing with a start that it's only been about a month with Joanie. Given the depth of my feelings for her, it feels like so much longer.

"Not long. Just about a month," I admit. "But that doesn't change anything. We're over, Hailey."

She leans forward, placing her hand on my knee. "See, but I've had the same problem. I can only date someone for a few months before I realize they're just not *you*. It hasn't been the same for you? Surely all our years together mean more than a month with this woman?"

I pull back and stand up. This is nuts. Why now? And I can't help but blurt that out.

"Why now? Why like this?"

"I get that this seems abrupt. But it's been *months* since I left that note, Greg. And when you called, I was thinking about you. That means something, I know it."

I shake my head, overwhelmed by the sudden strange turn to the day. My phone buzzes in my pocket, and I withdraw it only to see Joanie's name. And the time. Shit. She's probably wondering why I haven't let her know I was headed back already.

"I've got to take this," I murmur, answering the call.

Hailey stands up, clearly agitated, and just as I hear Joanie say "Hello?" in my ear, Hailey says, "Is it her? Does she really mean more to you than me? You wanted to *marry* me, Greg."

And then Joanie hangs up. I pull the phone from my ear and confirm that the call ended.

"Fuck," I curse. I look up at Hailey, trying not to let my anger get the best of me. "I don't know where this desperation is coming from, but you do not come into my house, *my life*, and make demands of me like this. The woman I love now probably thinks I'm cheating on her, thanks to you. Get out, Hailey. And move on, like I did."

Hailey draws in a breath. "If she thinks you'd cheat, she obviously doesn't know you," she pushes. "Not like I do."

I throw up my hands in disgust. "You have got to be fucking kidding me." I press my lips together and take a deep breath, so I don't go nuclear. "*You* dumped *me. Years* ago. You don't know jack shit about me. If *you'd* ever known me, you wouldn't have been worried about a bunch of pre-teen girls' crushes. But you know what? You haven't changed. You still need to grow the fuck up and stop living in a fantasy. Get out, Hailey. And don't ever contact me again." Hailey opens her mouth, and I can feel the protest coming before she utters a word. "Now," I growl in the harshest tone I can manage, cutting her off before she can start up again.

And thank God she finally has the sense to look worried. She scampers out the door and is gone. And the whole episode has given me whiplash and one big fucking headache. A headache that I know has only just begun.

I immediately try to call Joanie back, but she doesn't answer. Worry gnaws at my gut as I hop in my truck and drive back to Alpine Ridge. Hoping I can get there before Joanie decides to take off. Because I know my city girl, she's been afraid of committing this whole time. Afraid of telling me that she loves me too, of what that means for her future. And I'd bet every penny I have that this is the excuse she's been looking for to turn tail and run from her feelings.

I make record time getting back to my place, but it still doesn't feel fast enough. And when I walk inside, Joanie sits on the couch with her packed bag at her feet. My heart sinks.

"Joanie, please, let me explain," I plead.

She looks at me, her blue eyes guarded. But she nods.

So I launch into the whole story: how Hailey left a note, how I stupidly agreed to let her come over, how she wanted to get back together, but I turned her down unequivocally.

"I'm so sorry, baby. It was nothing, I swear," I finish, reaching for her hand.

She allows the contact and a fraction of the tightness in my chest eases.

"I know," she admits. And I swear my shoulders drop a foot. A small, sad smile pulls at her lips. "But it made me realize that there's *still* a lot I don't know about you. And that this —" she gestures between us "— is going *so* fast."

I let my head drop into her lap with a sigh. "Maybe, but every relationship goes at its own pace," I reply. I look back up into her eyes. "Tell me you're not falling as fast as I am, Joanie, and I'll give you all the space you need."

Her eyes shine in the dimming afternoon light. "I am. And honestly, I was trying not to freak out about it *before* I heard that you were planning to marry your ex once upon a time." She tilts her head back, blinking hard.

"That wasn't me," I explain. "That was all my parents. Or what I thought I was supposed to be doing to make them happy, anyway. When she broke up with me, I was just as relieved as I was upset, even though it took me a long time to realize it was because I *didn't* want to marry her. And I never felt about her the way I feel about you."

Joanie's head tips forward, and a manic laugh escapes her lips. "That. That right there is what I'm trying not to freak out about."

My brows slam together. "So you're not upset that it sounded like I was spending time with my ex behind your back but that I'm more in love with you than I ever was with her?"

She snaps her fingers and points at me. "Bingo." A single tear escapes her shimmering eyes and skitters down her cheek. "I don't know how to do this. I don't know if I *want* to do this or if I'm just caught up in how good it feels to be with you."

I pull back, stung by her words, but she grabs my hands before I can withdraw.

"That's not about you, Greg." She so rarely uses my name outside of orgasming. The few times she has, it's gone straight to my heart. But this time, it's like a knife.

"I know," I say thickly.

"Do you?" she asks earnestly, leaning forward. "I'm not sure I understood how much I prized my independence until you made me want to give it up."

I shake my head. "I would never ask that of you."

She shakes her head, and a few more tears skitter out. "*I know.* I wouldn't have even wanted to if you were the type of man who would. But it's because you are ..." She trails off, closing her eyes, pushing more tears down her cheeks. I reach up and wipe them away.

When she opens her eyes, I can see her resolve to leave. But I've listened, too. And I know she's closer than ever to giving in to this. I just need to push through this with her. However, she needs that to happen.

"Don't go too far for too long, city girl," I murmur, leaning forward and kissing away the last tears that fell.

She cups my face in her hand, leans in, and places the most tender kiss on my lips. It's so unlike her that it sends chills through me, both good and bad. One kiss that is somehow both comfort and fear. Love and loss. Fight and surrender. But that's Joanie and me. A contradiction that shouldn't make sense, yet somehow does. I hope.

"I'll see you soon," she promises, rising and picking up her bag.

I want to beg her to stay, but I force myself to nod instead. "I understand. I'll be here whenever you're ready."

She gives me a long look, then walks out the door. I sink onto the couch, my head in my hands.

How did things go sideways so fast? I can only hope Joanie will work through this and come back to me. Because the thought of losing her … it's unbearable.

I've never been one to run from a challenge. And I'm sure as hell not starting now. I'll give Joanie the space she needs. But I'm not letting her go. Not without a fight.

CHAPTER EIGHTEEN

JOANIE

As I drive away from Greg's place, my heart feels like it's being squeezed in a vice. I know I'm doing the right thing for myself by taking some space, but it doesn't make it any easier. The look on his face ... well, it was all I could do to leave.

With shaking hands, I pull out my phone and call Mia.

"Hey, Jo. What's up?" Mia answers cheerfully.

I take a deep breath. "I need a place to stay for a bit. Can I get a room at the B&B?"

There's a pause. "Of course. But why? Did something happen with Greg?"

I sigh heavily. "Things are just moving really fast, Mia. I need some time to figure out what I want."

"Ah. Well, there's definitely a room there for you, but on one condition. I meet you there for a girl's night," Mia replies.

Gratitude swells in my chest. "You know I'll never

turn down that deal," I respond. "Thanks, babe. I'll see you soon."

I make it to Gran's old place a few minutes later and wait in my car for Mia. It takes her nearly half an hour to make it down the mountain.

As soon as I step out of the car, she rushes over, wrapping me in a hug.

"God, Joanie, you look —"

"Don't you dare finish that sentence," I say threateningly.

She chuckles and leads me inside. "The place is all ours until tomorrow," she says, gesturing around.

Gran's former house mostly looks the same, but with newer furniture arranged in a more lobby-style sitting area instead of the old living room with its overstuffed couch and TV. A podium by the door has a logbook and a pile of brochures. A peek into the dining room gives me the same impression — newer, stuffier, and, well, more like a B&B. The kitchen, though, has been walled in completely with actual doors put in place. It makes sense, but it's still super weird.

"You don't do check-ins, cooking, and cleaning, do you?" I ask curiously, settling onto the closer of the two linen settees. It's decidedly less comfortable than Gran's old couch was.

Mia waves a hand and settles on the other one across from me. "Lord no. There's a property manager out of Ellensburg who comes as needed and a local who does the daily cooking, cleaning, and such. Though the bakery does supply pastries for breakfast."

I perk up a little at that. "Ah, so there's food here?"

Mia smirks. "There's food here, but I didn't bring any goodies. There is, however, always wine. And chocolates for the pillows, but I see no harm in plundering that stash." She rises and enters the kitchen, emerging shortly with a tray bearing a bottle of wine, corkscrew, two glasses, and a good-sized cardboard box of what I can only assume is chocolates.

I raise a brow at her. "Those look mass-produced," I accuse her in a teasing tone.

Mia rolls her eyes and sets the tray between us on the long, narrow wooden coffee table. "Since they're for the pillows, we need to keep a bunch of them on hand. Besides, candy-making isn't my thing. Candy eating, though, I'm here for." She winks at me and pops open the box, tossing me a chocolate while she unwraps one for herself. "Okay, now that we have provisions, spill," she demands as she pours us each a generous glass of red.

She hands me one, and I take a fortifying sip before launching into the story about Greg's ex showing up and my subsequent freak-out.

Mia listens intently, her brow furrowed. "Wow. That's a lot to process. But it sounds like Greg handled it well. He was clear with her that he's with you now."

I nod. "He did. And he was." I take a deep breath. "But hearing another woman trying to convince him to take her back because they'd once planned on getting married?" I shake my head.

Mia clears her throat. "I can't even begin to imagine what I'd think if something like that happened to me. And not to sound too much like a therapist, Jo, but … how did that make you feel?"

I bark a sharp laugh and drain the rest of my wine. "Like I wanted to claw her eyes out. Which scared me so much that I hung up. Because I've never thought of myself as the type to fight a bitch over a man."

"It wouldn't be a fight, and you know it. You'd crush her." Mia nudges me with her foot, and I laugh.

"Well, it sure wouldn't be a *fair* fight anyway," I agree. "But that was just my gut reaction. I wouldn't have done it. I think. Maybe." Mia gives me a skeptical look. "Okay, fine, there might have been some hair-pulling or something. Seriously, though, the fact that I reacted so strongly freaked me out. Because I had no idea they were talking about marriage. That he even wanted that. And here I am, falling for him, not having had those kinds of conversations. It just made me realize how fast we're moving. I mean, I was ready to tell him I love him."

Mia chokes on the chocolate she'd just popped in her mouth. "Excuse me?" she says around the mouthful. "You were going to do what now?"

I wrinkle my nose. "Did I forget to mention that part?"

Mia swallows and wipes the chocolate off her lips with a napkin. "Um, *yeah*," she replies. Her eyes soften. "You really love him?"

I draw in a slow breath before nodding. Tears prick at the backs of my eyes. "Yeah. I think I do." I tip my head back and blink them away. "Which is nuts, right? Who falls in love with someone they've only known a month?"

Mia snorts. "You, apparently, and I'm not the least bit

surprised. I knew it'd happen fast once you found the right guy."

I raise an eyebrow and give her a skeptical look. "Oh please, you did not."

Mia lifts her chin. "I did. You may be impulsive and reckless, but you know what you want and go after it. What made you think falling in love would be any different?"

I tip my head to the side and give her a look. "Oh, I don't know, maybe because once you do, it's not just you anymore? Having to consider another person in my plans for the future is huge. No more doing what I want, when I want. It's not just *me* anymore; it's *us*. How do you just ... make that switch?"

Mia reaches over and squeezes my hand. "I get it. Falling in love is a huge adjustment, which is scary. But you're looking at it backward. It can also be wonderful. You have someone there to do all the awesome things you want to do with. Someone to cheer you up after a shitty day. Someone to support you through the good and the bad. Doing everything alone may seem like freedom, but it can also be a burden. I won't tell you the transition is easy, but it's worth it."

"But what if —"

"It works out, and you get more than you ever dreamed of having?" Mia interrupts with a smirk.

"That's not what I was going to say at all," I reply drily.

She rolls her eyes at me. "Don't let fear rob you of something great, Jo."

I swallow hard. "I know. And I thought I was ready to make that leap. I left because I needed some time to wrap my head around it. To make sure I'm ready."

Mia nods understandingly and refills my wine glass. We sit in companionable silence, sipping our wine and eating chocolate.

"So, have you talked to Carrie about whether she's willing to file a report over the incident with Ned?" I ask, changing the subject.

Mia shakes her head sadly. "She said she didn't even know that was happening, and she's already overwhelmed between finishing her degree and dealing with our parents. But I'm pretty sure Nate is planning to."

"Good. That asshole needs to be stopped," I mutter darkly. I sigh heavily, unsure why I brought up another depressing topic. I rack my brain for good news, then remember my meeting earlier. "Oh, I met with the boundary definition expert today. He said he should have something preliminary for us in about a week. The boundary review committee will make changes anyway, but it's a start."

Mia smiles. "That's great news. Thanks for handling all of that, Jo. I know it's a lot of work."

I shrug. "It's what I'm good at. And I want to help." I don't deny that it isn't just for Nate and Mia's sake; Greg was a big part of my decision to take this on. My thoughts run in circles, so I decide distraction would be a better tactic.

"Is there still a place we can watch movies in this joint?" I ask.

Mia nods. "Your room has a TV with satellite cable. Come on. Let's go watch something that'll have us peeing laughing."

I pull a face and laugh. "As long as there's more wine and chocolate."

"What do you take me for? Of course there is," Mia assures me.

So we spend the rest of the evening watching old-school Jim Carrey movies and polishing off the wine and chocolate. And I know I gave her shit, but it's the exact combination of nostalgia, comfort, and easy companionship that I needed.

The next day, I wake up alone, Mia having ducked out at likely an ungodly hour to head into the bakery. I'm grateful because now that I'm rested and calm, I have the headspace to reflect on yesterday's events.

My conclusion? I'm a fucking moron.

I love Greg. I want to be with him. And yes, I'll be giving something up to do that. But Mia is right; I could gain so much more. If anyone is worth the risk, it's my mountain man. Even through what could've been a horrible, relationship-ending misunderstanding, he was nothing but apologetic, concerned, and considerate. And the man knows how to destroy my pussy in the best way possible. A combination I thought impossible, yet here we are.

Could this all blow up in my face? Sure. But anything

worth having is also worth the risk. And if anyone is worth that risk, Greg is.

Funny how a little distance and perspective can make you see through all of your bullshit.

Mia was also right that when I know what I want, I go after it. So I get my ass out of bed, throw on some tight jeans and a blouse that makes my small tits look luscious, and head out to drop in on Greg at the community center.

Though the late January midday temperature is a nipple-freezing cold — not literally thanks to a thick jacket — I'm once again bowled over by how gorgeous this place is. A light snow must've fallen earlier this morning; everything glitters as the sun reflects off the fast-melting crystals. I drive slowly because Greg's nickname for me is apt: I'm a city girl through and through, and driving in snow and ice is not my favorite.

Still, I'm nearly vibrating with anticipation and excitement when I get there, though the building is quiet as I enter. I peek my head in Greg's partially closed office door to find him at his desk, hunched over some paperwork. His chin is leaned on one strong forearm, a wayward curl gracing his forehead. His strong jaw is clenched, and I wonder if it's the paperwork or the tough conversation from yesterday evening.

"Hey," I say softly.

His eyes snap up, surprise evident on his face. He scans me from head to toe, and I suppress a shiver under his gaze. "Joanie. Hey. I wasn't expecting to see you today."

I step inside, closing the door behind me. "Do you have a minute to talk?"

"For you? Always," he says, gesturing for me to sit. I perch on the edge of the chair opposite his desk. "How was your night?"

I huff a small laugh. "Better than I expected it to be. Mia and I had a girls' night. Wine, chocolate, and Jim Carrey. It was great, actually. You?"

He pushes out a breath. "Honestly? Rough."

I grimace. "I'm sorry."

He waves a hand dismissively. "It's not your fault. It wasn't just what went down between us, anyway. This thing with my dad ... I guess it's affecting me more than I thought it would," he admits.

My mouth forms a small "O" of surprise. I don't know why I hadn't remembered that he had gone to Seattle in the first place to talk to his cousin about the lawsuit. And I didn't even ask. But then, the sudden reappearance of his ex forcing me to face my feelings was a little distracting.

"God, Greg, I forgot. Do you want to talk about it?" I ask.

He leans forward, steepling his hands under his nose. "Maybe later. What was it that you wanted to talk about?"

"Oh," I say, uncharacteristically sheepish. "Yeah. That." I take a subtle deep breath. "If you still want to, I'd like to keep seeing you. I feared committing to this would mean giving up parts of myself that I considered vital. But ... you're more vital to me." I shake my head, annoyed that I still can't seem to say those three words. I look up into his eyes. "This is just new territory for me. But I want to be here. With you."

He leans forward, his blue eyes earnest, and opens his mouth to respond, but he's interrupted by a sharp knock on the door. We both turn toward it to see an older gentleman looking in expectantly. "I'm sorry to interrupt. I'm here for my training appointment," he says.

Greg rises. "Of course, Bob, I'll be right out."

I stand up and step toward the door. "I'm sorry, I should've realized you'd be busy. I'll go."

Greg gently pulls me toward him as if waiting for me to protest. When I don't, he holds my hands and looks down into my eyes. "I am, but we can continue this later. If you want."

"This evening?" I offer.

"I'd like that."

"All right. Meet me at the B&B at six. I'll make dinner."

His eyebrows jump. "I thought you didn't cook."

I shrug lightly. "I said I don't cook, not that I can't."

Greg chuckles. "You never stop surprising me, city girl."

I bite into my bottom lip. "See you at six?"

"Wouldn't miss it for the world." His eyes drop to my lips, and my breath catches in my throat. But instead of kissing me, he pulls me into his embrace. The feeling I get with his strong arms encircling me is almost harder to resist than his lips on mine. "If I kiss you, I'm afraid I won't want to stop," he murmurs in my ear.

I nod against his chest before pulling away. "Later," I promise.

He dips his chin in response, and I turn to leave.

Once I get in the car, I let out a sigh of relief. I've taken the first step. And I'll take the next one tonight. I can do this.

Focusing back on the task at hand, I glance at the clock and realize it's just after one. If I wait until two, I can avoid Ned at the grocery store. But if I want to do the braised beef I'm thinking of, I'd need to get it going as soon as possible. Since it's the only thing I know how to cook that's both easy and impressive, I don't have another alternative short of asking Mia to cook something for me. But that would defeat the point. Cooking for him is a big deal for me. I don't cook for anyone, not even myself. And I want to show him that he's special.

That aside, I also refuse to let one creep deter me from my plans.

Mind made up, I start the car and head toward the grocery store.

A few minutes later, I park and step out, squaring my shoulders as I march into the store. I pass the register but don't see anyone in the store, not even another shopper. Ned must be in the back, and it seems it's not only the women of Alpine Ridge avoiding him these days.

With a smirk, I head to the refrigerated meat section at the back of the store.

I'm examining the few available chuck roasts when I feel a presence behind me.

"Well, hello there, beautiful." There's no mistaking

Ned's lecherous voice. And now that I know exactly what kind of predator he is, I'm not playing games anymore.

I whirl around to face him. "If it isn't the disgusting creep who tried to drug me and my friend."

Ned's eyes widen, and he lets out a nervous laugh. "I would never do anything like that to a beautiful lady like you." He steps closer, backing me up against the beef case. "I thought we had a connection."

"We definitely do not, and if you don't get away from me, you will regret it."

An unsettling, leering grin splits his wide mouth. "Oh, come on, baby, you don't have to play hard to get. I've got what you want right here."

He grabs my wrists, wrenching them down toward his crotch. His grip is so tight it hurts. The thought of being forced to touch his dick, even over his pants, almost makes me vomit on the spot.

I attempt to pull away, but he's stronger than I'd expected. While he may have strength, I have smarts. And training. So before he can force my hands where he wants them, I jerk upward just enough to duck under his arms, swinging my knee up as I move to his side. I aim for his crotch, but he bends forward, and I end up landing the blow to his stomach.

Even better.

It knocks the air out of him, and he releases me in surprise.

The thing is, taekwondo isn't about attacking. They train you to escape a dangerous situation first, whenever possible. But this guy? He needs to be taught a lesson.

And he's about to be taught one by someone he assumed was too small and weak to fight back.

It's all to ensure he can't do me more harm.

Really.

Because, in fact, my wrists are throbbing so badly from being wrenched around that I decide in the few seconds it takes him to get upright and whirl on me that a roundhouse kick to the chest is the only way to make sure he doesn't get back up next time.

As soon as my booted foot lands in the center of his chest, the "Oh shit, what the hell did I get myself into" look flashes across Ned's face. Well, for the split second he has before he goes flying backward, landing on the shelves behind him. The display crashes under his weight, sending dozens of wrapped cuts of meat tumbling over him as he, the shelves, and the broken stand collapse.

With Ned howling in pain and down for the count, I don't stick around to savor the moment. I race out of the store, adrenaline pumping through my veins.

As soon as I'm back in my car and on the road, I can see the angry welts and marks on my wrists that I know from experience are only going to get worse over the next few minutes. I take a few deep breaths before driving straight to the hospital in Ellensburg.

When I get there just over thirty minutes later, the intake nurse takes one look at my wrists and face, where there's a bruise I hadn't noticed — probably a glancing blow I didn't feel when I jerked Ned's arms up — and tells me that they'll get someone from the sheriff's office to come by after I'm treated.

Still, given the volume of higher-priority cases, it takes a few hours before they can get to me. Once they've assessed and photographed my bruises, I have to wait another hour for the sheriff to show up so that I can give an official statement. I make sure to tell him about today and seeing Ned try to drug Carrie on New Year's Eve. I even mention the coffee cup with his prints that I never drank from. I'd intended to find a way to get it tested, but I'm betting that's about to be taken care of.

"All right, ma'am. I'll get this report filed this evening, and someone should be up to collect the evidence you mentioned tomorrow. I assume you'd like to press charges?" He gives me a look that clearly says, "You'd better press charges."

"Absolutely," I say firmly.

He nods his approval, his lips pressed into a thin line that tells me exactly how he feels about men who abuse women. "With any luck, what you've given us will allow us to nail this bastard."

Once he leaves, I'm given my discharge papers. As I head back to the car, exhausted and realizing that making dinner for Greg is out, I check my phone to see if there's time to pick up something on my way back.

I find that it's after six, when I was supposed to meet Greg, and I have a few missed texts, one call, and a voicemail. All from Greg.

I contemplate calling, but this is a conversation I want to have in person, so I send him a text instead, letting him know that I'm okay and that I'll be there in a half hour or so to explain everything.

When I return to the B&B, Greg is pacing the sitting room. He takes one look at me and stops in his tracks. The anger on his face makes me take a step back.

"Who did this to you?" he demands. I can practically hear his teeth grinding together from here.

"Ned. But I'm betting he looks worse," I offer. The veins on Greg's forehead visibly flex, and I hold up my hands. "Let me explain. I'm fine, I promise."

The door opens, and a couple I've never seen walk in. They give us a friendly, though curious smile as they make their way through the sitting room and up the stairs, presumably to their room.

"Let's go to my room," I say, sliding my hand into Greg's and pulling him down the hall.

When we get inside, I find the bed made up and my things folded onto the armchair in the corner. I settle on the end of the bed and pull Greg down next to me. Then I tell him what happened at the grocery store. Greg grows even quieter as I talk, his jaw clenching and his hands curling into fists.

When I finish, he looks like he's ready to blow a fuse. "I'm going to fucking kill him," he grits out.

I close my eyes briefly and shake my head. "Don't you see? You don't need to do a damn thing. He's finally going to get his."

Greg's jaw grinds. "I fucking hope so." His unfocused

eyes finally zone in on me. "Why'd you go there, Joanie? You promised me you'd be more careful."

My brow furrows. "That's what you're focusing on in all of this?"

He shakes his head. "I'm glad you're safe. But I hate that you put yourself in harm's way like that. *Again*."

I bristle at his tone. "I can take care of myself, Greg. You know that."

He runs a hand through his hair. "I know. But I feel like you have this need to prove it. And promises mean something to me, Joanie."

I reel back like he slapped me. "So I'm just supposed to not go places I might run into someone unsavory because you're afraid for me? Even when I'm not?"

Greg's nostrils flare. "Maybe you should be a little more afraid. There's such a thing as being *too* fearless."

An ironic laugh escapes me. Given that I'd planned to use this evening to show him that I wasn't letting my fear of commitment stop me from being with him, I find this twist particularly infuriating. I was prepared to accept him for who he is and what we could be to each other. But maybe he's not ready to do the same. Maybe I had him all wrong.

"I think you should go," I tell him, standing abruptly and pointing at the door.

"I think we should talk about this," he insists, rising and putting himself in front of me.

"Talk about what, how you want me to become your cooperative little woman? Newsflash: I'm your city girl, mountain man. I come with self-defense training that I'm not afraid to use. I don't let creepy jerks who think they can get away with threatening women keep me from living my life. And I also don't let misogynistic assholes who think they can change me do it either."

"You know that's not who I am or what I'm saying," he responds.

I look at him like he's nuts. "Sounds like it to me."

"Then, obviously, we need to start over. I —"

I hold up a hand. "Don't bother. If you won't leave, I will." I grab my bag from the closet and shove the clothes from the chair into it.

And then I walk out without looking back.

One sleepless night later, I get a call from the sheriff's office asking to collect the coffee cup evidence. I arrange to meet them at the bakery. Since I hadn't felt like talking about it last night, I need to fill Mia in this morning before the town gossips do. Even though I still don't feel like reliving that awful, strange turn our relationship just took. Or former relationship? Either way, our fight in my room wasn't quiet, and apparently, all the other rooms were full. And if I've learned anything about Alpine Ridge, it's that news travels fast.

I meet the deputy outside the bakery, though as soon as I walk in, I can see the questions all over Mia's face. Rae at least has the good manners to pretend she wasn't watching.

I instantly put Mia out of her misery, telling her

everything that had happened since I last saw her: talking to Greg, planning to make him dinner, my run-in with Ned, the subsequent hospital visit, filing charges, and handing off the evidence to the sheriff's deputy just now. I leave out all the relationship stuff and our fight last night. I can fill Mia in on that later when it's just her and me.

To that end, since I need some distance from Greg to clear my head, literally and metaphorically, I decide to spend the weekend at Mia and Nate's. It gives me time to tell Mia everything that went on with Greg. However, I don't wallow in it or let her dissect it endlessly. I try not to think much about it at all. It's still too raw. And I still have no idea how to feel or what to do next.

On Saturday evening, Nate pulls me aside.

"Mia told me what Ned did," he says, his normally warm eyes hard. "I'm going down to the sheriff's office first thing Monday to give my statement about what I saw at the New Year's Eve party."

I give him the most grateful look I can muster, given everything that's going on in my head right now. "Thanks, Nate. Every bit helps."

Despite Nate and Mia's support, the week is torture. They work every day. I spend my days mostly with Simba, looking for jobs in Seattle. Something I've been putting off to see how things panned out here, but it's time to at least start thinking about my options again. Unfortunately, January isn't a great time to be unemployed, apparently, so that's a dead end for now.

Thankfully, at the end of the week, I get the proposed boundary definition from my contact. I immediately head to the county clerk's office and file the petition, a thrill running through me for the first time in a while. We're one step closer to helping Mia and Nate and to me taking a break from Alpine Ridge. I should have a few weeks until I need to be here for the initial boundary review meeting, so I think I might head back to Seattle. Hopefully being home and on my own for a bit will help me get my head back on straight so I can refocus on what I really want my path forward to look like.

I must not have had good reception as I drove as I notice a voicemail when I return from the county clerk's office. It's from the sheriff. The coffee cup had Ned's prints, and the coffee was spiked with ketamine. They're waiting on a warrant but plan to arrest him formally as soon as they get it. They also request that I remain available to testify when it goes before a judge.

I sit down heavily on the guest room bed, relief and anger and a million other emotions swirling inside me. Ned will face consequences for his actions. But my personal life is still a mess, and it looks like I'll be here for a bit longer. So no escaping to get back in touch with myself. For now, anyway.

In any case, I also realize that Greg should know that the coffee cup stunt worked. Not that I expect that to convince him the risk was worth it, but because it's his cousin, and there's bound to be more blowback once he's arrested. I may not be sure what is going on between Greg and me anymore, but I can't let this blindside him.

I shake my head, laughing at myself when I realize

how much I must really care about him to look out for him even when I'm angry.

Which makes me reflect on that anger a little more. Even though he made me feel like he doesn't accept me as I am, I know I probably overreacted. And because I've never been prone to overreacting or extreme emotions, that's when I know. I'm truly in love with Greg. Because only love is that irrational.

CHAPTER NINETEEN

GREG

I'm at the community center, trying to focus on paperwork, but my mind keeps drifting back to the fight with Joanie. The look of hurt and anger on her face when she told me to leave is seared into my brain.

I know I reacted badly. I was just so scared when I saw her injuries, knowing she'd been attacked. But she's right. She can take care of herself. Maybe I should trust her judgment, even though her actions scare me sometimes.

I'm jolted out of my thoughts by my phone ringing. And like my thoughts conjured her, it's Joanie. My heart leaps into my throat as I answer.

"Joanie, hi," I say, trying to keep my voice steady.

"I have some news," she replies, bypassing pleasantries. "The cup of coffee I gave to the sheriff? It turns out it was spiked with ketamine. And since it had Ned's prints, it was enough for them to request a warrant for his arrest. They're working on getting that as we speak."

I'm stunned into silence for a moment. Then I find my voice. "That's great news. I mean, I'm pissed that he's just as dangerous as I feared, but it's great that there's evidence."

"Yeah," she agrees. "I just thought you should know."

"Thanks," I reply. "And Joanie ... I'm sorry about our fight. You were right to get that evidence. I was being a jerk, telling you that you weren't being careful. Clearly, you know what you can handle and when taking a risk is necessary. I just worry because I care about you so fucking much."

There's a pause, and I hear her take a deep breath. "I know you do. And I'm sorry, too. I shouldn't have blown up at you like that. The truth is, before Ned attacked me, I was planning to make you dinner, as you know. What you don't know is that I was also going to tell you that I love you."

My breath catches in my throat. "You love me?" It's so Joanie to tell me that for the first time over the phone. I almost laugh. But my heart is too full right now to do anything but revel in hearing her say it.

"Yeah," she says softly. "I do. But then, when you got so upset about me going to the store, I started questioning if I could be with someone who didn't accept that sometimes I might seem reckless when I'm doing what I think needs to be done."

"Joanie, no," I rush to assure her. "It's not that I don't accept you. I love all of you, even the parts that sometimes scare me. I was just upset that you got hurt."

"I realized that," she says. "And I also realized that I

keep finding reasons not to commit to this, to us fully. But I don't want to do that anymore. Because despite what I said, I know who you are. And I do love you, Greg. I want to be with you."

I close my eyes, emotion welling up in my chest. "I want that too. More than anything. Where are you right now?"

"I'm at Mia and Nate's because the B&B is fully booked this weekend. Why?"

"Because I need to see you," I tell her honestly. Her answering silence unnerves me. "That is, assuming you want to see me."

A breathy laugh escapes her. "Of course I do. I was just trying to figure out if I could get to you faster than you could get here."

I grin. "Well, that's easy. I'm on my way."

I make it up the hill in record time. When Joanie opens the door, the sight of her takes my breath away. And it's not even her long, dark hair up in a messy bun that shows her slender neck or the tiny shorts and tank top she's wearing. It's her inner beauty radiating through the stunning exterior. She may drive me crazy, but it's also what makes us work. She smiles at me like she knows, and I sweep her into my arms and hold her tight.

"Hey, baby," I murmur into her hair.

She pulls back to look at me, her blue eyes shining. "I missed you."

I lean down and kiss her, pouring all my love into it,

showing her how much I missed her too. She responds with equal enthusiasm, her hands fisting in my shirt as she pulls me inside and upstairs to the second-floor guest room.

We stumble inside, shedding clothes as we go. Her top goes first so that I can lick those pert little nipples. While I do that, she unbuckles my belt. As soon as her fingertips graze my cock, I growl and shove her back onto the bed, ripping the tiny shorts off of her. I likewise tear off my shirt.

Looking down at her naked and gorgeous, I wish I had the patience to worship every inch of her body slowly. But something about our reunion, even after such a short time, has me desperate for her.

"Fuck me, Greg," Joanie demands, obviously right there with me.

Her words travel through me, making me impossibly hard for her. So much so that I can't be bothered to finish undressing. Instead, I shove inside her, hard and fast. I lean in so I can take her mouth as I take her pussy.

"I love you," I tell her as I move inside her. "God, I love you so fucking much."

"I love you too," she gasps, arching into me. She scrapes her fingernails down my back, and my cock pulses.

"Fuck," I groan. She grins and does it again. Something about the sharp pain contrasted against her tight heat wrapped around my cock has me ready to explode. "If you keep doing that, I'm going to come inside you, baby." A small gasp escapes her, and her pupils dilate. I raise an eyebrow. "You want that?" She nods desperately. "You want me to come in your tight little pussy?" Joanie groans and spasms around me as her orgasm crashes into her impossibly fast. I barely have time to mentally take note that the dirty talk makes her squeeze my cock harder than ever before I'm doing exactly what I promised.

Joanie's final moan in my ear is another "I love you." My vision blurs as we come apart together and are forever remade with pieces of each other.

We lay tangled together, basking in the afterglow, our newly declared feelings, and the fantastic sex that went with it.

"Shit," I curse, panting into her neck. I place a gentle kiss on her clavicle. "That was different."

Joanie tilts her pelvis into me, and my cock twitches in response. "It was," she agrees with a giggle. "I'm going to need more of that seriously sexy dirty talk."

"Yeah? Like how? You want me to tell you what a good girl you are?" I tease, pumping gently, setting her shivering under me.

"God, no," she groans, wiggling her hips. "I want you to tell me I'm your naughty girl. Your dirty, naughty little whore."

My balls tighten, and my cock thickens. "Fuck, Joanie, you're making me hard again already," I warn her.

She flicks her hips. "Good. Fuck that cum into me harder then," she challenges.

My breath catches, and arousal shoots through me like

fire. I haven't gotten hard this fast again so often since I was a teenager. But this woman …

I work my hips, giving her a small taste. "Like that?" She nods. "You want me to fuck you with both of our cum all over us?" She groans and tips her head back. "You want me to get harder and harder and fuck your dirty little cunt until it's covered in me, baby?"

"Of fuck, yes, God, yes," she groans, arching so her tits push up. I hitch back to free my hands and grab both nipples, tweaking hard so she gasps and bucks on my cock, bringing me back to full mast. Our centers are still joined but slippery with cum and her fresh arousal. It's next-level hot.

"Then brace yourself, baby." I grab her hips hard. "Because I'm going to fuck you like the dirty little slut you are. My dirty little slut."

I've never spoken to a woman this way during sex — or ever — but somehow, it's the biggest turn-on of my life. And as I pound her beneath me, the keening moans coming out of her tell me it's working for her, too. I continue to pour out a filthy stream of encouragement until I'm coming so hard I can barely stay upright, until Joanie's moans take a sharp turn into "dear God, someone's murdering her in there," and she comes so hard on my cock that I see stars as I empty into her once more.

"Jesus fucking Christ, Greg," Joanie screams as she convulses under me. "God, baby, yes, fuck, yes."

I cover her body with mine, the pace of our bodies colliding slowing as our orgasms fade. Sticky, sweaty, messy, and unbelievably sated, I cover her lips with mine as she wraps her legs around me.

"I love you, Joanie," I say softly onto her lips. "I'm crazy, recklessly in love with you."

Joanie giggles and presses a gentle kiss to my lips. "I love you too, Gary."

I pull my head back to give her a look of incredulity, but I can't maintain it, and we both burst out laughing.

"Oh good, you're done fucking," Mia's voice calls from downstairs. "Next time, close the damn door."

The admonition makes us pause for a split second before we laugh again.

"Payback's a bitch!" Joanie calls loudly to Mia.

Unfortunately, she yelled so loud it took ab muscles, so it pushed my cock, and everything else, out of her. I look down between us and back up at her with a smirk.

"Shower for my dirty girl?" I ask teasingly.

She grins and nods. "Definitely in order. But maybe after that, we can go to your place," she suggests.

My eyes darken at the idea of having her back in my bed. "A quick shower, then."

After a night filled with more dirty talk and dirty sex than I've ever had in my entire life, I, unfortunately, have to go into the community center for some scheduled training sessions. But I can't bear the thought of being far from Joanie, so I ask her to come with me.

But when my aunt and uncle barge in between appointments, I realize that was a huge mistake.

"You bitch!" my aunt screams, pointing at Joanie. "Our baby is in *jail* because of your lies! We're going to have you arrested for filing a false report!"

"And after you're done serving your time, we'll be suing you for defamation!" my uncle adds, his face purple with rage. "How *dare* you?"

Before I can even react, my aunt is in front of Joanie, shoving her. Joanie stumbles back, shock on her face.

And just like that, I see red, which snaps me out of my shock. I step between them, forcibly moving my aunt away. "Are you fucking kidding me? Get the hell out of here," I snarl. "Before I call the cops on *you* for assault." I advance on them, forcing them back toward the door as they continue to hurl insults at Joanie.

"This isn't over," my uncle threatens as I push the door closed behind them. "You'll pay for this!"

I turn to Joanie, and in a few long strides, I'm cupping her face in my hands, my eyes searching her for any physical damage. "Are you okay?"

She nods, but I can see she's shaken. I am, too, honestly. That all happened so fast. "I'm fine," she assures me. "I just … I'm a little blindsided."

"Me too," I admit. "On the bright side, it sounds like Ned was arrested, so there's that. Still, let's report this."

Joanie's shoulders rise as she steels herself, and her shaking stops. "I agree. Let's go down to the sheriff's office. And then I guess it's back to the County Clerk's office on Monday." She presses her lips together grimly.

My brow furrows in confusion. "Why?"

"To file an order of protection against Ned *and* his parents." She squeezes my hand. "Just to be careful."

My chest aches in both a good and bad way. Bad because this whole thing with Ned just took an even more fucked-up turn. Good because somehow she's managing to show me that even in a shitty situation, she wants to reassure me that she heard me, that she's trying.

I pull her into my arms and stroke her hair. "Thank you," I murmur. She wraps her arms around me and rests her head on my chest. For a brief moment, the world stops, and there is no Ned, no bullshit with my father, nothing standing between Joanie and me. It's just us. It feels so fucking good that I never want to let go.

Still, I have to, so we close the center and head to the sheriff's office, where we give our statements. Joanie mentions the orders of protection. Given their history, I mention that I doubt they'll care about a piece of paper. The officer assures us it's a good idea to have everything on record.

When we return to Alpine Ridge, we stop at the bakery so Joanie can tell Mia what's happening if she hasn't already heard.

But as soon as we walk in, I know she has. Mia removes her apron and darts around the counter to envelop Joanie in a hug.

"Are you guys okay? We heard Ned was arrested last

night. And that his parents were seen outside the community center this morning."

Joanie rolls her eyes, presumably at the speed and accuracy of the rumor mill around here.

"We're fine. His mom just had some choice words for me. And a good, hard shove."

Mia pales. "Oh no. Did you shove back?"

Joanie smirks. "I would've if I weren't so fucking surprised to see them. We didn't even know Ned had been officially arrested."

Mia smirks in return. "Maybe if you guys hadn't been so *busy* ..."

From behind the counter, Rae coughs to cover her laugh.

A small blond woman sitting at one of the small tables on the other side of the bakery hesitantly approaches.

"Excuse me, are you the one who reported Ned Tyler for assault?" she asks.

Joanie nods. "Yes, that's me."

The woman takes a deep breath. "I just wanted to say thank you. And that ... he assaulted me, too. A few months ago. I was too scared to say anything then, but hearing about what he did to you ... I filed a report this morning."

Joanie's eyes widen. "I'm so sorry that happened to you. But thank you for coming forward now."

The woman gives a small smile. "Of course. Everyone knows his parents always get him off the hook, and I don't want to see that happen this time. I hope he gets what he deserves and isn't allowed to hurt anyone else."

"I hope that too. I'm Joanie, by the way," she offers, holding out a hand.

"Meg," the other woman responds shyly, shaking it. "Guess I'll see you around?"

Joanie nods, and Meg waves goodbye to Rae before heading out.

Once she's gone, Rae clears her throat. "She's not the only one," she says quietly. "Lots of other women have come to me, telling me Ned assaulted or harassed them too. I encouraged them all to file reports."

We're all silent for a moment, processing the enormity of the situation. The phrase "lots of other women" loops through my mind, and my stomach churns with anger and disgust.

"At least they're speaking up now," Mia finally says. "With more victims coming forward, there's no way Ned's getting out of this."

"He better not," I say through gritted teeth. The thought of what he's done to Joanie and so many others makes me want to bring a world of hurt down on his shoulders. But Joanie is right again; I need to let the law handle this. And trust that justice will be served. And if it's not, then I'm sure Nate can help me find a suitable place to bury his body where no one will ever find it.

That idea shouldn't give me so much satisfaction.

I wrap my arm around Joanie, holding her close. "You're amazing, you know that?" I murmur. "Your bravery, your strength in all this ... I'm in awe of you."

She leans into me. "I couldn't do it without you," she

says softly, then looks around. "Any of you. Knowing you've all got my back —"

"We've got each other's backs," Nate corrects from the doorway, where apparently he'd been leaning. "I came in when Meg went out, so I caught the gist," he adds with a wink. Mia goes to him, and he wraps her in his arms.

I press a kiss to Joanie's temple. "Come on, guys," I say, trying to inject a lighter energy into the room. "It's Saturday night. Let's go blow off some steam."

"But I made a roast back at the house," Mia objects, looking stricken.

Nate and Joanie laugh. "Sounds like a party to me," Joanie responds.

"Ooh, and we can play Scrabble," Mia adds excitedly.

"I'm not playing Scrabble with this guy," I say, gesturing at Nate. "He's a fucking doctor. He knows way too many big words."

Nate's answering grin makes me chuckle, but Joanie pipes up. "Um, lawyers," she says, pointing between her and Mia. "I think we can take him."

Mia shakes her head. "Trust me, we can't."

Rae folds up her apron and walks around the counter. "I'm willing to give it a shot."

All four of us turn to her with raised eyebrows. Joanie gives her an appraising look. "My money's on Rae. That voice of hers came out of nowhere for me, too, so I'm betting she's got some other mad skills she's hiding."

Now it's Rae's turn to wink, and we all laugh.

"Bring it on," Nate says, rubbing his hands together. "You bringing some pastries home, babe?"

Mia rolls her eyes and trudges into the back.

"We'll meet you guys there, okay?" I pipe up. Nate nods, and we wave goodbye.

When we get out into the cold, fading afternoon, I press Joanie up against the passenger side of my truck.

"I meant what I said in there. You amaze me, city girl."

She grins up at me, trailing a finger down my chest. "You haven't seen anything yet."

I shake my head and smile down at her. "I love you, Joanie. Exactly as you are. And I'm so damn proud to be yours."

She tilts her face up to mine. "I love you too, mountain man. More than I ever thought possible."

I lean in and kiss her, not holding back. Our tongues meet, and I groan into her mouth. And as I lose myself in her kiss, I know that whatever comes next, we'll face it together. Through all this, I realize she's not just my love; she's so much more. For the first time, I'm picturing what it would be like to share my life with someone. To grow old together.

Despite all this drama, I want to be with this woman. To protect her. To take care of her. Despite all the obstacles that have been thrown our way. Because a love like this? It's worth fighting for.

I'm there for Joanie when she tackles the next obstacle first thing Monday morning at the County Clerk's office.

She files the protection order and is informed that she'll be on the docket this afternoon. When she comments on how quickly she'll get in, the clerk shares that Ned's arraignment will immediately follow her appointment in a courtroom across the hall. In case we're interested in attending that as well.

Obviously, we are.

Given that information, I'm much less surprised when neither Ned nor his parents personally appear at the protection order hearing and instead are represented by an attorney. Probably not even their main attorney, as Joanie speculates they'll be helping Ned prepare for his arraignment.

But the protection orders are a slam dunk either way. With the evidence and our statements, Joanie is granted temporary protection orders against Ned and my aunt, given that they both assaulted her, even though Joanie has declined to press charges against my aunt. Since my uncle didn't touch her and didn't make direct threats of bodily harm, that order is denied. The temporary orders will be in place until a hearing they schedule for next Wednesday to make the orders permanent.

It goes so quickly that we have to wait a few minutes before entering the courtroom across the hall.

When we're allowed in, Joanie sits toward the back to avoid notice, and I sit beside her, wrapping an arm around her protectively.

"Why didn't they tell you the arraignment was today?" I ask in a hushed tone.

She shakes her head. "They'd only bring me in if they

needed me for the pre-trial hearing. Given the mounting evidence against him, I doubt they will."

I open my mouth to ask another question, but the judge calls the matter to order. My eyes scan the front and land on Ned's greasy head next to an older gentleman, who I presume is his lawyer, with my aunt and uncle seated behind him.

"Are you supposed to be in the same room with them, given the protection orders?" I can't help asking quietly.

Joanie smirks at me and points to the heavily armed bailiff. "I think we're good," she murmurs.

We listen as the judge reads the list of charges against Ned. It's a whole fuckload longer than I thought it would be and is filled with legal jargon, not all of which I understand. But I catch "sexual assault," and I'm floored when the judge lists crimes against minors. One look at Joanie's face tells me there's more going on here than just the charges she filed. When the judge is done, he asks Ned to enter an official plea.

His lawyer stands. "My client pleads not guilty, your honor."

My mouth opens to protest, but Joanie immediately shuts me down with a look. "That's standard procedure," she says soothingly. "Don't worry."

They move on to reviewing bail, and I'm pleasantly surprised when the judge denies Ned bail. But again, looking at Joanie's deep frown, I know there's something else I'm missing here. Once they set the pre-trial hearing for this Thursday, Joanie grabs me and quietly pulls me out of the courtroom.

"Based on the look on your face, I'm going to guess Ned is in some deep shit?" I hazard as we head back to the car.

"Deep, *deep* shit," she confirms. "The good news is, he's likely to go away until he's a very old man. Going after women was bad enough. But Federal charges for involvement in the sexual exploitation and assault of minors ... that's one of the deepest levels of shit there is."

My jaw drops. "I'm sorry, he did what now?" Minors. The words rattle through my head, and my stomach turns. Not even knowing exactly what she means by that, I'm already disgusted by the thought that I could ever be related to someone who would hurt kids.

Joanie stops at the car and turns to face me. "On top of drugging and raping both adult and minor females, they're accusing him of being involved with criminals that sell kids for sex." My jaw drops even further, and she holds up a hand. "I doubt he's *that* dumb. Or that far gone, as it were. But who knows? Anyway, my guess is he used their services, and, in turn, the legal system is using him to flush out the people behind that operation."

Fuck. Holy fuck. Holy fucking shit fuck. I take a long, deep breath as I process that. The depth of his depravity is ... astounding. That his parents have denied and covered up his behavior all these years has clearly only fed his sick nature. This is exactly the kind of thing I've been worried might have been going on. Still, now that he's been caught, there's an end in sight. And I'll focus on that so I don't beat myself up over what I should've done sooner. As the shock passes, Joanie's words sink in.

"They're trying to scare him into taking a deal," I realize out loud.

"Bingo," Joanie confirms. "Even if he's not involved with organizing it, for them to find evidence that fast that he was involved …" Her face takes on an uncharacteristically furious look. "However that went down, he deserves whatever he's got coming to him."

"Well, now I'm doubly glad they denied him bail," I murmur angrily.

She shakes her head grimly. "Can't have him alerting anyone. Or assaulting anyone else." We share a heavy look.

"Come on," I say, opening the passenger door for her. "Let's go home."

One side of her lips tips up ever so slightly, but I can tell it will be a while until the clouds that have formed over her break up — probably not until at least after the pretrial hearing in three days. It's a feeling I understand. I've long felt responsible for him knowing he was a creep — even if I didn't know exactly how much of one – and not being able to do a damn thing about it.

Unfortunately, when Joanie contacts the court for the exact time and location, she's told it's a closed hearing. Which means we won't know what goes down until after the fact. Joanie doesn't seem surprised. I guess I shouldn't have been either, given her suspicions. There are some serious stakes here, and I can see how sensitive information might come out that they'd want to keep a lid on.

But we don't talk about it. We don't talk about much.

Joanie seems withdrawn, and God knows I've got enough on my mind between keeping momentum at the community center and surreptitiously researching my luxury town idea. It's slow going, with intrusive thoughts of Ned getting off the hook breaking through constantly.

I can tell Joanie is anxious, though. And God knows I am, too. Everyone wants to see Ned go away for a long time so he can't continue terrorizing the women of Alpine Ridge. He likely will, though the waiting and anticipation leave plenty of room for doubt.

Finally, Thursday, the pre-trial hearing day, arrives. If the past three days have felt long, it's nothing on waiting out the day for news. But we don't hear anything. Well, not until Friday anyway, when someone from the sheriff's office calls.

Joanie answers and listens intently for a few minutes, asking very few questions that don't reveal anything. Her face is blank when she hangs up.

Her shoulders sag with either relief or despair.

"Ned has accepted a plea bargain. He'll be held at the county jail until he's transferred to federal prison in a few weeks. And that he'll be in for a minimum of twenty-five years." She huffs a wry laugh as tears start to spill down her cheeks.

It was relief. Definitely relief. She climbs into my lap and wraps herself around me. I hold her tight.

"Thank God," I murmur, squeezing her against me. "Thank fucking God."

CHAPTER TWENTY

JOANIE

As news of Ned's sentencing spreads through Alpine Ridge, a collective sigh of relief seems to wash over the town. The dark cloud over us all dissipates, and life feels normal again. Better than usual, even.

I'm further bolstered by the finalization of the protective orders against Ned and Greg's aunt and the news that the initial boundary review meeting for the incorporation will be held at the end of the month. Things are moving forward on all fronts, and I can't help but feel a sense of excitement and possibility.

My relationship with Greg is blossoming, too. Today, Valentine's Day, he surprised me by taking the day off and suggesting we hike back to our special lake. The weather is still brisk, but the sun shines, and the snow sparkles like diamonds as we make our way through the pristine wilderness.

When we arrive at the lake, Greg pulls out a picnic basket he'd stashed in his backpack. He spreads a blanket, and we settle down, enjoying the sandwiches, fruit, and chocolates he packed.

I can't help but reflect on how we got here as we eat. And there's still a question I haven't had the courage to ask until now.

"So, about that whole thing where you were planning to marry your ex," I say, trying to sound casual.

Greg smirks. "What about it?"

I shrug nonchalantly. "Is that something you want? Marriage, I mean?"

Greg takes a moment to consider. "Honestly, I've never felt strongly about it one way or the other. I'm not against the idea, but it's never been a driving force for me. I think I only discussed it with Hailey because I knew she wanted it, and my parents were all for it. What about you?"

I lean back on my elbows, looking out over the serene water. "I never thought I'd find someone I wanted to marry," I admit. "I always figured I'd be the perpetual bachelorette, married to my career. That was the plan, anyway."

Greg's eyes meet mine, a hint of a smile playing at his lips. "And now?"

I bite my lip, feeling suddenly shy. "Now ... I can see myself being swayed toward it. If the timing was right."

His smile widens, but he doesn't press further. Instead, he asks, "Since we're on heavier topics, what about having kids? Is that something you've ever considered?"

"I'm open to it," I reply slowly. "But again, it's not

something I've yearned for. I guess I've always been a bit ambivalent about the whole motherhood thing."

"I get that. It's a big deal," Greg says. "And it's funny that even though I've never cared much about marriage, I've always known I want kids someday. "

I let his words roll around in my mind for a few minutes. "I don't think deciding to have kids is something you should do to please someone else," I finally say. "If I had them, it would be because I wanted them too. Would it be a deal breaker if I never felt that way?"

Greg licks his lips and leans back. "That's a good question," he replies, his eyes scanning the towering evergreens on the opposite side of the lake. "I honestly don't know." He pauses before meeting my eyes. "When you asked me that just now, all I could picture was a little girl with your face. Your sass. And how much she'd have me wrapped around her little finger."

Oh fuck me, my uterus just did a little somersault. Who knew that was a thing? But picturing Greg as daddy to a little girl … holy shit, I'm so screwed. He'd be a fantastic father, of course.

Then, the idea of a little boy with Greg's curls and bright blue eyes pops into my head. I nearly faint at the thought of contending with two beautiful men who take my breath away. Albeit in very different ways, of course.

"Fucking, hell, mountain man, don't say things like that," I reply in a husky voice I don't recognize.

Greg grins mischievously in response. "Sorry?"

I fan myself. "You should be. It's all I can do not to

jump you so we can start making beautiful babies right now."

Greg tips his head back and laughs. "So obviously, you could be convinced. Noted." His tone is so smug and *male*. It should make me angry, but it makes me even more soaking wet.

Down, Bev. Down. Since we're neck deep into the heavy stuff, as he said, I have one more for him before I get to tearing off his clothes.

"There's something else we should probably talk about," I venture, picking at the edge of the blanket. "I'm a city girl, Greg. And you love the mountains. How do we make that work long-term?"

Greg reaches over and takes my hand, lacing his fingers through mine. "I've thought about that," he says. "And the way I see it, we have homes in both places. We can split our time and travel back and forth. Oh, and speaking of travel, I've always wished I had done more of that. I'd love to explore the world with you, Joanie."

Jesus H. Roosevelt Fucking Christ. If he gets any more perfect, I might lose my mind.

"I love to travel," I tell him, even though it's something I'm pretty sure he already knows. "There are so many places I want to go. And so many places I've been that I'd love to show you."

"I could deal with that. I think I play it a bit too safe most of the time. I could use a dose of patented Joanie recklessness to liven things up," he says with a chuckle.

I raise an eyebrow at him. "Oh yeah?" I rise to my feet, taking off my jacket. "I think I can bring some of that to you right here, right now. Didn't you say something about skinny dipping here?" I lift my sweater off and toss it at his feet.

"Are you serious?" Greg asks, laughing.

I unclasp my bra and throw it on top of my sweater. "Does that answer your question?" I tease, starting to shimmy out of my fleece-lined leggings, turning so he gets a view of my bare ass. "Come on, mountain man. Live a little."

I look back to see him stripping and grin. "Let's do this, baby," he agrees, racing past me. Hot on his heels, I follow him in.

We both yelp as we plunge into the icy water, but the exhilaration is worth it. The cold makes me feel alive in a way I've never experienced before.

Greg ducks under the water, and I follow. My lungs seize from the cold, and I come back up spluttering. Nope. I was wrong. The cold is going to kill me.

"Okay, okay, this was a horrible idea!" I shriek, laughing as I race back to the shore.

Greg follows, cackling at my sudden change of heart. Dripping wet and shivering, he pulls another blanket out of his pack and wraps us in it, and we settle back onto the picnic blanket.

His hands rub up and down my arms. "Skin to skin, baby, that'll warm you right back up," he murmurs. His hot breath on my neck and the shell of my ear sends a different sort of shiver through me.

My hands skate down his back as I wrap my legs

around him. My core grazes his cock, and Bev weeps with happiness.

"Fuck, city girl, how are you so hot and wet after that?" he groans.

I grind against him. "What can I say? Bev loves you."

Greg's head pulls back, and he gives me a bemused look. "Bev?"

I raise an eyebrow. "My beaver?" I say with a very "duh" tone.

Greg's head tips back as he lets out a deep, loud laugh so full of joy and amusement that I'm soon laughing with him. The shaking does interesting things to Bev *and* his cock. Soon, our laughs dissolve into kisses. And as the heat builds between us, Greg slips inside me. I'm so wet that he slides in to the hilt before I realize, stretching me pleasurably.

"God, yes," I breathe.

Greg's lips trail up my neck, and he takes my mouth with his as he tilts his hips to drive in and out of me gently. "That good, baby?"

I swirl my hips with him, the soft strokes stimulating in a way I've never experienced before. The press of his chest against mine, our hearts beating in tandem, is almost overwhelming. "So good," I agree.

His lips gently pry mine open, his tongue stroking against mine. Greg runs his fingers down my back as his cock slides deeply and firmly inside me. The tight fit of him against me has my clit rubbing the base of his cock with every push. My orgasm builds inch by inch as our bodies stay locked together. I can't help the low moans that slip out of me.

"Damn, Joanie, how is making love to you just as good as fucking you senseless?" Greg whispers in my ear.

My core tightens, and I arch into him, pushing him deeper inside. It takes him a fraction of a second to realize he should keep talking.

"Your pussy feels so good around me, baby," he continues. "So wet for me. So beautiful. You're beautiful." He kisses under my ear as he gradually ramps up his pace. "Hearing how much pleasure I give you? Such a fucking turn-on." He pumps harder, and I groan.

"Yes, just like that. I want to hear you come on my cock. I want to love you until you come apart and squeeze me, baby. Ride me, Joanie. You own this dick. You own me."

I buck my hips hard at his sweet, dirty words. I look into his eyes as I chase my orgasm. The love and lust in them nearly undoes me. "You're mine," I tell him.

He nods and bites my bottom lip, sweeping his tongue into my mouth. "Ride me like I'm yours. Because I am. Every fucking inch of that cock is yours." He reaches a hand down and squeezes my breast gently, flicking his thumb over my nipple. "Every inch of my body is yours. Take it, Joanie." He tilts his hips faster to meet mine. My breaths turn shallow and rapid, and I feel myself hanging on the edge. "I love you, Joanie Morris. You're all mine." He punctuates his words with thrusts, and I'm a goner, tumbling into ecstasy. And he tumbles with me, moaning and biting my shoulder gently as he comes apart with me.

Afterward, as we lay tangled together, Greg strokes my hair and says softly, "I meant every word, you know. I can't imagine my future without you in it. I love you more than I've ever loved anyone."

Tears prick at my eyes, and I bury my face in his chest. "I love you too, Greg. So much it scares me sometimes." I look up into his eyes, deciding to let him see the love and fear in mine. "But you know that never stops me."

He chuckles and kisses my forehead tenderly. "Good. Because I want you to move in with me," he says. "I know you have to go back to Seattle at some point, and I understand that. But I want my home to be yours whenever you're in Alpine Ridge. It feels empty now when you're not there." He strokes a thumb over my cheek as he looks into my eyes.

I swallow hard, emotion clogging my throat as I envision nights spent fucking this man in every way possible. Mornings in his arms. And so much more in between.

"Okay," I agree. "Yes. I want that, too."

Greg's answering grin crinkles the corners of his eyes, and we seal it with a kiss. Amazingly, I'm not even a little bit afraid. Instead, I feel a sense of rightness settle over me. I'm not running from commitment for the first time in my life. I'm running toward a future with this incredible man by my side. It's like winning a big court case, Christmas morning, and a dozen orgasms all rolled up into one amazing feeling.

The high of it lasts the whole hike back. The time is filled with laughter and stolen kisses, our hearts light and full of love. And as we make our way down the trail, hand in hand, I can't help but marvel at how much has changed in such a short time.

When I first came to Alpine Ridge, I was adrift — wondering what was next after escaping the confines of my crappy job, unsure of my next steps. But now? Now I have a purpose, a passion project in helping to incorporate the town. I have friends who have become like family. Most importantly, I have Greg.

My mountain man. My partner in every sense of the word. That idea would've had me running for the hills just months ago.

But now?

Together, we're building something beautiful. A life that blends both of our worlds, celebrates our differences, and strengthens us both. And damn if that doesn't feel like hope.

As we return to his truck, I squeeze Greg's hand and smile at him. "Thank you," I say softly.

"For what?" he asks, cocking his head.

"For being you. For loving me. For showing me what it means to truly belong somewhere."

He pulls me into his arms. "You never have to thank me for that, Joanie. You deserve it and so much more."

I bury my face in his chest, breathing him in. And for once, I don't feel the urge to run or push him away. For once, I'm exactly where I'm meant to be.

I know there will be challenges. The incorporation process will be long and complicated. I'll have to figure out how to balance my time between Alpine Ridge and

Seattle since there isn't a permanent, full-time job for me here, and my condo and parents are there. Greg and I will undoubtedly have our share of ups and downs as we navigate this new phase of our relationship. Because let's face it, even though I'm in this, I still come with heaps of drama.

But I'm not afraid anymore. Because I know that whatever comes our way, we'll face it together.

Alpine Ridge is more than just a quaint mountain town to me now. It's where I found myself and learned to open my heart and take a chance on love.

It's the place that finally feels like home.

God, Mia is going to flip. The thought makes me laugh, and Greg looks at me as we climb into the truck.

"What?" he asks curiously.

I shake my head as he starts the engine and navigates back onto the road home. "I was just thinking about Mia."

Greg cocks an eyebrow. "And?"

"She's not going to believe that I, of all people, fell in love with this place too."

His hand reaches over and wraps around mine. "Why not?"

I run my thumb over the back of his hand. "Oh sweet, innocent, Greg," I tease. "I've spent years jumping around, doing whatever and whoever struck my fancy." He frowns jokingly, and I laugh. "I agreed to spend the holidays in a tiny mountain town, assuming I'd have a sexy romp in the snow with the hottest man I could find before going back to my selfish little world. And here I am, planning a future with said hottest man in said town."

I shake my head. "You came out of nowhere and turned my world upside down, mountain man."

A grin spreads slowly over Greg's face. "You know you love it, though."

I tip my head back and laugh, squeezing his hand.

"Yes, I do. Take me home, Greg."

This time, when he turns to look at me, there's no teasing. His face is serious, his eyes brimming with heat. "Say it again."

I grin. "Take me back to our home, mountain man, and make love to me all night long," I croon teasingly.

Greg gives an exaggerated shiver. "With pleasure."

CHAPTER TWENTY-ONE

GREG

The news that Ned has officially reported to prison brings a sense of closure, and I find myself breathing a little easier. With one major hurdle behind us, Joanie and I focus on the next challenge: the initial boundary review meeting.

The meeting is held at the Central Washington University student union in Ellensburg, and as we walk in, I can't help grumbling. "They could've handled this at the community center. We only have a few hundred people here."

I'm sure the large ballroom is great for functions, but the rows upon rows of chairs aren't close to filled.

Joanie gives me a wry look. "The county has to account for a certain percentage of the town being able to attend, even if they don't show up."

I huff out a breath and nod, conceding her point. As we take our seats, I scan the room, and my gaze lands on my father. He's sitting quietly, not speaking to anyone. My chest tightens, knowing he can't be up to anything good.

The meeting itself goes smoothly. The county official presents the proposed boundaries, fields questions, and opens the floor for public comments. Surprisingly, very few people speak up, and we wrap up in under an hour. I should've known it went too smoothly because as everyone files out, my father approaches me. "Gregory, may I have a word in private?"

I exchange a glance with Joanie before nodding reluctantly. "Fine," I say tersely to my father. And then to Joanie, "I'll meet you outside in a minute, baby."

She gives me a supportive wink and squeeze of the ass before leaving. I chuckle as I watch her go before turning back to my father. Who looks like he just sucked on a lemon.

And with no preamble whatsoever, my father hands me a thick envelope. "I think you should take a look at this. It's about your … *girlfriend*."

Frowning, I ignore the disdain in his voice when referring to Joanie and open the envelope, perusing its contents. My stomach drops as I do. It's evidence that Joanie had an affair with one of her former law firm's managing partners and was using it to blackmail him for a promotion and other perks. Text message conversations, emails, performance reviews, and even a few photographs of Joanie looking flirty and touching an older, albeit not unattractive, man.

"Where did you get this?" I ask, my voice tight.

"Since your girlfriend made such an … interesting impression at our first meeting, once I heard she was spearheading the town's incorporation and that you two have been seen about town looking rather cozy, I took it upon myself to learn a bit more about the woman my son was getting into bed with. Literally and figuratively, as it were. Luckily, my attorney knows one of the other managing partners at the firm she worked for," he explains. "Listen carefully, Gregory. If you do not end this relationship with her and relinquish your interest in our joint property, her former firm and I will release this information to every law firm in Washington. She'll never work in law in this state again. I will not have you prancing about with a harlot while doing everything in your power to sink this family's legacy."

Anger surges through me, but I force myself to stay calm. "I'll look at the evidence and think about it," I say evenly, but even that amount of deference chafes against my pride. Still, I know my father, and he doesn't make idle threats.

My father nods, a smug smile on his face. He thinks he's won. But I know playing this card means he expects to lose his lawsuit against me. He's getting desperate. Still, if what he says is true, Joanie's career is now in my hands. As soon as my father walks away, I allow myself a moment to feel the despair that's already tearing me apart. But I pull it back together. I need to walk out of these doors and pretend everything is fine in front of Joanie until I can decide what I'll do next.

Back at home, I pour over the documents alone, searching for chinks in the story that's laid out in front of me, my mind racing. I'm upset, but I need to talk to Joanie about this. I don't want to believe it, but it's all laid out in black and white.

When I call her into the room, I can see that she wonders why I've been locked away in here. But when her eyes land on the documents spread over the desk, her face pales.

"Is that what was in the envelope your father gave you?" she asks gravely.

I nod. "Yes," I reply simply.

Her eyes turn glassy, and her shoulders rise with the deep breath she takes as she settles into the chair across from me. "I can explain."

"Please do," I say, gesturing for her to go ahead while trying to keep my voice neutral. "Because I don't want to believe this, but it's hard to ignore."

She takes another deep breath, but I can see her hands shaking. It hits me right in the gut. Even knowing she may have done these horrible things, my heart still reaches for her.

"When one of the managing partner's sons was promoted to junior partner, even though I'd been promised the position, I threatened to sue for gender discrimination. I'd been building a case against them for years, noticing patterns in their promotions. In response, they fabricated this story and evidence to discredit me if I ever proceeded with a lawsuit. They asked for my resignation."

I lean forward, listening intently as she continues. "Their story wouldn't stop the lawsuit, but it would ruin my reputation and prevent me from getting a job at any law firm in Western Washington. So I decided I didn't want to work there anymore. But instead of quietly resigning, I chose to have sex with the recently promoted son and get us both fired. A final 'fuck you' to the partners." She blinks her eyes and barks a harsh laugh. "The joke was on me because even though I've tried to pretend it never happened, it's been difficult to move on from. "

My brows jump. "How so?"

She rubs at her forehead. "I don't like to focus on the negative. I'm all about what's next, what I can do, not what I can't do. It takes a lot to keep me down, but after years of dealing with their shit … it just wore me out. And then they made up all this —" she gestures at the documents "— and I knew even if I could prove it wasn't true, the damage would be done by the time I could get anyone to listen. It made me hate the industry. Because this is how it is. Lies and fabrications and mind fuckery. They sure don't tell you about all that in law school, and it's why I was having such a hard time deciding what to do next with my life." She shakes her head like it doesn't matter, but I can see her breaking from here.

I gesture for her to come to me. With a sniff, she rises and rounds the desk. I pull her into my lap and wrap my arms around her. She rests her head on mine, and I kiss her neck where it meets her shoulder.

"I'm so sorry, Joanie. I'm sorry they mistreated you. I'm sorry they made up a pack of lies to keep you quiet. But I'm mostly sorry that I didn't instantly see this for the complete bullshit that it is," I apologize. I tilt my head up and look her in her ice-blue eyes. "And I'm sorry my father has gotten his hands on this information."

Joanie snorts. "Hey, I'm the one who called him powerless. I was practically baiting him to do something like this." She shakes her head, anger written in the tight lines around her mouth and eyes.

"This isn't your fault," I assure her. "But the fact remains that my father could destroy your career over this. So I think … as much as I hate to let him think he's won even for a moment, I think we should at least appear to break up for now. Just until I figure out what to do."

Joanie's eyes flash with hurt, but she nods. "You're probably right. Except about one thing."

I give her a half-hearted smirk. "What's that?"

She nuzzles into me and places a gentle kiss on my lips. "Until *we* figure out what to do."

I don't contradict her that this is my father, my battle to fight. Instead, I run my hands up and down her arms. "You need to be here for the incorporation. I have some ideas that I can look into in Seattle. I'll keep you in the loop as much as I can."

Joanie cups my face in her hands, looking deep into my eyes. "I'll go stay with Mia and Nate for a while."

"You can stay here while I'm gone if you want to," I assure her.

She shakes her head. "It'd make me miss you too much."

Overwhelmed with affection at her words, I lean in for another kiss, soaking her in, knowing that no matter what, I'm going to miss her like crazy.

"I'll spend the rest of the afternoon clearing my calendar for the next few weeks. And then I want to have you for dinner," I growl into her ear.

She arches against me, stroking a hand down the back of my head. I bury my face in her breasts and sigh.

"When will you leave?" she asks quietly.

I kiss her clavicle. "Tomorrow morning." Her chin rests on my head, and I wrap my arms around her. "This is just a bump in the road, baby. We'll get through this."

She slides off my lap and heads toward the door. She turns back from the doorway and smiles sadly. "I know." Her gaze drops to the desk. "Thanks for believing me."

I shake my head, angry at the idea that someone believing her is something to be grateful for like the alternative is even remotely acceptable. And again, I'm angry at myself for the small window of doubt my father's delivering this package instilled in me. I'm an asshole.

"You deserve all the faith in the world, Joanie. Believe that."

Once she's gone, I clear my schedule and put the documents back in their envelope to take to Seattle. Somehow, I'll figure this out. I just hope I do it before my father gets tired of waiting for my complete submission.

After making love to Joanie twice the next morning, it takes everything I've got to walk out the door, bag packed for fuck knows how long away from her. With a heavy heart, I start the trek, letting my mind sift through everything as I drive.

By the time I get to the house in Queen Anne, I don't have any brilliant ideas—save calling Sera and asking her advice. At the very least, she asked for updates on the property stuff, and it would be good to talk to someone about this.

I call her, and we arrange to meet for lunch near her office the next day. That done, I make up a bed and head to the grocery store. If I'm going to be here a while, I may as well get settled in.

The restaurant Sera wants to meet at near her office is in the heart of downtown Seattle, and it hasn't been long enough since my last trip for the stress of the city to leech entirely out of me. So it's even more overwhelming this time. It probably doesn't help that I'm already on high alert, given everything that's going on.

Once I step into the burger joint, the noise level falls considerably, and my shoulders drop from around my ears. The inside is done in the 1950s diner style, with bright colors and period-appropriate posters. It's cute, if not a little kitschy. And I'm a bit early, so I wait in the entryway until Sera breezes in a few minutes later, looking pretty in a khaki shirtdress.

"Hey, you," I greet her, going in for a hug.

She squeezes me briefly before putting me back at arm's length. "You look even more stressed out than before," she comments drily.

I give her a wry smile. "Thanks?"

A hostess leads us to a small booth, and we settle in.

"So, what's daddy dearest up to now?" Sera asks as she flips through her menu.

I snort. "I'm going to need beer for this conversation," I joke. Thankfully, the waiter shows up and takes our drink orders, bustling back with them before I can so much as take another breath.

"Well?" Sera asks after he takes our orders and rushes off again.

"He dug up some dirt on my girlfriend, Joanie, and threatened to kill her career with it if I don't stop seeing her and sign over my share of the property," I summarize succinctly, knowing Sera's fondness for getting to the point.

"Shit," she says. "What an asshole."

I chuckle. "Yep. Speaking of assholes, how's your mom doing?" I tease.

She rolls her eyes. "Don't even get me started," she grouses jokingly. She taps the table. "I did have an idea after our last meeting, though. I was going to hold onto it until the right time, and this seems like it."

I raise an eyebrow. "This I've got to hear."

"I'd like to buy you out of your interest in the property you own with your father," she replies.

Not that I had any idea what I expected her to say, but

I'm still shocked by her suggestion. "Sera, I can't ask you to take that on. And I'm not even sure it would work that way ... legally, I mean."

She smiles. "I looked at your draft proposal and I've done my research. Your type of ownership allows you to sell your interest. I'll buy in and use cash to build facilities for the city, which I'll then lease to them. Once the initial city planning is done, I'll use the remaining land to build luxury retail and residential spaces to promote town growth. Your father won't see a penny, and if he's smart, he'll let me buy him out, too, which will be hard for him to turn down as I plan to make him a very generous offer. You won't have to fight him anymore, and the town wins."

"Sera ... I appreciate the thought, but I think I'm just going to give in and let him have the property. It's not worth fighting over, and I don't need to drag you into it."

"It's cute that you think that'll stop his reign of terror," she comments lightly. "You don't think he'll use full ownership of prime real estate in your new hometown to lord every little decision he makes over you? To terrorize you into doing exactly what he wants?"

I let out a frustrated growl because she's right. "Okay, fine, you may have a point."

Sera laughs. "Sorry. I understand wanting to fix things on your own. But you can lean on me, Greg. That's not weakness. That's what family *should* be for."

"Damn. I forgot what that's like," I say, breathing a sigh of relief. "Thank you, Sera. You're brilliant and amazing, and I'm forever in your debt. Yes, let's do it."

She beams at me. "Excellent. I'll start the paperwork. Full disclosure: I plan to clean up on that investment as Alpine Ridge grows, so don't worry, I win, too."

I shake my head and laugh. "I would hope so. It's an amazing plan and one only you could pull off. If you're sure, I'm in. Though I still don't know how I'm going to deal with what my dad's got on Joanie."

Sera tips her head to the side as our burgers arrive. "Tell me about it."

I take a huge bite of my bacon cheeseburger as I consider how to frame it. Then I remember who I'm talking to, and I just tell her about the firm's fabricated evidence to stop Joanie's discrimination lawsuit.

"Wow, they've got some seriously big balls," she says, irritation lacing her tone, her nose wrinkled in disgust. "But I have an idea on that too."

I huff a laugh and finish off my beer. "Well, aren't you a jack of all trades?"

She shakes her head before popping a ketchup-laden fry into her mouth. "Oh no, my idea is to point you at someone who will have real ideas." She swallows and takes a sip of water. "Remember I told you my husband owns a corporate security firm?"

My eyebrows pull together, but I nod. "Yeah, I remember."

She looks at me with a glint in her eye. "Trust me. Bryce will know exactly what to do." She whips out her phone and starts composing a text.

"Really?" I ask skeptically. "I thought his company

protected other companies from spies and hackers, like he did for you."

She nods as she sends the message, setting her phone down and looking back up at me. "He does that. But they handle threats of all kinds, too. I'll put you in touch with his assistant so you can get the packet your dad gave you to him. He'll let you know if he needs anything from there."

I push out a breath. "I don't know what I did to deserve all this help, but you have no idea how much I appreciate it," I assure her.

Sera nods sagely. "Been there. And I wouldn't be here to help you if I hadn't had help, too. So just say thank you and take it, Tyler," she teases.

I laugh unreservedly. "Thanks, Sera. You're the best."

She winks at me. "I know. Now, that was a good burger, but how do you feel about coconut cream pie?"

I spend the next couple of weeks waiting for Sera's husband to do his thing. But thanks to Sera, I walk to the Dahlia Bakery daily for a coconut cream pie. Because damn, those things are good. She offers to take me on a chocolate walking tour that's offered downtown, but I decline. It's bad enough that I don't have access to the community center gym right now. I have to be extra purposeful about cardio and strength training, and even then, I'm getting creative since I don't have any equipment with me.

Joanie and I talked every night for the first few nights, but it started to get difficult to be so far from her and with nothing new to report, so we talked less frequently as the days passed.

The only day this week we've talked was Monday after Sera had me sign the ownership transfer paperwork. The relief I felt was real, and Joanie and I had some seriously hot phone sex that night. But right after, she asked me to come home. And I had to tell her I couldn't. I could tell she was upset, but there wasn't much to be done about it. So, I promised to call again when there was something to share. It's been radio silence from us both since. Me, because I didn't have anything to report. Her … well, she's probably busy, but I also know it's probably mostly because she's upset. Hopefully less at me and more just at the situation, but it still leaves me on edge.

Finally, Bryce's assistant calls asking me to come in the next day. I was starting to get antsy given that St. Patrick's Day is two days away, and last I spoke to Joanie, they were full steam ahead on organizing an event as a cover to get signatures for the incorporation petition. I've used that to convince myself she's been too busy to call. Either way, I miss her like crazy, and I was hoping I could be there.

So I'm glad to finally get moving again on solving this last sticky issue. I'm taken aback as I walk into Sera's husband's office. Bryce, with his height and muscles, reminds me so much of Nate, save Bryce's hair, which is short and chestnut brown instead of tawny, and his eyes, which are blue, not hazel. But they both have that intimidating air. And suddenly, strangely, I miss Nate too.

Though to be fair, dressed in crisp khakis and a light blue button-front shirt, Bryce is much better dressed than Nate usually is. I fight a smirk at the thought and extend my hand.

"You must be Greg," he greets me. "Nice to meet you."

"Nice to meet you, too, Bryce. Sera has told me a lot of good things about you," I say.

"She's my biggest fan," he jokes. "And obviously, she's told me things about you. Including the threats your father's made against your girlfriend."

I huff a sharp sigh and shake my head. "Yes, unfortunately. I'm sure she's also told you it was part of his bid to regain complete control of the family property. Thankfully, your amazing wife was able to help me with that."

"Sera's good at what she does," he replies with a glint in his eye. "And luckily, so am I."

My brows raise. "You've got something? Already?"

"Oh, I've got what we need," he assures me. "And while sharing the details with you would be unethical, let's just say it didn't take much digging to find evidence of serious misconduct by Joanie's former employers that is related to the evidence they fabricated. And that releasing said fabricated evidence would also end up revealing their indiscretions."

I choke down a laugh. "You're going to blackmail them right back?" I ask incredulously.

Bryce contemplates that for a moment. "Strictly speaking, it isn't blackmail. I'm simply pointing out to them that if they choose to disseminate false information about former employees, they will inadvertently be drawing attention to other information that *isn't* false. You'd have to look closely, but it's not hard to find. Thankfully, I'm under no legal obligation to report what I noticed, nor am I in any way guaranteeing it will never be revealed. Just not by me." He smirks.

And there's no better word for it: I'm gobsmacked. If Sera is a real estate whiz, this guy is her security counterpart. If what he's saying is true, it sounds like he knows the exact line he shouldn't cross and uses it fully to his advantage.

"Well, I'm glad you're on my side," I finally reply. "So what happens now?"

"The next step would be to approach the law firm."

I ruminate on that, but I'm still unsure since I don't know what information he has or if what he says is true; that this is all on the up and up.

"You're sure there's nothing illegal about this?"

Bryce leans back in his chair and crosses his legs. "I'm sure. I wouldn't risk my company, you, or Joanie," he assures me. Despite hardly knowing him, he's got a very confident, reassuring air about him, and it's hard not to trust him. Still …

"What would you do if you were in my shoes?" I ask.

"If it was Sera in this situation, there's nothing I wouldn't do to protect her," Bryce says without hesitation.

His words remind me that he's done exactly that in the

past and that he's the reason my cousin is alive today. Moreover, he's right. There's nothing I wouldn't do to protect Joanie. So I nod resolutely. "Do it."

Bryce smiles sheepishly. "Would you be mad if I told you I already did?"

I can't help it; I burst out laughing. "Hell, no," I assure him. "Are you serious?"

He shrugs, grinning now. "It was time-sensitive, so I had to act fast."

"Damn," I say, shaking my head and laughing. "I'm guessing it went well then?"

Bryce dips his chin in agreement. "They've agreed to destroy all the false evidence against Joanie. The partner who gave the information to your father's attorney has warned him that if it ever gets out, they'll ruin him — their words. And just to be safe," Bryce adds, "I had the firm issue a public statement disclaiming any erroneous information about former employees that may have been leaked."

I lean back in my chair, scrubbing my hands over my face. "Holy shit," I say with a laugh. "I can't even begin to thank you enough, Bryce."

"I'm glad I was able to help," he replies sincerely.

"I'm just having trouble wrapping my head around this. It's over? Just like that?"

The corner of Bryce's mouth tips into a smile. "Well, there was some posturing and threatening, but … yes, pretty much just like that," he replies. "We take care of our clients, Greg. Especially ones that are related to my wife."

I chuckle. "Well, I'm grateful for that, but you haven't

asked me to pay you anything yet, so am I really a client?" I point out.

Bryce grins. "Buy me a drink, and we're even."

"Right now?"

Bryce cocks his head to the side. "You know what? Yes. Right now. You game?"

I spread my arms and stand up. "Absolutely," I reply. How can I turn him down after that?

Over whisky, Bryce gets me talking about Joanie and encourages me to return to her as soon as possible.

"I'm afraid she's too mad at me," I confess. "She asked me to come back a few days ago, but I said I couldn't. I haven't heard from her since."

Bryce clasps my shoulder. "Life is short, Greg. Never let your woman forget how much you love her."

He's right. I've been an idiot. I've been aching to get back to Joanie; I just wasn't expecting things to wrap up so quickly here. But I'm more than ready to go back. I resolve to head back to Alpine Ridge first thing in the morning. I'll miss the St. Patrick's Day event, but Joanie will be busy anyway. Better to show up after and grovel for forgiveness.

As I settle into bed that night, my heart feels lighter than in weeks. The obstacles ahead don't seem so daunting anymore. I have a plan, allies, and, most importantly, Joanie.

I just hope she can forgive me for pushing her away, even if it was to protect her. I drift off to sleep, dreaming of her smile, her sass, and the feel of her in my arms.

Tomorrow, I'll make things right. Tomorrow, I'll remind her that she's my everything. My partner, my love, my future.

And come what may, I'll never let her doubt that again.

CHAPTER TWENTY-TWO

JOANIE

As Mia and I get ready to head to the town square for the St. Patrick's Day event, she's practically vibrating with excitement. At first, I assume it's just because of the event, but then she turns to me with a huge grin.

"Nate and I finally set a date for the wedding," she announces. "We're getting married on September twenty-third!"

I squeal and pull her into a tight hug. "Oh my God, Mia, that's amazing! I'm so happy for you both."

And I am. Truly. But as we pull apart and I see the pure joy on her face, I can't help the pang in my chest. It makes me miss Greg even more, seeing Mia and Nate blissfully in love and planning their future.

I push down the feeling and focus on the day ahead. We've got a lot to do, and I need to be on my A-game.

When we arrive at the town square, there is a flurry of activity. Mia heads to the pastry booth, where she sets out a mouth-watering array of shamrock cookies, Irish apple cakes, and soda bread. I'm running the costume contest with a gift basket for the best-dressed leprechaun. It's silly, but people seem to be getting into the spirit of things.

Ever the peacemaker, Nate has convinced Jerry to set up a booth serving green beer and limeade. I'm not sure how he managed that feat, but I'm impressed. Nate oversees the shamrock scavenger hunt in the field behind the community center, with kids and adults alike racing around, laughing and shouting.

And then there's Rae manning the all-important petition-signing booth. Beyond festivity, the whole point of this event is to gather those crucial signatures for the incorporation.

As the day goes on, I get swept up in the fun. There's something about the camaraderie, the laughter, the sense of community that warms me from the inside out. For a few hours, I almost forget the ache of missing Greg.

Toward the end of the event, Rae comes running over to us with a huge smile. "We did it!" she exclaims. "We have more than enough signatures!"

Mia, Nate, and I erupt in cheers and hi-fives. With the event winding down, it was just in time. It's a major victory, and everything feels right in the world for a moment.

But the joy is short-lived. As we're cleaning up, Rae comes rushing back, her face stricken. "The signatures," she pants. "Someone stole them when my back was turned."

My stomach drops. "What? How?"

She shakes her head, looking distraught. "I don't

know. I just turned around for a second to put the clipboards in a bin, and when I looked back ... they were gone. I'm so sorry, you guys. This is all my fault. I should've been keeping a closer eye on them."

Mia immediately pulls Rae into a comforting hug. "Hey, it's okay. It's not your fault. That could've happened to any of us. We'll figure this out. If we can't find out who did it, we'll get the signatures again. It's not the end of the world."

Mia's right. It's not the end of the world. But after weeks of missing Greg, of waiting to know if my career is out of my hands, if Greg's father is going to ruin both of our lives, Mia and Nate's wedding plans reminding me of what I don't have, and now this... I'm at my limit. My chest tightens as all the stress I've been suppressing rushes to the surface. And even though we're outside, I feel like I just can't breathe.

I pull Mia aside while Nate continues to reassure Rae.

"Mia, I'm sorry, but I need to leave," I tell her.

She puts a hand on my shoulder and smiles reassuringly. "Of course. I'll catch up with you later?"

I huff out a breath and shake my head. "No, I mean, I need to go *home*," I say, my voice cracking. "I've been trying to stay strong and act normally, but I just … can't. I feel like I don't know which end up is anymore. All this waiting and worrying … I think I just need to get out of Alpine Ridge for a little while."

A look of understanding dawns on Mia's face. "I was wondering when this would all hit you. But you seemed to be doing so well. God, I should've known you were faking it," she says, frustration evident in her voice.

"Hey, this is on me. I should've spoken up sooner. Before I started having a mental breakdown," I joke.

Mia's eyes go wide. "Are you really having a mental breakdown?"

I open my mouth to deny it, but ... "Yeah, kind of?" I admit. "For a while, everything seemed too perfect to be true. But when Greg's father showed up with those documents ... well, it all just unraveled, and I've been going downhill since." Mia reaches out and squeezes my hand. When I'd finally told her about why I'd really lost my job, she was furious on my behalf. Even with her and Greg's support, I'm only now realizing how much it affected me. "I feel like ... Fuck, I don't know how to feel anymore. And I can't wait around forever for Greg to fix things for me. Who knows if he can or how long he'll be gone."

"He hasn't said when he'll be back?" she asks, pressing her lips together in concern.

"Nope. I even asked him to come home," I admit in a small voice.

"Oh, Jo. He said no?" she asks incredulously.

I close my eyes and nod. "I tried not to see it as a rejection. I really did. I know he's doing what he can. But that doesn't mean it'll work. And I feel like I'm hanging over the edge of a cliff right now, and I need to do something to pull myself back. Does any of this make sense?"

Mia sighs and nods. "Actually, yes," she admits. "If I were you, I'd be going out of my mind."

I give her a small smile. "I think I just need to reconnect with my real life. Since Greg is off doing his thing, maybe I should be too."

Mia's brow furrows, and I know what she's thinking. She thought Alpine Ridge and Greg had become my real life. I'd thought so, too. Now, everything seems like a mess that I don't know how or have the energy to fix.

Still, ever supportive, Mia steps forward and hugs me tightly. "Okay," she murmurs. "I understand. We'll look into the signatures issue and take care of everything here. You focus on taking care of yourself, okay?"

I nod against her shoulder, grateful for her support even as I feel like I'm abandoning her, abandoning all of them.

But I can't think about that now. I need to go, breathe, and clear my head. So I give Mia one last squeeze, wave goodbye to Nate and Rae, and head for my car. I stop by Mia and Nate's house only long enough to get my things, and then I'm back on the road.

Driving out of Alpine Ridge, I feel a sense of déjà vu. It wasn't that long ago that I was fleeing Seattle, running away from my old life and all its problems, if only for a little while. And now, here I am, running back to it.

The difference is that I'm not sure what I'm running toward this time. Seattle doesn't feel like home anymore, but neither does Alpine Ridge without Greg.

Greg. Just thinking his name makes my heart clench. I know he's been busy trying to fix this mess with his dad and protect me, but the silence this past week after not seeing him for so long on top of it has been torture. I miss him so much it's like a physical ache.

But I can't think about that now either because Greg was clear about why we needed to be apart. So, all I can do is focus on myself and what I should do now.

I let out a harsh laugh. Who am I kidding? I have no idea what I should do. But I have to do *something*.

As the snowy peaks of Alpine Ridge fade in my rearview mirror, I feel a sense of loss. But also, strangely, a flicker of hope. Maybe this really is what I need. A chance to regroup and gain some perspective.

Maybe it's time to remember who Joanie Morris is, separate from this town and these people I've come to love. It's time to rediscover my strength and figure out what I really want.

Again, who am I kidding with this? Because what I really want is a certain mountain man with eyes like the summer sky and a heart as big as the Cascades.

I know that sooner or later, we'll figure things out. I'd hoped for sooner, but clearly, that's not meant to be. It's a good opportunity to focus on myself for now, anyway.

Seattle isn't quite how I left it; it's somehow busier. Fuller. As I drive through the rain-soaked city, a sea of umbrellas skim the sidewalks.

When I let myself in, the condo feels impersonal. The quiet is deafening. I drop my bag on the floor, and it echoes through the small space.

After I've unpacked a bit, I flop onto the couch with a sigh. Funny how a place I once loved can seem so different now.

Maybe I should try harder. Maybe getting back to work would make me feel more like myself. I can still handle the incorporation project from afar, and Greg and I agreed we'd split time between Seattle and Alpine Ridge. It could work.

My eyes slide to my laptop on the dining room table, but I'm too restless to look at job listings right now. Maybe later.

I decide to finish unpacking first, methodically putting away my clothes. But as I do, I realize my wardrobe no longer feels like me. It's all sharp angles and power suits, remnants of a life that no longer fits.

On impulse, I start pulling things out and making a pile for donation: skirts I can't imagine ever wearing again, blouses that feel too constricting, towering heels that now seem impractical. It's cathartic, shedding these layers of my old self.

When I'm done, my closet looks bare. But somehow, I feel lighter.

Next, I wander into the kitchen, opening cupboards and the fridge. They're all depressingly empty, so I decide to brave the rain and do some grocery shopping. Hopefully, the normalcy will help snap me back to myself.

But as I walk the store's aisles, I miss Alpine Ridge — the friendly faces that were becoming familiar. Here, everyone avoids eye contact, and I feel lost and faceless in the crowd of shoppers.

I shake off the melancholy and focus on the task at hand. I grab some essentials — coffee, eggs, bread, butter, and cheese — to get me through the next few days until I can figure out a plan.

Back at the condo, I put away the groceries and make myself a grilled cheese sandwich. I purposely wanted to feel closer to Greg by remembering when he made me one, but all it does is make me miss him more. I eat at the counter, staring out the window at the grey Seattle skyline — a far cry from the snow-capped forest and majestic mountains of Alpine Ridge.

As I do the dishes, my mind starts to wander. What am I doing here? Running away from my problems? From the best thing that's ever happened to me? The thought makes me pause, sudsy water dripping from my hands.

Am I really going to let Greg's father dictate my life? Let my former employer's threats push me away from the man I love, the friends who have become family, and the town that's started to feel like home? What is there for me here, really? Coming home to no one from a job in an industry that now chafes? It's not like I spend much time with my parents either. Even before they retired to travel the world, we were never close, all three of us being uber career-focused. And I don't have true friends here anymore, either, merely a professional network of barely-acquaintances.

I think of Mia and her unwavering faith in love, Nate and his quiet strength, Rae and her resilience, and Greg, who loves me for exactly who I am, flaws and all.

They're worth fighting for, and this life I've started to

build with them is worth fighting for because it's so much better than anything I ever had here. Fuck the law firm. And fuck Everett Tyler.

I finish the dishes, my mind spinning. I need to talk to Greg. I should've called him before I left Alpine Ridge, before I freaked out and ran. Again.

Which makes me remember … he's here in Seattle.

How did I not think of that until now?

I reach for my phone, my heart in my throat. But when I place the call, it goes straight to voicemail. Shit. Shit, shit, shit. I'd never even asked him where he was staying, either. I mean, I know he has a house here, but where, I have no clue.

So now I'm back in Seattle, wishing I was with a man I met a hundred miles from here, who is also somewhere in this city. I just can't win today.

CHAPTER TWENTY-THREE

GREG

As I drive back to Alpine Ridge from Seattle, my heart feels lighter than it has in weeks. The weight of my father's threats, the worry about Joanie's career, the uncertainty of our future together—it's all been lifted from my shoulders. I can't wait to share the good news with Joanie, to take her in my arms and tell her everything will be okay.

When I arrive at my house, the first thing I do is call Joanie, but it goes straight to voicemail. A knot forms in my stomach. It's not like Joanie to be unreachable.

I wait a while, unpacking and making a cup of coffee before trying again, only to get her voicemail once more. And now I have a feeling in the pit of my stomach that something's not right, so I call Nate.

"Hey, man," he answers. "What's up?"

"Is Joanie with you guys?" I ask, trying to keep the anxiety out of my voice.

There's a pause. "No, she's not. She, uh... she went back to Seattle, Greg."

My heart sinks. "What? When?"

"Right after the event. Apparently, she needed some space. She told Mia she needed to reconnect with her real life."

I close my eyes, a mixture of confusion and hurt washing over me. Why would she leave without telling me? Then again, it's not exactly like I told her I was coming back, either. I shake my head at my idiocy.

"Thanks for letting me know," I manage to say. "Hey, can Mia give me Joanie's address?"

"Going after her, huh?"

"That's the idea," I confirm.

"All right, hold on a sec."

I hear muffled voices in the background; then Mia comes on the line. "So what's your plan, hot shot?"

I can't help but laugh despite my nerves being on edge right now. "I'm going to apologize for not being able to come back sooner, beg her forgiveness, then spend the rest of my life making her feel like a fucking queen if she'll let me. Good enough?"

"It'll do," she replies primly. "I'll have Nate text you the address."

"Thanks, Mia."

"Don't make me regret it." And with that, she hangs up.

I can't even be mad at her for protecting Joanie because it's what I've been trying to do, too.

As soon as I have the address, I'm back in my truck,

heading for Seattle once again. My mind races the whole drive, trying to decide what to say. It's hard because I'm just guessing what's going on with her. Is she angry with me for being gone so long? Hurt that I didn't come back when she asked? Or is it something else entirely?

When I finally arrive at her condo, my nerves are completely shot. I take a deep breath and knock on her door.

It swings open, revealing a surprised Joanie. She looks tired, her usually bright eyes shadowed. But she's still the most beautiful thing I've ever seen, and I want to wrap her in my arms. I hold back, though, to see where she's at first.

"Greg," she breathes. "I just tried to call you. Why didn't you answer?" She steps back, and I cross the threshold with a sigh of relief as she closes the door behind me.

"I was driving back from Alpine Ridge. I went back because the thing with my father is over, Joanie. You know Sera bought out my ownership in the property, but her husband also worked a fucking miracle and got both your old law firm and my dad to destroy the fabricated evidence and issue a public retraction in case it went any further. I went back as soon as I could to tell you, but you were gone."

Her brow furrows. "He did what? How? But wait … you're not mad at me?"

I laugh at the backward question. "Why would *I* be mad?" I ask.

"I bailed on Alpine Ridge, on *you*. I knew you'd be back eventually. I just … God, I can't believe it, but I freaked out and ran away from everything. The waiting and wondering was just … I couldn't handle it anymore. So I thought I'd come home and just … breathe, I guess." She buries her face in her hands. I gently pull them away and wrap my arms around her. She slides into my embrace.

I shake my head. "I could never be mad at you for needing space. I'm just sorry you felt like you had to leave in the first place." I take her hands in mine. "Are you still upset with me?"

Joanie's eyes fill with tears. "I was never upset with you. Your dad and my former bosses? Hell yes. But mostly, I just missed you so much. Phone calls weren't enough anymore. And then Mia and Nate set a wedding date, and the petition signatures were stolen —"

"Holy shit," I exclaim. I feel my anger rising, but I try to push it down. That can wait. First, I need to make sure Joanie and I are okay because that's much more important. I shake my head, shaking it off. "That's awful, but we can deal with it." I cradle her face in my hands and look deep into her eyes. "What matters most is that I missed you like crazy, too. I don't ever want to have to be away from you like that again."

Joanie's top teeth sink into her bottom lip. "Then don't," she replies. "I think I'm done here, Greg. I came back thinking I could get a handle on my emotions by plugging back into who I was. But I'm not the woman I was when I left. And I don't want a job in Seattle, though it's good to know I don't have to worry about those bastards potentially sabotaging me. Either way, this isn't who I am anymore. This isn't where I want to be."

My breath catches as I stare at her in disbelief. "You're … are you serious?"

She looks at me with pleading eyes. "Yes. I left because Alpine Ridge didn't feel right without you, but it turns out neither does Seattle. Actually, I think it really turns out that I don't do so well being away from you. Who knew so much could change in a few months? But it has. I want to be with you, in the place you love … like, permanently. But if that's too much, then I can —"

I cut her off with my lips on hers. Because like hell am I going to let her think I want it any other way.

I back her against the door and plunge my hands into her silky hair, tugging her head to the side so I can deepen the kiss. Her hands skate down my back to my ass, squeezing me closer. My cock swells as she rubs her hips against me.

I break away, panting. "It's not too much. I want you to come live with me, too, Joanie. You're sure? Really sure?" I have to ask because I just can't believe it.

She nods. "That's all I want."

I can see the truth in her clear blue eyes. So many emotions swirl through me. I shake my head and let out a disbelieving laugh. This is really happening. "Guess I can't call you 'city girl' anymore, then," I murmur.

Joanie rubs me through my jeans. "Just call me yours, Greg. Only yours."

My heart sings, and I need this woman. Now. I push into her hand, and she takes the cue, unbuttoning my jeans to free my cock. She makes to drop to her knees, but I grasp her by the arms and turn her around, roughly yanking her leggings to her knees before bending her forward until she's pressed against the door, and I enter her from behind.

We fuck hard and fast and possessive. Her hand reaches back for mine. I hold on while we both work our hips together. Until she's convulsing with bliss, and I'm spilling inside her. I lean onto her back, kissing her neck.

"I missed that too," she says, breathing hard, her cheeks rosy.

I chuckle and straighten up, smacking her ass cheek. She yelps in surprise and grins at me. "Like that?" I tease as I pull out of her.

"Mhm," she murmurs. "We can explore that later. First, shower."

Once we've thoroughly cleaned ourselves, gotten dirty again under the water, and cleaned ourselves again, we get dressed and head back to the living room.

We settle onto the couch, and Joanie puts her legs in my lap. I stroke them gently, glad she's relaxed and more herself again.

"So it's really over?" she asks, presumably referring to the mess with my father and her former employer.

I take a steadying breath. "For the most part. I imagine my father will throw a tantrum now that he has no way to control me anymore. But that's nothing new." I look up at her. "Either way, your career is safe now. You can do whatever you want without fear of retaliation."

"Whatever I want, huh?" she asks in a sultry tone, running a finger down my arm.

"Whatever you want," I reply huskily.

Joanie smirks. "Well, after I'm done having my way with you here and we go back to Alpine Ridge, I want to see this incorporation through and figure out if there's a way I can keep helping the town. That's what I want."

I smile and squeeze her calf. "Well, considering that a lot of running a town involves legal matters, that seems like a viable option. But is that enough for you?"

Joanie shrugs but has a thoughtful look on her face. "I could always start my own practice and take on private clients if I need more," she muses, then meets my gaze. "But if you're asking whether *you're* enough ... yes, Greg. You're more than enough. While I never saw myself living in a small town in the mountains with a man who swims naked in ice-cold lakes, I apparently didn't dream big enough. I'd be insane to turn down that life."

I lean in and kiss her softly. "If I get to keep you, I'll swim naked wherever you want, Joanie."

She tips her head back and laughs. "This just keeps getting better and better."

I cover her lips with mine and give her a real kiss. One that leaves her — and me — a little breathless. "That. That right there is my new life goal. To make you say that every damn day."

Joanie's expression softens, and she puts a hand on my

chest. "I love you, Greg. Being with you, the life we can have, it's more than I ever thought to dream of. All you need to do is love me, and I'm there. For as long as you'll have me," she says. The uncharacteristic seriousness pierces me right in the heart, in a good way.

"Forever okay with you?" I ask softly.

Joanie smirks at me. "I could be convinced," she says nonchalantly.

I chuckle. "Shall I attempt to convince you right here, or would your bedroom be better?" I tease.

Her pupils dilate, and she grins. "Yes to both," she teases back. "And you can keep convincing me every day, in our bed, in our home. Deal?"

I extend my hand for her to shake. "Deal. But for the record? My home is wherever you are."

She nods in agreement. "And my bed is our bed now. Care to get started?"

Instead of answering with words, I scoop her up and take her to the bedroom. To show her I mean it.

Because she is my home. My heart. My everything.

And I'm never letting her go again.

EPILOGUE

JOANIE

As I stand in the wildflower field behind the community center, getting ready to watch my best friend marry the love of her life, I can't help but reflect on the whirlwind of the past six months.

After Greg and I reunited in Seattle, everything quickly fell into place, surprising even me. I moved in with him in Alpine Ridge, and a few months later, I sold my condo in the city. Though we still use Greg's Queen Anne house for our Seattle getaways, my heart is firmly rooted in the mountains.

The incorporation efforts hit a snag when the petition signatures were stolen, but Rae, ever the determined force, took it upon herself to collect them again. Within a couple of weeks, we were back on track. The final boundary meeting in June went smoothly, and now we're just six weeks away from the election that will officially make Alpine Ridge a town.

Mia's sister, Carrie, has been another surprising but

welcome addition to our little family. After graduating and having a massive falling out with their parents, she moved in with Mia and Nate in July. She's been doing remote work for Western Washington politicians as we enter election season, and she's also agreed to spearhead our upcoming elections since while a few folks in town were willing to help, none were willing to run the show. It's a win for everyone; I won't have to handle something I know nothing about, Carrie's resume will be even more impressive afterward, and the town will benefit, too.

Greg's father did try to stir up trouble at the 4th of July celebration, but the town made it clear he wasn't welcome. He hasn't been heard from since. To my knowledge, he's also still holding out on Sera's buyout offer.

Ned's parents have likewise found Alpine Ridge less than hospitable now that the truth about their son's crimes and their cover-ups has spread. They recently put their grocery store up for sale, and Sera pounced on the opportunity. She has grand plans to turn it into something reminiscent of a Trader Joe's, much to everyone's delight.

But today is all about celebrating Mia and Nate. The setting couldn't be more perfect — a sea of purple fireweed, white asters, and lingering yellow buttercups, framed by trees just beginning to don their autumn colors. Mia looks ethereal in her flowy white gown and aster crown, like a fairy bride straight out of a storybook. And Nate, dashing in his light grey slacks and crisp white shirt, can't take his eyes off her.

The guest list is small but meaningful. Greg and I, of course, along with Rae and Carrie. Nate's parents and brothers. Everyone is surprised to discover that Nate's youngest brother is the famous Evan Edwards, one of the hottest action stars in Hollywood. Carrie seems particularly mesmerized by him, and the feeling seems mutual from how he's flirting. And a handful of our closest friends from town round out the group. Mia's decision not to invite her parents was difficult, but seeing the pure joy radiating from her and Nate, I know she made the right call.

Nate's other brother, Dylan, officiates. He's a musician, but apparently, anyone can become an officiant. When he calls the ceremony to order, Mia gives me a joyful but nervous smile. I squeeze her hand and push her toward the front of the crowd.

"Thank you all for coming today to share in uniting Nathan Edwards and Mia Anderson in marriage," he begins.

Everyone quiets down, and Nate and Mia join hands in front of Dylan, eyes locked on each other, grins on both of their faces.

"Now, the bride and groom have elected to do their own additional vows privately after the ceremony, so everyone pay attention because this is going to go fast. Which is good because there's Chantilly crème chiffon cake waiting for us," he jokes. My mouth fills with saliva at the thought of one of Mia's best cakes, so I don't chuckle with everyone for fear of drooling all over my new lilac-colored tulle gown.

Dylan turns to Nate. "Do you, Nathan Edwards, take this woman to be your lawfully wedded wife, to live together in matrimony, to love her, comfort her, honor and keep her, in sickness and in health, in sorrow and joy, to have and to hold, from this day forward, as long as you both shall live?"

"I do," Nate says thickly.

Mia choke-sobs, and I hold a hand up to my mouth to stifle a similar noise. They've both already been through so much between Gran's death, struggles with Mia's parents, and opening their businesses. Not to mention all the recent drama.

Nate smiles down at her, but I can tell he's about to lose it, too.

Now Dylan turns to Mia, and just the look on her face has me blinking back tears. Even as a sobbing mess, she's beautiful and radiating joy. "Do you, Mia Anderson, take this man to be your lawfully wedded husband, to live together in matrimony, to love him, comfort him, honor and keep him, in sickness and in health, in sorrow and joy, to have and to hold, from this day forward, as long as you both shall live?"

Mia nods for a moment as she swallows another happy sob. "Yes." Dylan looks at her with raised eyebrows. She's only confused for a moment before she laughs and chokes out, "I do" around giggles.

I facepalm and shake my head, laughing. Only Mia would forget the *one line* she's supposed to nail. Thankfully, Nate is chuckling, too.

Dylan smirks. "Nate and Mia will now exchange the rings they've chosen for each other as a symbol of their unending love." He turns to Nate, who fishes a ring from his pants pocket. "As you place this ring on Mia's finger, please repeat after me." Mia offers her hand, which Nate takes, carefully sliding the simple band onto her finger next to her blindingly huge engagement ring. "With this ring, I thee wed and pledge you my love now and forever."

And that's the line that does Nate in. Tears pouring down his face, he manages in a thick, joy-filled voice, "With this ring, I thee wed and pledge you my love now and forever."

Tears are pouring down Mia's face, too, as her hand shakes in his. And I wish I'd brought a towel to mop these two up afterward. I brush away a few of my own tears, realizing I probably also need one. An elbow gently nudges me from the side, and Nate's mom slips me a tissue. I gratefully accept it, hoping she has more of those on hand.

"You ready, Mia, or do you guys need a minute?" Dylan teases.

Mia laughs and shakes her head. "I'm so ready." She takes Nate's hand and reveals the ring she'd had tucked in her palm.

Dylan smiles patiently and prompts her, "With this ring, I thee wed and pledge you my love now and forever."

Mia takes a shaky, deep breath and slides the ring onto Nate's finger, looking lovingly up into his face. "With this ring, I thee wed and pledge you my love now and forever." And I think the worst of the tears have passed for her because she's far steadier than Nate was. Nate, however, continues to cry unabashedly.

I'm not usually one for emotional displays, but seeing Nate, a steady rock of a man, cry like this is getting to me. Almost as much as Mia's tears are. I can feel Greg's eyes on me, but I don't look. If I do, I know I'll see his love and concern there, and then I'll lose it, too. We can't have the *whole* wedding party be a blubbering mess.

Dylan grins at the happy couple and spreads his arms out. "By the authority vested in me by the State of Washington ... I now pronounce you husband and wife!"

The small crowd, myself included, claps, hoots, and cheers as Nate leans in and kisses Mia sweetly. And I can't help it; I lean into Greg and whisper in his ear. "You can bet your gorgeous ass if that were us, there'd be a whole lot more tongue."

Greg chuckles and leans toward me. "And probably some groping." He winks at me.

I grin and give him a "guilty as charged" shrug because we both know he means me.

Nate and Mia turn to us all and are passed around for hugs before Rae leads us back to the community center, where the reception is held. It's full of laughter, love, and more pastries than even I can handle. The cake is out of this world, and I'm pretty sure I'm going to be ordering this on the regular just because it's practically orgasmic. Light, fluffy, and buttery, the cake itself is bliss even without the decadent vanilla-flavored whipped heaven. But watching Mia and Nate's joy is the cherry on top. It's the perfect day for my best friend, and my heart is so full of happiness for her and Nate.

As the happy couple departs for their Hawaiian honeymoon – a nod to the trip Mia was forced to abandon, ultimately allowing them to meet in the first place – Greg pulls me aside. We walk hand in hand to the pond on one side of the community center, settling on a bench overlooking the tranquil water.

I smile to myself remembering ice skating last winter when Greg and I showed off for each other before our first real heavy-petting session in his office.

"Well, it seems like that went off without a hitch. That might be the first event here that has," Greg teases, running his hand through the layers of tulle of my skirt.

I turn toward him with a smirk. "I'm glad. They deserved it. Though I half expected her parents to show up and start some shit."

"God, I hadn't even thought of that," he admits. "I hope my parents don't do that when we get married."

A laugh spills out of me. "When we get married?" I tease. "I don't remember you even asking."

Greg smirks and looks down. I follow his gaze. And in his hand is a small velvet box. My heart stutters as he opens it to reveal what appears to be a stunning diamond ring that's the same shade of blue as my eyes.

"Joanie," he begins, his eyes shining with emotion. "You came out of nowhere and made me feel alive. Being with you has made me a better man, one who wants everything out of this life with you by my side. As your husband, if you'll have me. Joanie Morris, will you marry me?"

"You know," I muse, looking away so he doesn't see the sheen of tears in my eyes, "I always pictured you proposing during sex."

Greg tips his head back and laughs loudly. Then he leans in and kisses me. "Then let's go home, and I'll try this again."

I shrug lightly and gesture for him to give me the ring. He shakes his head, chuckling as he withdraws the ring and slides it onto my finger. I hold my hand out, examining the gorgeous jewelry exaggeratedly as I pretend to contemplate it and his question.

"Wait ..." he says before I can say anything else. "You just said you've pictured me proposing."

I give him a sly smile. "Maybe."

He grins. "And did you see yourself saying yes to that proposal?"

My grin widens. "Maaaaybe."

Greg laughs. "Joanie?"

And I can't keep it up anymore. I laugh and grab him by the shirt, pulling him toward me. "Yes. Make me Mrs. Mountain Man, stud."

Greg laughs against my lips, pulling me into his lap. And I don't give a shit that I'm wearing a dress; I wrap my legs around him. He runs his hands up my bare thighs and groans into my mouth.

"I might get to propose again sooner than I thought," he murmurs, pulling my core against his hard length.

"Public sex?" I gasp in a scandalized tone. "For shame."

Greg sucks hard at the spot under my ear, and I moan. "You know you love it, dirty girl," he teases.

I lean back and put my hands on his face. "I know I love you," I reply sincerely. No snark, no teasing. "And I'd be honored to be your wife, Gregory Tyler." And I seal it with a tender kiss so there's no question that my "yes" is for real.

When his mouth breaks away, he rests his forehead against mine. "Ready to go home, fiancée?"

I nod, my heart soaring at the new title. At the idea of being his forever. Because he's most definitely mine.

As we walk back to the community center, hand in hand, I can't stop smiling. The future stretches out before us, filled with promise and possibility.

It's wild that I've finally found my home. My happy ever after. I never imagined that path would lead me here, to this incredible man, to this life that feels like a dream come true.

But that's the beauty of life, isn't it? The unexpected detours, the surprises that catch us off guard and change everything.

Alpine Ridge brought me a better life than I'd had planned. It gave me love, purpose, and a sense of belonging. And now, it will be the setting for the next chapter of my story. Our story.

And I can't wait to see what adventures await us. Mountain man and (former) city girl. Ready to take on the world. Together. Forever.

Thank you so much for reading! Please take a minute to leave a review on any retailer, goodreads, and/or BookBub. Even if it's just a couple of sentences, your opinion is important to potential readers and to me.
Thank you!

Want more Alpine Ridge? Get ready for Carrie and Evan's story, *Unscripted Love,* coming November 1st and available for preorder now at https://melanieasmithauthor.com/books-unscripted-love.html

Oh, and if you're curious about Sera and Bryce, their story starts with *The Safeguarded Heart*, which you can check out at:
https://melanieasmithauthor.com/books-the-safeguarded-heart.html

Sign up for Melanie A. Smith's newsletter to get a FREE book plus all the latest news and more
https://melanieasmithauthor.com/newsletter.html

ACKNOWLEDGMENTS

My first and deepest thanks go to my husband and son. Their unwavering support and their ability to give me space when inspiration strikes are truly remarkable. I am endlessly grateful for their acceptance and encouragement in all aspects of my life, especially in my writing journey.

To Erin, without whom, I would have given up writing long ago. Being an author has its ups and downs, but your cheering me on is what gets me through the lows. I'm truly blessed to have found you.

To my #morewordsmay homies, my beautiful betas, Eve Kasey and Jen Morris, thank you for your words: words of encouragement, words of support, and, of course, the words you write. You and your books are an inspiration to me!

To my *Naughty List* readers, your anticipation for the completion of Joanie and Greg's story has been a source of motivation during a challenging dry spell. I sincerely hope you enjoy the rest of their journey as much as I enjoyed writing it!

And to all of my readers, old and new, thank you for being here. I truly hope you enjoyed this story. Stay tuned; there is so much more to come.

ABOUT THE AUTHOR

Melanie A. Smith is an award-winning, international best-selling author of steamy romance with smart, self-sufficient heroines and strong, swoony book boyfriends with hearts of gold. A former engineer turned stay-at-home mom and author, when Melanie is not lost in the world of books you'll find her spending time with her husband and son, crafting, or cross-stitching.

facebook.com/MelanieASmithAuthor

x.com/MelASmithAuthor

instagram.com/melanieasmithauthor

BOOKS BY MELANIE A. SMITH

The Safeguarded Heart Series

The Safeguarded Heart

All of Me

Never Forget

Her Dirty Secret

Recipes from the Heart: A Companion to the Safeguarded Heart Series

The Safeguarded Heart Complete Series: All Five Books and Exclusive Bonus Material

Life Lessons

Never Date a Doctor

Bad Boys Don't Make Good Boyfriends

You Can't Buy Love

The Heart of Rutherford: Life Lessons Novels 1 – 3

L.A. Rock Scene Series

Everybody Lies

Finding His Redemption

Alpine Ridge Series

Tough Love

Recklessly in Love

Stand-alones

Last Kiss Under the Mistletoe

Vegas Baby

Pompous Paramedic: A Hero Club Novel

Short Stories

Cruising for Love

Hot for Santa